The Fire

by

NICOLE PYLAND

The Fire

Twenty years ago, Ripley Fox's entire family was killed in a fire. After years in the foster care system and trying to rebuild her life, she's once again confronted not only with the horror of what happened that night, but also with the truth about who was responsible.

Kenna Crawford is the very definition of a hard-nosed reporter. She always gets her story, never takes no for an answer, and never lets go once she's got something or someone in her sights. When she comes across the story of Ripley Fox, she's not only intrigued by it, but also by Ripley herself.

As the two women attempt to discover if there's something between them, they're forced to deal with the realities of what happened to Ripley and how Kenna's career doesn't make it easy for Ripley to let go of what she's tried to forget for the past twenty years.

To contact the author or for any additional information, visit: **https://nicolepyland.com**

Subscribe to the reader's newsletter to be the first to receive updates about upcoming books and more: **https://nicolepyland.com/newsletter**

BY THE AUTHOR

Chicago Series:

- Introduction – Fresh Start
- Book #1 – The Best Lines
- Book #2 – Just Tell Her
- Book #3 – Love Walked into The Lantern
- Series Finale – What Happened After

San Francisco Series:

- Book #1 – Checking the Right Box
- Book #2 – Macon's Heart
- Book #3 – This Above All
- Series Finale – What Happened After

Tahoe Series:

- Book #1 – Keep Tahoe Blue
- Book #2 – Time of Day
- Book #3 – The Perfect View
- Book #4 – Begin Again
- Series Finale – What Happened After

Boston Series:

- Book #1 – Let Go
- Book #2 – The Right Fit
- Book #3 – All Good Plans
- Book #4 – Around the World
- Series Finale – What Happened After

Sports Series:

- Book #1 – Always More
- Book #2 – A Shot at Gold
- Book #3 – The Unexpected Dream
- Book #4 – Finding a Keeper

Celebrities Series:

- Book #1 – No After You
- Book #2 – All the Love Songs
- Book #3 – Midnight Tradition
- Book #4 – Path Forward
- Series Finale – What Happened After

Holiday Series:

- Book #1 – The Writing on the Wall

- Book #2 – The Block Party

- Book #3 – The Fireworks

- Book #4 – The Sweet Escape

- Book #5 – The Misperception

- Book #6 – The Wait is Over

- Series Finale – What Happened After

Stand-alone books:

- The Fire

- The Disappeared

- The Moments

- Reality Check

- Love Forged

- The Show Must Go On

- The Meet Cute Café

- Pride Festival

CONTENTS

PROLOGUE

PEOPLE always assume the smoke is noticed first. They assume that they would wake with the smell, or maybe they would wake up choking for air. Ripley didn't wake with the smoke, though; she woke up to the heat. Her skin was coated in sweat, which wasn't uncommon for her; Ripley often kicked off the blankets at night, and her mom would always put them back in place for her when she came in each morning to kiss Ripley's clammy forehead and tell her it was time for school. So, when she woke up sweating that night, there was nothing out of the ordinary. She had even closed her eyes again, seeking slumber, only to have them shoot back open upon seeing the flames.

The deep-red, near-purple flames were slinking under that tiny gap between the floor and the door to her bedroom. So many times, she had played with their family cat in that same gap and watched Tiger reach his brown and gray paw through the space in search of her hand and dancing fingers. She would giggle as she gripped his paw lightly. He'd pull it away. He'd slide it around and around, searching for something else to play with, and she'd just laugh and laugh. Ripley didn't know it then, but Tiger had been lucky: he'd died the year before the flames seeped in somehow so slowly yet so quickly at the same time, seeking another source of oxygen to keep it alive.

The heat was upon her in an instant, but then she felt

1

more than saw the smoke. The room was dark, save only her night light that she had plugged into the corner outlet. Then, even that light flickered and went out. She coughed and coughed, suddenly unable to breathe. It smelled like the campfires her dad used to build them when they went camping each summer. The next thing she noticed was how the fire sounded. It was crackling in that way those same campfires used to crackle. In that moment, Ripley recalled how it was roasting marshmallows at those campfires. Her mom would bend old coat hangers, let them sit over the fire first, and slide the marshmallows over them with ease. She would pass one to Ripley's older brother, Ethan, and then she'd pass the next one to her other brother, Benji. Ripley was next. Her mom would scold the two boys, who would inevitably start sword-fighting with their skewers. Their mother would threaten them with no s'mores if they didn't stop. Their father would be preparing the graham crackers and chocolate. He'd laugh while he watched his boys play. Then, he'd smile at his youngest child and only daughter as her mom passed her the marshmallow to roast.

The fire didn't smell like roasted marshmallows now, though. It attacked the small pile of books she always left on the floor by the door. It moved swiftly to the stuffed bunny her grandmother had given Ripley for her sixth birthday before it made its way toward the Care Bears comforter her parents had gotten her for Christmas that past year. The sound changed then. It wasn't crackling anymore; it was seething. That was how she would describe it much later, years later. The fire seethed in anger as it tore through her possessions, like they weren't even there, and appeared to be reaching out for her as she folded her legs into her tiny body and pressed as close to the back wall of her bedroom as possible, only to realize that the wall behind her was hot as well.

She felt bad later, once she was older and had time to reflect on the events of that night, because she had never thought about the other members of her family as she clutched at her skinned knees and felt the sweat trickle down her forehead and into her eyes. She never even screamed. She never called out for her mother or father. She also never yelled for her older brothers, who shared the bedroom next to her. She didn't even scream out for her favorite and only grandmother, who had moved in with them a few months prior and lived in the basement apartment her father had built specifically for her. Ripley screamed for no one. She just sat there, picking one of the scabs she'd earned on the playground at school the previous week, while the flames slid elegantly across the image of Good Luck Bear.

She didn't think about burning or dying. She didn't understand enough about death yet. She didn't consider how the burning of her skin might hurt or that she would be in incredible pain until the fire took her from her body and her soul would enter the great unknown. She didn't think about heaven or hell or anything her parents had taught her about, either.

The man in a yellow jacket and a black helmet came in just before the fire reached her toes. She actually felt it there for a second before she coiled them further into her body. He had a mask on his face, so she couldn't make out what he was saying, but before she knew it, he had opened her bedroom window, which she had forgotten about entirely. He yelled something outside, and Ripley was quickly lifted from her bed as the flames engulfed it. He took her to the window where another man in a yellow jacket and a black helmet was waiting on a ladder.

A few moments later, she was standing on the ground with a silver blanket around her and a mask on her face. A woman stood in front of her, searching her skin for burns and asking Ripley questions she didn't know the answers to. It was only then that she thought to ask one of her own.

"Where's my family?"

CHAPTER 1

SOMETIMES, the nightmares woke her up, and other times, the dreams did. People often tend to confuse the two. Dreams, to Ripley, were good things. In her case, she dreamed of her family, of the ways things were before she lost them. She dreamed of those camping trips and the times her older brothers would jump into their backyard swimming pool, yelling 'Cannonball!' at the top of their lungs. Ripley dreamed of standing next to her mother and licking the spoon when she made brownies. She would dream of her grandmother knitting in the chair they'd moved into the living room when she started living with them. Sometimes, the dreams woke her up, and she'd smile into the morning.

Other times, the nightmares took Ripley back to the night she lost them. She would feel the fire on her skin again. She would taste and smell the smoke. She'd hear it crackle, and, in its hunger, she'd hear it consume all her worldly possessions. She would also see things she hadn't seen that night. She would see the fire burning Ethan and Benji's skin. She would see her mother and father standing in the hallway, outside her bedroom, with their skin partially covered in soot and the other parts peeling away. It was usually that vision that caused Ripley to nearly fly out of bed and into the bathroom, where she'd typically vomit into the toilet. She'd cry into the morning then.

Today was a nightmare kind of day. That made sense – the anniversary was coming up. Ripley always had more nightmares like this the closer it got to the date of the fire. She brushed her teeth after flushing the toilet, as was her custom, and made her way into the bedroom again to shut off her incessant alarm. Her first therapist had suggested working out as a way to take her mind off the past. Ripley had resisted at first, but since the nightmares got worse instead of better with time, she decided to give it a try and had been working out briefly every morning for the past ten years.

She stretched first before she did her morning sit-ups and push-ups. She also did a few yoga poses and hit the treadmill she'd bought a few years ago at a garage sale. She ran only for ten minutes before she hopped into the shower and readied herself for the day. Nightmare-days were always harder to get through. Part of that was because the visions were more prevalent in her mind, but the other reason was that she often had to deal with nightmares in her job as a social worker.

"Hey, Rip." Officer Jeff Wonder approached her desk. "I got a new one for you."

Ripley looked away from her laptop and at the police sergeant. She pushed the image of her dying mother out of her mind as she focused on the portly man in front of her.

"What's up, Wonder?" she asked.

"Nine-year-old boy just showed up. His mom died in a hit-and-run this morning. We've got him in Interview 2. He was in the car with her, and we can't get him to talk. We pulled her up, but there's no next of kin outside of the kid, and the kid doesn't have a dad on the birth certificate."

"You need me to try to talk to him?" she asked.

"Would you mind? It would really help us out. You're so good at this stuff. I think he's scared of all of us." He shrugged. "The uniform does that to them sometimes."

"I was just about to head out of here for a home visit," Ripley replied. "I can stop in, but I can't take the case or escort him. You still have to call it in."

"Understood, Rip." He mock-saluted her. "I'll call it in right now. You do your thing."

Officer Wonder walked off toward his desk. She watched him pick up the phone, likely to call it into social services. Ripley closed her laptop, slid it into her messenger bag, and made her way to Interview 2. Before she entered, she hit up the vending machine and paid for a bag of salty chips, a chocolate bar, and a soda. She probably spent at least a third of her take-home pay on snacks for kids, but she did it for them. She did it because she had been one of these kids about twenty years ago. Actually, it would be exactly twenty years ago in two weeks.

She entered the interview room and noticed a boy with dark, bowl-cut hair and dark eyes that were red-rimmed likely due to exhaustion and tears. He met Ripley's eyes immediately and then lowered his head again. He looked so small in that metal chair. Ripley glanced outside into the station proper and noticed at least fifteen officers. The room the boy was in was bare and gray. It had one sign on the wall that explained a suspect's rights and another that said "No Smoking." Outside of those decorations, it had one rectangular metal table and four metal chairs. In the middle of the table was a bar that handcuffs could be attached to, and to Ripley's right was the two-way mirror. It was a standard interrogation room, and it was a bad place for this young boy to be after losing his mother.

"Hi there," Ripley greeted softly. "My name is Fox." She sat down at the table across from the boy, leaving her bag over her shoulder and the snacks in her hands. "What's your name?"

The boy looked up at her, considered for a moment, and said, "Dustin." He paused and then added, "Your name is Fox?"

"My first name is Ripley," she replied. "My last name is Fox."

"My last name is Erickson." Dustin slid his hand under

his nose as he sniffled.

"It's nice to meet you, Dustin Erickson. You can call me Fox or Rip."

He gave a shy smile before it disappeared.

"Rip is a funny name."

"I know." She smiled at him. "Listen, I was wondering if you'd like to get out of here for a few minutes with me."

"They told me I can't go," he replied and glanced at the metal door.

"I got their permission. It'll just be a few minutes. I was thinking we could go to the park on the block to talk."

He didn't say anything for another moment. Then, he looked back at her and at her hands.

"Is that for me?" he asked.

"I thought you could have it outside, away from all these police officers. How does that sound?"

Dustin nodded, and Ripley smiled at him again. He stood and picked up his Spiderman backpack. It was then that she realized the boy had been on his way to school when the accident happened. Ripley helped him slide the straps over his shoulders and walked him out of the room and then, the building. It was spring, so the weather was nice. They were able to walk around the corner and locate the park she'd frequented with other children in similar situations. Ripley sat on a bench, and Dustin joined her. He kept his backpack on and leaned forward on the bench while he wiped his hands up and down his jeans. Ripley handed him the chocolate bar, which he took and opened immediately.

"Thank you," he said between bites.

Ripley sat there and watched him eat while looking at a few kids that were too young to be in school, play while their parents looked on. When he finished the candy, she passed him the soda. She knew she was contributing to cavities, but the kid probably hadn't eaten in hours and could use a little sweetness right now.

"So, Dustin, what's your favorite thing on the

playground? Are you a slide guy? Do you like the swings?" she asked.

"I'm too old. That stuff is for little kids." He took a long drink of the soda.

"Really? I love the swings, and I'm way older than you." She chuckled. "I try to swing whenever I can."

"You do?" He looked up at her quizzically.

"I do, but it's hard to find the time when you're a grown-up, and you have to work all the time. What do you want to be when you grow up?" she asked.

"Basketball player. I'm a point guard at school."

"Really?"

"We're undefeated. There have only been three games, but we're the best team."

"I bet you are." She laughed to herself while he took another drink. "I was terrible at basketball. I did play soccer for one year."

"I'm good at soccer, too," he replied. "I play that in the summer. My dad even said he'd come to a game next year, since he couldn't last time."

Ripley waited a moment, like she always did when she was trying to get a kid to open up. She'd found when she first started working that if she jumped right on comments like that, it usually caused the kids to clam up on her, and she'd get nothing.

"Yeah? That's awesome. What position do you play?"

"Forward."

"I was a goalie," she said. "You would have been my sworn enemy." She gave him a playful glare, which he returned and then giggled.

"I would have scored on you a million times," he said.

"I'm sure you would have. I wasn't very good," Ripley laughed. "My dad was, though. He played in college."

"He did?"

"He did. That's why I started playing. My big brothers played, too. They were much better than me, though."

"I don't have any brothers. It's just me." He shrugged.

"Did your dad play soccer or basketball?" she asked and looked away toward the slide to make it appear as if she didn't really care about the answer.

"He played football, but Mom says I'm too young for that." Dustin took another drink of his soda.

Ripley wondered if he understood the difference between present and past tense and when he would start using the past tense to talk about his mother. It took her a few months, and she'd been only a little younger than him at the time.

"Football, huh? That's cool." She tried to move the subject back to his father. "What's your dad's name?"

The boy looked at her like she was crazy for a second and said, "Dad." He shrugged again. "But Mom calls him Rick. I'm not allowed to call him that, though."

"Oh, right. Do you have his last name like I have my dad's last name?"

"I don't know." He shrugged again.

"What's your middle name?" Ripley asked him.

"Allen. I hate it." He shook his head from side to side.

"Mine is Elizabeth."

"That's better than Allen," he said.

Ripley laughed at him as he took another drink of his soda.

"Is it your dad's middle name, too?"

"Yeah."

"So, his name is Rick Allen?"

"He drives a truck; that's why he's never around. That's what my mom said."

"He's a truck driver. That's an important job."

"I guess," he replied.

"He helps deliver important things to people."

Dustin placed his half-empty soda can between their bodies and stared ahead at the children playing.

"They said my mom died."

Ripley knew what would happen.

"I'm very sorry, Dustin."

9

"Can I see her?" He kept watching the children.

"Not right now."

"Why not?"

"You know how grown-ups can make silly rules sometimes, like you have to go to bed at a certain time or no watching TV until you do your homework?"

"Yeah."

"Well, you were in an accident this morning. And when an accident happens, us, grown-ups, have rules we have to follow."

"Like what?"

"Like, I bet they took you to see a doctor after it happened, right?"

"Yeah."

"And they checked you out to make sure you were okay?"

"Yeah."

"Well, there are other rules, too. It's important, just like what your dad does with driving his truck. That's why the police officers were asking you those questions earlier; they were following their rules."

Dustin didn't say anything for a long moment before he looked up at her.

"What happens to me now?"

"Now, we'll go back into the police station, and someone from where I work is going to pick you up. They'll take you to get some real food, and they'll have some more questions for you, too."

"Like what?"

"Like, about your family."

"It was just my mom and me."

"Okay. That's okay." Ripley squeezed his shoulders. "There's a place where they'll take you. It's not far, and there will be kids your age that you can play with."

"How long will I be there?" he asked as his dark eyes connected to her hazel ones.

"I don't know, Dustin. But we're going to make sure

you're okay," she replied. "I promise. Just remember that no matter what happens, everything will be okay. Can you do that for me?"

"I guess." He shrugged again.

Ripley sat there with him for a few more minutes before she returned to the station and left Dustin with the officers after telling them what she'd learned about his father, which should be enough for them to find the man. She gave Dustin the chips she had bought and a side hug on her way to her next appointment. Ripley was what the officers of the Pleasant Valley police force called "a specialist." All social workers had to be able to handle working with children, but Ripley seemed to have abilities beyond the normal social worker. She could get just about any kid to open up to her or give her the information she sought. Sometimes, she had to resort to telling them at least part of her own story, but other times, like with Dustin, she was able to sit still for a moment, ask a few questions, and get what the officers needed.

She had a feeling her next appointment, a home visit with a mother who was a recovering drug addict with three young children in a one-bedroom apartment, would not go as well as her conversation with Dustin. The last time Ripley had visited, she'd given the woman one more chance to find employment. She'd been fired from her last job the month before and hadn't reached out to file for unemployment or put in any effort to find a job. Her kids were living off of bread that Ripley had found mold on during her inspection.

When Ripley arrived, she found the apartment empty. The superintendent had to unlock the door for her after telling her the family had moved out in the middle of the night the previous week. While she was glad she wouldn't have to pull the children away from their mother when they had no idea why, Ripley wasn't happy to find out that they had disappeared. She would report that back to the office, and there would be an investigation. With her extra time, though, Ripley made one more home visit. This one was to a foster home where she knew several of the young children because she'd placed them there herself. While she hated that the older kids so rarely got adopted, she did find a small amount of enjoyment in being able to check in on them from time to time and make sure they were getting what they needed.

Later, when she tucked herself in, alone, and in her full-sized bed, Ripley wondered if that night she'd have nightmares or dreams. She didn't have to wonder, though. With the anniversary of the death of her entire family fast approaching, she knew only the nightmares awaited her tonight.

CHAPTER 2

KENNA Crawford couldn't stare at the screen a moment longer. She had been doing so for the past ten hours. She had recorded her audio for over three hours earlier in the day and had to then stare while in the editing bay with her favored editor, Trey. They'd gotten what they needed done for the day at the sacrifice of her eating lunch or dinner and surviving only on the muffin she'd grabbed at the coffee shop on her way in. That was how it was to be a reporter sometimes. Whenever she was working on a good story, she would spend hours and hours researching and interviewing, hours recording the footage itself, and then hours in the ADR booth, adding clean audio before she put the finishing touches on it in editing. She was a control freak, but it was her face, her voice, and her hard work going out to the masses. She wanted it to be perfect.

As she headed home for the night, she couldn't believe this story was finally finished and would run next week. She had been working on it for the better part of six months, and she had spent the past ten years after journalism school working her way up to this. She was a featured reporter for the Channel 8 News, which was an NBC affiliate. She had done the grunt work; she'd put in the hours and the work. And she was finally here: she was able to pick her own stories, for the most part, and work on them how she saw fit because her producer trusted her. She had earned that trust, and she was ready to find that next big story.

Kenna grabbed tacos at the food truck outside the station, ate them as she walked to her car, and drove home to take two heartburn pills and try to get some sleep. She had tomorrow off, which meant she would spend the day surfing the web for possible new stories. She would also meet Bella for lunch, like she always did on her days off, and they would talk about Bella's job, her husband, and the kids. Kenna would talk about her job. She'd talk about the date she went on last Saturday that went so horribly, she had asked Bella for an out call. Then, she would take a walk to work off all the calories she'd just eaten, come back home, do some more research, and have a TV dinner before she'd Netflix and chill for the rest of the night.

***

When Kenna woke up the following morning, she made her coffee, set her laptop up in her home office, and got to work on research. She had a few potential stories lined up, but there was one that had been drawing her attention the most recently. She'd been putting off diving into it until she could wrap up the other one, but she clicked on the first article she had read that caught her eye several months ago, and reread it for the fourth or fifth time. It was about a social worker in Pleasant Valley that had both an interesting name and an interesting story. Her name was Ripley Fox, and she, somehow, had a magical ability to get children in difficult situations to open up. The woman had had a blog article written about her on just that topic from one of her colleagues. The blogger had interviewed police officers, other social workers, and attorneys along with a few foster parents regarding Ripley's abilities. It caught Kenna's attention all those months ago not only because of the story, but also because of the picture that went along with it. Ripley Fox was incredibly attractive. She was in her mid-twenties, if Kenna had to guess, which made her only a few years younger than Kenna's thirty-two. She had long, very straight dark brown hair and these bright, hazel eyes. She also had a ski slope nose and skin that looked clear and was probably very soft. It wasn't pale, but it also wasn't very tan. Ripley was smiling in the photo, but it wasn't a bright or a wide smile. It was a smile that showed shyness. One side of her mouth was lifted while the other remained somewhat straight. She also had a strong but not too strong jaw, and she was beautiful.

"What's the next story going to be?" Bella asked as she took a bite of her penne pasta.

"I don't know. I have a few small ones I've been working on, but I still have to pick my next full feature." Kenna took a long drink of her iced tea. "I have an idea, but I'm not sure there's much to it. It may just be a one-and-done."

Kenna called her short-term stories her "one-and-done" stories. They would only be a five to ten-minute piece on the nightly news, and that would be the end of it. Her one-and-done pieces tended to only take a couple of weeks, at most, to put together and produce. The longer pieces took months and a lot more work.

"What's it about?" Bella asked.

"I don't know exactly," Kenna replied to her sister and best friend. "There's this social worker who is, apparently, amazing with kids."

"Isn't that part of the job?"

"She had this blog piece written about her, and there were tons of comments. Everyone said she's basically a miracle worker."

"Like the second coming of Mother Teresa?" Bella sipped her water.

"I guess." Kenna finished her own pasta and pushed the plate away. "I don't know. I think there's something to it."

"Then, you should do it."

"I read something else about her that caught my eye. One of the comments mentioned she'd been raised in the system."

"Foster kid?"

"Yeah. I thought it was interesting. She was a foster kid, and now she's helping them. There's something there, right?" she asked.

"Could be," Bella replied. "If you're into it, you should follow it. You've always had good instincts." The woman pushed her own plate away. "Hey, Brady was wondering if you were coming to his wrestling thing on Saturday. It's an all-day thing. I don't think he expects you to be there all day, but he would love it if his favorite aunt were there."

"I'll be there." Kenna smiled at her sister. "He's got that cute thing going for him."

"And you're a big softy, even though you pretend you're not," Bella replied. "Hey, speaking of that… I was thinking about setting you up with this woman from work. She seems like she'd be a big fan of that rough-exterior-but-soft-interior thing you've got going on."

"First of all, how is that a *speaking of*? Secondly, I do not have a rough exterior and soft interior."

"Please. You're all badass most of the time, but if I checked your phone right now, you'd have pictures of my kids, cute baby animals, and just about nothing else," Bella said as she laughed.

"I don't want another date from your job, Bell. The last three didn't go well. What makes you think another one would?"

"I have to keep trying. You're almost thirty-three and have no prospects, Ken." Bella used her nickname for her younger sister.

"I'm not a leper, Bell. This was all by choice."

"No one said you're a leper, McKenna. You just only go on dates with decent women when I'm involved. Outside of that, you meet these young twenty-somethings in gay bars, and you have no idea where they've been."

"You sound like Mom," Kenna replied.

"That's not nice."

"It's the truth." Kenna chuckled. "You're, like, seven years older than me, Bell; you're supposed to have your life together. I'm just at the point where my career is finally stable, and I'm picking my own stories."

"Right. Now, you can make the time to find a nice woman to settle down with."

"Mom!" Kenna pointed at her and laughed.

"Fine. See if I try to help you get some anytime soon."

"Get some? I have no problem getting some whenever I want. I can walk into any lesbian bar and find a woman who is willing to give me some." Kenna laughed at how terrible that sounded. "I don't, though, because I don't want one-night stands, Bell. Isn't that mature of me?"

"Well, it's better than when you were in your early twenties and just figured out girls liked you."

"I knew I liked girls long before then," Kenna replied.

"I said when *they* figured out they liked you. Once you realized all the ladies wanted you, there was no stopping that cocky attitude and an endless stream of women coming out of your apartment each morning."

"And you just assume I had sex with all of them?" Kenna smiled at her sister as the waiter brought their check. "I'll have you know, some of them were too drunk, and I just gave them a place to crash for the night."

"Yeah? What percentage of them was that?" Bella lifted an eyebrow at her.

***

Kenna had done her research and knew that the office of social services was on the fourth floor of the municipal building on Hallow Street. She stood outside the building for a few minutes after her walk. A few people walking past recognized her from the news. She smiled and thanked them for watching, as always. Then, she walked into the building, hit the elevator, and made her way up to the fourth floor.

"I'd like to see Ripley Fox, please," she told the woman at one of the many desks in the wide-open space.

"Do you have an appointment?"

"No." Kenna looked around the room to see if she could spot the woman she actually needed. "My name is Kenna Crawford. I'm a reporter for Channel 8."

"Miss Fox isn't here right now. She's on a home visit. I'd suggest you make an appointment."

"When will she be back?"

"I don't know. That's why I suggest you make an appointment."

The woman looked to be in her sixties and clearly wasn't interested in answering any of Kenna's questions. Kenna had taken a chance that Ripley would be here. She thought she'd spend a few minutes with her, see if there was a story to tell, and leave right after if she was unimpressed. If something came out of it for work, great. If nothing came out of it for work, but she found Ripley Fox interesting beyond just her physical beauty, that would be okay, too. She nodded politely at the woman who probably needed to retire about five years ago and made her way back outside.

"Oh, sorry," Kenna said as she bumped into someone just outside the door to the building.

"Excuse me," a soft voice came back to her. "I wasn't looking where I was going."

"Ripley?" Kenna asked when she realized she'd just bumped into the woman she had come to see.

"Do I know you?"

"You don't watch Channel 8, do you?" Kenna gave her a TV smile.

"I don't watch a lot of TV, no." Ripley still stared at her quizzically. "Did you need something?"

"I was hoping to talk to you." Kenna continued smiling as she took a step to the right to get away from the door.

"About?" Ripley shuttled her bag from one shoulder to the other.

"I'm Kenna Crawford."

No reaction to the introduction followed. Ripley just

stared at Kenna with those gorgeous hazel eyes and then lifted an eyebrow at her, wordlessly asking Kenna to continue. Kenna didn't, though. She just kept staring.

"I'm sorry. I have to go. I have an appointment," Ripley said and made a move back toward the door.

"I'm sorry," Kenna put a gentle hand on Ripley's arm and added, "I did this wrong. I didn't expect to bump into you. Let me start over."

"I have, like, five minutes to get upstairs." Ripley hooked a thumb in the direction of the door.

"It took me only four minutes to get back down, so that gives me sixty seconds then." Kenna smirked this time.

"I have to go all the way to the conference room. I'll give you thirty seconds," Ripley replied.

Kenna's usual charm wasn't working for her. She'd gotten herself many good interviews in her career with a smile and a few strategically placed words, and she'd also gotten a lot of dates.

"I was hoping I could talk to you about a story."

"A story?"

"I wanted to interview you about your uncanny ability to connect with the children you help. I read a blog piece-"

"That thing? I told her not to write that," Ripley said mostly to herself. "I don't talk about my cases."

"Is that why she didn't interview you? Your colleague, I mean. It seemed like she interviewed everyone else except for you."

"I don't do interviews, Miss Crawford." Ripley gave a fake smile and turned to the door.

"Why not?"

"Because I wouldn't want to talk about a child's case."

"It would be confidential. You wouldn't have to reveal any names."

"Can I just say *no, thank you?*" Ripley asked with a concerned expression.

That stood out to Kenna. Ripley didn't have to be polite right now. She could've just turned her down and gone inside. It's not like Kenna hadn't been refused before. She had been shoved into a car by a politician who didn't want to comment about his affair; she'd had hot coffee thrown on her by a business owner who was caught stealing the identities of his customers. She always prepared herself for that kind of reaction, but Ripley was giving her a polite 'no, thank you.'

"Can I ask why?" Kenna asked.

"I don't talk about my cases."

"This isn't about your cases, Miss Fox. This would be about you," Kenna reminded. "About how you're able to get through to these kids."

"It's part of the job," Ripley replied. "We all do this." She pointed to the building. "My colleagues and I do this for those kids. I don't want to exploit them."

Kenna watched those concerned hazel eyes flicker to the door and then back to Kenna again, as if Ripley was considering running away.

"I don't want to exploit them, either. Can I ask you a question?"

"Isn't this whole thing about you asking me questions?" Ripley replied. "And you're down to about five seconds."

"That's it?" Kenna smiled at her.

"Three. Two," Ripley counted down.

Kenna didn't have time to think. She knew that once Ripley was through that door, she'd lose her, and Kenna wanted the story. She wanted to know Ripley's story, and she had one second left; she had to act.

"Go out with me?"

"What?" Ripley's eyes went wide.

"I had one second left." Kenna shrugged and smiled. "I went for it."

CHAPTER 3

"YOU went for it?" Ripley asked. "You don't even know me."

This woman, this reporter person from some local news channel, had interrupted her day to first ask her about some story, and then she had asked her out. She had just asked Ripley out on the front steps of her workplace.

"Is that a rule? People can only ask you out if they know you?" Kenna asked.

Her eyes were kind, and they were a deep shade of blue. She had this warm, blonde hair with touches of golds and reds. Her smile was gorgeous. Ripley could understand how this woman was on television; she had this presence about her that both put Ripley off and also intrigued her to learn more.

"It's not a rule," Ripley replied. "But-"

"I'm sorry. I shouldn't have just done that."

Ripley watched Kenna somewhat deflate, and she started looking around at the other people moving in and out of the building.

"I really do need to go," Ripley said into the awkward silence between them.

"Did you grow up in the system?" Kenna blurted out.

"Excuse me?" Ripley took a step away from her.

"Can we try again?" Kenna asked. "I am not doing this right at all. This isn't me."

"I hope not." Ripley shifted the bag on her shoulder, which she knew was a nervous habit. "I'm going to get back to work now. I don't want a story about my cases or my life to be on any news show."

"I came on strong. I do that." Kenna held up her hands in supplication. "I'm sorry."

"It doesn't matter. I am now late for my next appointment."

Ripley moved to the door and pulled it open.

"Miss Fox, I don't apologize often. It's not something someone in my line of work does regularly, and I've now apologized to you four times. That's more than I think I've apologized to my sister for being late to my nephew's baptism."

Kenna moved to hold the door open for Ripley. When her hand clasped the door handle, it grazed Ripley's hand for only a moment, but a shock registered through Ripley's fingers before it moved into her palm and up her arm. She could have sworn it landed somewhere in her heart.

"Sorry," Kenna added. "That's the fifth time." She shrugged. "I'm a reporter." She then seemed to consider something for a second. "We're aggressive; it's part of the job. But I am sorry."

"Six," Ripley replied.

"Yeah." Kenna's eyes moved from Ripley to a man who exited the building through the door she was still holding. "I pick my own stories, you know. I basically produce my own content. I found the blog about you, and I thought it would be something nice for the world to see. The news is all bad these days. Maybe, there's one three-minute piece about some schoolkid raising money for his mom's cancer research or something, but that's it. I think the world needs more good news." Kenna paused and ran a hand through her long hair. "My sister, Bella, tells me I'm like a bull in a china shop sometimes."

"I do have to go, Miss Crawford."

"Kenna, please."

"Kenna, I wasn't just trying to blow you off when I said I had a meeting in five minutes."

"That's good to know, I guess." Kenna motioned for Ripley to walk through the door with an open hand. "Can I buy you a cup of coffee sometime?"

"Is this for the story or a date?" Ripley turned back to ask her.

Kenna's smirk rapidly appeared as she said, "Would you be interested in either?"

Ripley hated that she liked the way that smirk looked on Kenna's face.

"I might be interested in one." Ripley smiled at her, turned, and walked toward the elevators.

"Which one?" Kenna asked, but Ripley didn't respond.

***

Kenna had fallen into one of her patented research black holes. She had spent the entire rest of the day – after her altercation with Ripley – trying to uncover as much as she could about the woman. She even asked the investigator the station had on retainer to look into Ripley Fox. She fell asleep that night, and for the first time, she wasn't one hundred percent certain she should be diving into Ripley's life like this. The woman was obviously a private person. It had been difficult for Kenna to find much beyond the blog she had already discovered. She worried that digging into Ripley's life might not be the best thing for her to do, but she always had that part of herself to consider.

There was a fire in Kenna. It had always been there. From the moment she was born, her parents had referred to her as their little spitfire. Kenna said what was on her mind all the time, she rarely held back, and she never got nervous. She won her first writing contest at age eight. Then, she won another at age eleven and two more by the time she was fifteen. She joined the daily announcements crew at her high school, and that was where she had discovered her love for being on camera.

Kenna was ambitious, and she made no apologies for it. She worked hard because she wanted to; because she liked how it felt to earn something she really worked for.

Instead of going for the easy stories, the quick-to-wrap-up stories, or the typical stories a local reporter would take on, she hunted like a predator seeking its prey until she found the one story she thought might help her make her mark. She had no idea why, but she felt it in her bones that Ripley Fox was just that story.

"Mal, what do you have for me?" she asked as she sat in one of the station's conference rooms across from the investigator.

"I just started on this, like, eighteen hours ago, Crawford," he replied.

The station was an open floor plan with small desks for their reporters, researchers, fact-checkers, and copy editors. Only the senior editorial staff had real offices, and most of the time, that didn't bother Kenna. She was rarely at her desk for more than an hour anyway. Today, though, she wanted some privacy, and the conference room was the only place on the floor to get it.

"You're the best in the business, Malcolm. I know you have something."

"This girl's squeaky clean." Malcolm tossed a manila file folder in her direction. "She's a saint, according to everything I've found so far."

"I guessed that."

Kenna picked up the file as she rolled her eyes. Malcolm had always been an old-school kind of guy. He could have easily emailed her whatever he had found, but he liked the hard copies. The guy had two rooms of file cabinets back at his office. Kenna thought it redundant and not exactly environmentally friendly, but she wouldn't tell the man how to run his business.

"There is one little blip, though." He pointed at the folder. "Page three."

Kenna flipped to the third page in the folder, removed it, and placed the folder back on the table while she read the copy of the newspaper article in her hand.

"So, this is how she ended up-"

"A foster kid, yeah," he interrupted. "She was in until she aged out at eighteen."

"Ten years?" Kenna said mainly to herself. "She lost everyone," she breathed out. "I had no idea."

"I assumed that was why you asked me to look into her." Malcolm stood. "I'll keep digging, but I'm not sure there's much more to find."

"No, don't." Kenna stood, clutching the piece of paper. "This is enough."

"Are you sure?"

"I'm sure."

Malcolm nodded and left the room without saying anything else. That was just his way. Kenna sat back down and stared at the piece of paper in her hand. She was again being pulled in two different directions, and it was because of a woman she'd spent all of five minutes with the day before.

She went back to her desk. The article had been copied from the Pleasant Valley Voice, and it was dated almost twenty years ago exactly. With that information, Kenna pulled up the article on her computer. She had it physically in her hand, but it was as if she needed to see it in the newspaper's digital archive to ensure it was real. She read the words and leaned back in her chair.

"That poor girl," she muttered to herself.

A few hours later, she found herself at her sister's dinner table, along with Bella eating leftovers. Bella was a nurse and worked odd hours. Kenna was a reporter and worked odd hours. This often meant that they had some alone time late at night, once Bella's husband and kids had gone to sleep. Kenna made her way over to her sister's house for a late-night dinner at least twice a week.

"Her whole family?" Bella asked as she dipped her chopsticks into chow mein.

"Her mother, father, two brothers, and her grandmother," Kenna replied. "She was the only one that survived."

"And she didn't have any other family to take care of her?"

"The article didn't say that, but Mal found some other stuff. Her other three grandparents died prior to the fire. Her father had a brother, but he'd died in some military training exercise two years before it happened. That was it. Her mother didn't have any siblings. He said there was a great aunt that lived in Michigan, but that she had some problems and couldn't take her in."

"So, what are you going to do?" Bella asked and took a drink of her water. "Are you going to try to change her mind?"

"I don't know," Kenna replied. "Something's different about this one."

"How so?"

"I got nervous," Kenna said. "When I was talking to her, I kind of spewed word vomit at her."

"You don't get nervous."

"I know," Kenna stated.

"But you spew word vomit at people all the time; that's kind of your thing," Bella continued. "It's a reporter thing, isn't it? You confront someone outside their place of business and rapid-fire questions at them."

"That's true, but it was different."

"You said that already." Bella glared at her in that sisterly way that said she was annoyed.

"Bell, I asked her out."

"What?" Bella leaned forward in her seat and clasped her water glass in both hands. "Before or after you told her you wanted to do a story on her for the six o'clock news, Ken?"

"Kind of in-between." Kenna shrugged. "I have never done that in my life, Bell."

"Asked a woman out? You ask women out all the time."

"Ask the subject of a potential story out while I'm trying to convince her to actually let me do the story."

"Is she really that hot?" Bella lifted an eyebrow but calmed her initial excitement.

"It's not about that," Kenna replied.

"But she is, right?"

"The woman is gorgeous. Are you satisfied?" Kenna glared back at her sister. "But I just saw something in her. I don't know what, and I can't explain it; it was so strange. I was in the middle of charming her with my usual methods, but she wasn't falling for it. I worried she'd run off."

"Because you really want to do this story?" Bella asked.

"I don't think so." Kenna leaned back in her chair. "I mean, yes – I do really want to do a story on her. She's, apparently, a God's gift to social workers, has an amazing track record with kids and her coworkers, she grew up in the same system, and has a tragic backstory. She's perfect."

"But?" Bella said.

"There was something in her eyes. Plus, even though she was trying to get away from me, she was nice about it. I don't think she wants the story, and I want to respect that."

"Did I just hear my baby sister say she's backing off a story because she wants to respect the subject?" Bella chuckled.

"I didn't say that."

"You asked her out, Ken."

"I know." Kenna put her face in her hands.

"What did she say?"

Kenna lifted her eyes to her sister and dropped her hands. She knew her smirk had returned to her face the moment her sister started laughing at her.

"What?" Kenna laughed out.

"She said yes? Even after all that?"

"No." Kenna laughed again. "She said she might be interested in one of my asks."

"Meaning?"

"That she might want to go out with me or do the story."

"Well, that's ambiguous," Bella replied.

Kenna crossed her arms over her chest as she leaned farther back in her chair. She turned her eyes away from her sister for a moment and looked to the digital picture frame that was on the counter. The first photo she saw was of Bella and her husband. The second that showed up a few seconds later was of Bella and Brady when Brady was around five. The next was Bella and her two boys together. It was from last year at one of Brady's wrestling matches. He was ten in the picture, and Cody would have been eight. It made Kenna think about Ripley: the woman had been eight when she'd lost everyone she cared about. Kenna loved her oldest nephew, but Cody was still clinging to his mom's side consistently. He was still at that age where he wanted his parents around and wasn't worried if it made him less cool. She knew that in a few short years, Cody would pull away entirely, but while he was eight, he still very much needed his parents. She wondered how Ripley had managed to lose everyone and not only survive but thrive. She made a decision then that she had to know more.

CHAPTER 4

RIPLEY completed her second surprise home visit of the day, and it had been a long one. The foster parents were not on her most-liked list. They had eleven foster children living in a four-bedroom house. The five girls all shared one room, while the six boys had been divided into two rooms. The two foster parents were the classic example of people trying to get money by taking in foster kids, and Ripley hated them for it. She had choked down the bile in her throat when she'd entered and found two girls on the floor of their shared bedroom. One of them had on a shirt that was about three sizes too small for her, while the other was sleeping on the mattress with what looked like a dirty sheet on top of it. If Ripley were in charge of the system, this kind of people would not have been allowed to take in foster children. Unfortunately, she wasn't in charge. She also knew the realities: not everyone wanted to be a foster parent. With limited adults willing to take on the burden, to begin with, it often meant children ended up in places like this.

"What do you want me to do, Rip?" her boss, Jessica, asked. "They're technically not violating any laws. There was food in the fridge, right? The heat was on; the place wasn't a disaster, according to your report."

"More," Ripley replied. "I want you to do more."

"With what money? What resources? We're cash-strapped as it is. When was the last time you got even a cost of living raise?"

"I don't want a raise." Ripley sat across from Jessica's desk in their open office. "I want at least five of those kids moved."

"Where?" Jessica tossed the folder containing Ripley's report onto her desk. "Is there a house I don't know about with two loving parents and five spare bedrooms? Do they each make a million a year and have a swimming pool, basketball court in the driveway, and caviar in the fridge?" Jessica leaned forward and clasped her hands together. "Rip, I know this is hard. This job is already the absolute worst sometimes." She lowered her voice. "And I know that for you, it can be even harder. Plus, it's that time of year."

"That's not what this is about," Ripley replied.

"Fine. But, Rip, there's not much we can do about this."

"If I can find another place for them, can we move them?"

"Where is this fictional house that can fit half a dozen kids?" Jessica asked.

"I don't know," Ripley admitted. "I'll figure something out."

She stood and left Jessica sitting at her desk like she always did when Ripley proposed taking kids away from a house she was concerned about. It happened at least once a week. Jessica was used to it by now, this dance they did together, but it didn't change the outcome. Ripley hadn't been successful in moving any child away from any home that was in borderline violation of the fostering rules. She had only seen success when the foster parents were in clear violation, and even then, sometimes, it was an uphill battle.

"Miss Fox?"

Ripley crossed the street to get to the parking lot but heard a voice calling from behind her. She turned to see that Kenna Crawford was walking briskly through the crosswalk before the lights changed, trying to catch up to her. Ripley rolled her eyes and shifted her bag on her shoulder. She hadn't seen Kenna in a week, and she'd been hoping the reporter had moved on to a different story by now; but she'd be lying if she said she never wanted to see Kenna again.

"Miss Crawford, I didn't think I'd see you again." She turned back around to head to her car.

"I asked you to call me Kenna." The woman caught up with her and held out a cup for Ripley to take. "Coffee."

"You brought me coffee?" Ripley asked and took the cup from the outstretched hand. "Is this a bribe?"

"Bribe for what?" Kenna smiled over at her.

"You know what."

Kenna smirked at her and then looked ahead at the parking lot.

"It's just coffee. It's black, and I'm sure it's not good; I got it at the cart on the corner. I thought I'd have more time to pick up my peace-offering before seeing you, but my last appointment ran over. I'll get you something better next time."

"Next time?" Ripley clicked the button on her fob and heard the beep of her car unlocking.

"Next time," Kenna repeated and then swiftly moved in front of Ripley, effectively blocking her from getting into the car. "I'm about to apologize again. Are you ready?"

"What is this, the tenth time?" Ripley lifted a mock-concerned eyebrow.

"Seventh," Kenna corrected with a smile. "And I'm sorry," she added.

"Fine. Accepted. Can I drive home now?"

"Do you have dinner plans?" Kenna asked.

"I do not," Ripley replied.

Kenna smiled at her, and Ripley didn't know why. Maybe Kenna just thought that Ripley's lack of plans gave her an opportunity to ask about that date again, or maybe she just wanted to interview her for a story.

"You're honest to a fault, aren't you?" Kenna asked

while continuing with that smile.

"What? No." Ripley shifted her bag on her shoulder.

"You could have told me you had plans. You could have told me you were exhausted from the long day at work. You could have also shoved me aside, gotten in your car, and driven away. And you didn't."

"I don't go around shoving people."

"I do," Kenna replied, and her smile dimmed a little. "Not physically – my cameraman did that once, and he had to take anger-management classes – my shoving is verbal."

"I guess that's the reporter in you," Ripley said.

"I've kind of always been like this," Kenna replied, took the coffee from Ripley's hand, and slid the bag off Ripley's shoulder. She then passed the coffee back to her and slid Ripley's bag over her own shoulder. "Come to dinner with me," she said softly.

"I would prefer not to," Ripley replied.

"Did you read *Bartleby* in high school?" Kenna asked with a laugh.

"I read a lot of things in high school," Ripley replied.

"I can see you are not about to make this easy on me."

"I don't even know what *this* is," Ripley said. "What do you even want from me, Kenna? Are you after a story? Are you asking me out? Are you asking me out just to get a story?"

"Why are you assuming I have ulterior motives?" Kenna fired back.

"Because you approached me a few days ago asking to do a story on me."

"Because you have a story to tell, Ripley," Kenna said. "You have a great story to tell."

"Great? What do you even know about me? You know I'm a social worker and I was raised in the system; that's it. What do you know about my story?" Ripley shot back. "Can I just take my bag and go, please?" she asked and reached out for her bag with one hand. "And you can take this back. I only drink decaf after five." She held out the coffee cup.

"You lost your whole family, made it through the system, then graduated college – hell, the fact that you even made it to college is a story, Ripley. With what you went through, I don't even know how you made it through high school; and you went to grad school! You have multiple degrees, and you're great at your job. You could be an inspiration to other kids who-"

"I just want to go home." Ripley dumped the coffee onto the pavement and tossed the now empty cup into the trash can nearby. When she returned, she held out her hand again for her bag. "Please."

"You don't like fighting with people, do you?" Kenna lifted an eyebrow as she passed Ripley's bag back over to her.

"I fight when it's important," Ripley said as she took her bag and slid it over her shoulder again. "Good night, Miss Crawford."

"Back to last names now?" Kenna asked as she stepped aside. "I guess all I can say then is have a good night, Miss Fox."

Ripley nodded, opened the car door, tossed her bag into the passenger's seat, and climbed into the car. Then, she closed the door and put the key in the ignition. When she finally looked to her left just to see that Kenna was still standing next to her car, the woman knocked on the driver's side window with her closed fist. Ripley knew she could just drive away. All she had to do was put the car in reverse, and she would be home in fifteen minutes, eating a TV dinner in front of her laptop while she reviewed case files. She didn't have to roll the window down to talk to Kenna. She didn't have to, but she did.

"Yes?" she asked without looking at Kenna.

"Your work ID fell off your bag," Kenna stated as she passed Ripley's work security badge through the now open window.

"Oh. Thanks," Ripley said.

She reached to the side and took the badge from

Kenna's hand, which pulled away abruptly. Then, Ripley turned her eyes to watch Kenna walk away as she, herself, shoved her badge into the outer pocket of her bag and leaned her head back against the headrest. What exactly had she been hoping for? She had told Kenna no to the story and the date multiple times. Was she expecting the woman to be a masochist and keep trying? Ripley finally rolled up the window, put the car in reverse, and drove home.

After she prepared her TV dinner of grilled chicken and vegetables, she moved to the bed with her laptop in tow. She'd planned to review some case files but found herself searching for the name 'Kenna Crawford' instead. A Wikipedia page gave Ripley some basics. If the information was correct, Kenna was thirty-two. She had grown up in Freemont, which was one town over. Kenna had only moved to Pleasant Valley after school when she'd gotten the job at Channel 8. Ripley watched several clips of the attractive and competent reporter, including one where she had somehow gotten a city councilor to admit on camera that he'd siphoned money from the budget to pay for his new summer home in the Bahamas. Kenna was good. She was very good.

Ripley fell asleep to one of the longer interviews Kenna had done the year prior. When she woke up, it was to a cold sweat on her skin. She had seen them again. This time, she had not only seen them; she'd felt them. She had felt the heat on her skin, and it was as if she was still trapped inside that house nearly twenty years ago. Ripley shook them out of her mind, did her normal workout, and then showered before she closed her laptop, packed it up, and headed to the office. When she finally made her way into the building and sat in her uncomfortable desk chair, she glanced up to see Jessica talking to none other than Kenna Crawford.

CHAPTER 5

"AND the story would be on social work?" Jessica asked Kenna while leaning back in her chair. "I'm not exactly sure what the appeal is there."

"It would be on a few social workers and their jobs. I'm trying to highlight the work you all do to help these kids." Kenna leaned forward and clasped her hands on top of Jessica's desk. "I think it's important that people see the long hours, the struggles, the impact you make on the lives of these children. I have a few people already lined up to talk to me."

"People here?" Jessica seemed surprised.

"I have a few kids I've reached out to."

"You reached out to children?" Jessica lifted a concerned eyebrow.

"They're all over eighteen. They were in the system and agreed to be interviewed about it."

"Who, exactly?"

"One has asked to remain anonymous, so we'll use a pseudonym for them and block their face, obviously. The other two – I'm not prepared to give their names out yet until they tell me it's okay. They've agreed to the interview, but not to being on camera yet."

"So, you have three former foster kids that you're going to interview about their time in the system? This is a good story? You're not just trying to get my buy-in so that you can rake us over the coals?"

"No, I promise you, this story will have a positive spin to it. It's not about railroading. It's about making sure your people get the credit they deserve," Kenna explained.

"What are you doing here?"

Kenna turned to see Ripley Fox standing behind her chair.

"Do you two know each other?" Jessica asked.

"Yes," Kenna replied before Ripley had a chance. She turned back to Jessica and added, "I've approached Miss Fox about an interview as well."

"As well?" Ripley asked her while moving to the other side of Jessica's desk and folding her arms over her chest.

"Kenna was asking for my approval to do a story on a few of our social workers. She's already spoken with a few of our former kids," Jessica spoke to Ripley but remained looking at Kenna.

"You did? I told you-"

"Former, Ripley," Kenna said. "They're all adults now. I haven't talked to a single kid that's still in the system."

"Why is this so important to you?" Ripley asked.

"Because it's important, period," Kenna explained. "People should know how hard you all work and how you benefit so many children."

"I think this is a good idea," Jessica said. "I'd love it if the news actually said something good about us and the kids we try to help. Maybe it will get some people to step up and foster."

"It's not just about you." Kenna knew what Ripley was concerned about. "It would be about a few people."

"But it would include me?" Ripley asked. "You went to my boss?"

"What's going on here? You two obviously know each other." Jessica rolled her chair to the side so that she could look at them both at the same time. "Is there some history here I should know of before I agree to this?"

"So, you're agreeing?" Kenna asked with a hopeful smile.

"I'm considering." Jessica pointed at her. "Rip?"

Ripley stared at Kenna. Kenna tried to keep up her smile, but the look in Ripley's eyes told her she'd gone too far. It was an expression Kenna knew all too well. She'd seen it time and again when she encountered resistance.

"I don't want to be a part of it," Ripley stated. "If you

choose to involve others, though, Jess, there's not much I can do about it. I'll be at my desk."

Ripley uncrossed her arms and moved back around to the front of Jessica's desk before moving across the room to her own desk. Kenna watched her sit down in her chair and try to bury her face behind a file. She also watched Ripley's eyes lift high enough to see that Kenna was staring at her. It was kind of hot. Ripley stared at her with heat in her eyes. Sure, it was the heat from anger, but it was sexy as hell. Kenna knew smirking back at her was a horrible idea because she'd already pissed the woman off, but she did it anyway, more out of instinct than anything else, before she turned around to continue her conversation with Jessica.

***

Ripley was seething. Kenna Crawford had just walked out of the office after talking to Jessica for over an hour. She had even taken notes. She'd written things down. That could only mean that Jessica had agreed to the story and that Kenna would be getting started soon. Ripley could only hope that Jessica wouldn't make her be a part of it. Jessica was her boss, after all. If the woman insisted, Ripley would have no choice, but as she tried to think of ways to get out of it anyway, Jessica approached her desk.

"It's after six. You should be gone by now," she said as she sat on the edge of Ripley's desk.

"Did you agree to do a story?"

"I did," Jessica replied. "It's a good deal for us, Ripley. We could always use a little good publicity. You remember Christopher Marshall. He did a number on our reputation when he got arrested."

Christopher Marshall had been a seventeen-year-old boy who had been placed with a foster parent at age sixteen. Unfortunately, he had been abused by that foster parent, and to prevent future abuse, Christopher had stabbed the man and gotten himself arrested. Ripley hadn't been involved in his case, but it had opened a whole can of worms. People wanted to assume every foster parent had an ulterior motive. There also had been several investigations. Jessica's old manager, Ripley's director, had resigned and taken full responsibility for missing the signs. The social worker that had been assigned to the case had been terminated.

"But do I have to be a part of it?" Ripley asked.

"Not if you don't want to." Jessica stood and held out a piece of folded paper. "She left this for you."

"For me?" Ripley took the piece of paper that she could tell had come from Kenna's notebook.

"I don't know what's going on with you two, but she did tell me that she'd already reached out to you about the story featuring you."

"She did." Ripley unfolded the piece of paper. "I told her no."

"I get it, Rip. We're going to do the story, though. I'll pick a few people that will look good on camera and represent us well. I'll leave you out of it."

"Thank you," Ripley replied.

She stared down at the piece of paper in her hand and smiled for a moment.

"What did she write?" Jessica leaned in a little.

"Nothing."

Ripley tucked the piece of paper into her pocket.

"Are you okay with this? I'll do my best to make sure there's no impact on you."

"I'll do my best, I guess." Ripley stood and began packing her things. "I should get out of here. The cleaning crew comes at seven, and they hate having to work around me."

"We're usually the last two here, aren't we? What does that say about us?" Jessica asked wistfully. "Want to come by for dinner? Carter is cooking tonight, so you know it will be good."

Jessica's husband was a private chef. Ripley had been

to their house several times to enjoy his cooking, but tonight was not a night she planned to spend with her boss and her family.

"I think I'd rather head home."

"Okay. Have a good weekend."

Jessica made her way back over to her own desk, packed up, and was in the elevator before Ripley had finished organizing her desk for a fresh start on Monday. She hit the elevator herself moments later and made her way to the parking lot, where she found Kenna Crawford standing next to her car.

"Are you stalking me, Miss Crawford?"

"That depends… Are you for or against stalkers?" Kenna asked with a smirk.

"Against," Ripley replied as she arrived at her car.

"Then, I'm just standing outside, waiting for a friend."

"Who's that friend?" Ripley gave a smirk right back to her.

"Dave. He works on the third floor." Kenna pointed to the building behind them.

"Oh." Ripley crinkled her eyebrows in confusion.

"I'm totally kidding." Kenna laughed. "You should see your face. You're cute when you're confused."

"I was just leaving." Ripley changed her expression. "And I'm kind of mad at you, so I don't know why I'm even talking to you right now."

"Because I passed you a note in study hall," Kenna replied and, once again, took Ripley's bag off her shoulder. "Did you read it?"

"Yes, it was the world's greatest prose," Ripley replied. "I'm sorry. I'm sorry. I'm sorry," she said the words that Kenna had written out loud.

"I just wanted to get ahead of it; figured I'd owe you a few after today," Kenna replied.

"You don't plan to let this drop, do you?" Ripley asked.

"Which part? The story or the date?"

"Either one." Ripley squinted. "Both." She glared at Kenna, who was still smirking at her. "You're annoying."

"You're right." Kenna slid Ripley's bag over her own shoulder. "I owe you a drink."

"No, you don't."

"I feel like I owe you a drink," Kenna corrected.

Ripley considered for a moment.

"If I go for one drink with you, will you leave me alone?"

"If you go for one drink with me, I'll agree to play it by ear," Kenna suggested.

"I'm not much of a drinker."

"Come on, Ripley." Kenna laughed. "I'm trying here. One drink. You can have water, if you want."

"Fine. We can walk. There's a bar down the block." Ripley pointed to the left.

"Of course, there is. This block is filled with municipal buildings and government employees that need booze."

Ripley laughed. She wondered how long it had been since she had laughed. The sound felt foreign coming from her body, but she did her best not to let Kenna see that it was unfamiliar to her as they began walking.

"You don't have to carry my bag," Ripley said after a few moments of silence.

"I've been trying to carry your bag for like a week." Kenna laughed out. "You kept turning me down."

"Why?"

"Why did you keep turning me down? I don't know. If I knew that, I probably would have figured out a way to change your mind," Kenna said and glanced at her with a smile.

"Why are you pursuing this?" Ripley asked.

"You or the story?"

"Can we please stop this and just separate our topics? Why are you still pursuing the story? Then, you can answer the other question."

"Okay." Kenna laughed lightly as they passed a

bookstore. "I am pursuing this story because I think there is a story. It's as simple as that."

"But you're okay with me not being involved? With it not being about me?"

"No, but I'm hoping I'll be able to change your mind."

"Kenna, I don't-"

"If you don't, you don't," Kenna interrupted. "There's still a good story here, Rip."

"Rip?"

"I heard Jessica call you that." Kenna moved a few steps ahead of her and opened the door for Ripley to enter the bar. "Anyway, I'd love to write a story about you. Whether it's this one or another one, it doesn't matter. I just think you have a story to tell."

"I don't." Ripley turned to wait for Kenna to join her.

"Everyone has a story to tell, Ripley." Kenna stood in front of her and gave Ripley a shy smile. "I'd love to hear yours. It can be for a story, or it can be off the record. Come on, let's sit over there." She pointed to a booth in the corner.

Ripley walked behind her as they made their way through the semi-crowded bar. Kenna had been right: it was filled with men in suits and ties and a few women in business-casual or professional clothes. Kenna sat down, resting Ripley's bag beside her in the booth. Ripley followed on the other side and felt a bit naked without her bag next to her. They didn't say anything as they settled. A bartender approached and tossed two cardboard coasters with a beer logo onto the table.

"What can I get you?" she asked.

Kenna nodded at Ripley, and Ripley said, "Water, please."

"And I'll have water, too," Kenna added.

"Should I bring you a menu or something?"

"No, I think we're okay for now. She only agreed to a drink." Kenna pointed at Ripley while glancing at the bartender.

"You can't take up a table for water," the bartender

stated.

"Are you sure you don't want anything?" Kenna asked Ripley.

"One drink, remember?" Ripley said. "A quick one."

"Manhattan for me then, and a shot for her." Kenna pointed at Ripley again. "I'm thinking something sweet." She winked at her, and Ripley rolled her eyes. "Yeah, give her a pineapple upside-down cake."

"A what?" Ripley asked.

"I'll be right back." The bartender returned to her post.

"What is a pineapple upside-down cake?"

"Vodka, pineapple juice, and grenadine; very little alcohol in the thing."

"I told you I wasn't-"

"Much of a drinker; I remember. You also said one drink, and then you added the condition that it had to be a fast one. There's not really a faster drink than a shot," Kenna said. "Can I answer your other question now?"

"What other question?"

"You asked if I was going to stop pursuing you."

"That's not exactly what I asked," Ripley reminded.

"Sure, it was," Kenna stated. "Here's the truth." She folded her hands on the table and leaned in. "I'm going to say one thing you might like and probably some things you'd hate. I need you to listen to all of it, though."

"Why? Why is this so important to you?"

"I don't know," Kenna replied. "That's the truth. I honestly don't know. I just know that I want to tell a story, and I'd like that story to be about you."

"That's the thing I'll hate?"

"No, Ripley. The thing you'll hate is that I've done a lot of research on you in the past week. I had the station's investigator track information down. I know about the fire."

Ripley swallowed.

CHAPTER 6

KENNA tried to figure out what Ripley was thinking. Ripley's expression showed frustration but also, somehow, a little relief. The woman was silent, though, and hadn't spoken in the past several minutes. The bartender dropped their drinks in front of them and set the check on the edge of the table before walking away. Ripley took the shot glass with the yellow and red liquid swirling inside and tipped it back along with her head as if it was the strongest shot she'd ever taken. She set the empty glass on the table and pointed at it.

"Can we have another?" Kenna half-yelled to the bartender. "Do you want something stronger?"

"No," Ripley said and took a drink of her water.

"I guess we should get up to eleven apologies now," Kenna said.

"Why are you doing this?" Ripley mumbled as she set her water glass down.

Kenna saw the hurt in Ripley's eyes then, as the bartender dropped a second shot in front of her. Ripley downed it and took another drink of water. The shot was sweet, Kenna knew, but if Ripley didn't usually drink much, the alcohol would hit her fast if she kept going at that rate.

"I'm not trying to hurt you," she replied softly.

"Well, you're failing." Ripley reached across the table for the Manhattan Kenna had yet to touch. She tipped it to her lips and took a long swallow. The expression she made upon tasting the drink was so adorable, Kenna couldn't help but smile at her. Ripley set it back down on the table and slid it slowly back to Kenna.

"I'm sorry if bringing it up causes you pain. That's not my intention."

"Then, why bring it up at all, Kenna? For some stupid story?" Ripley asked.

"At first, yes. I was following a lead I thought could turn into a story. I had heard of you. I knew you were great at your job and that you'd been a foster kid. I didn't know why, so I kept digging. That's what I do, Ripley; I'm an investigative reporter. My job is to dig until I find what I'm looking for, and I won't apologize for doing my job well." Kenna paused. "But I will apologize if I've hurt you."

"Do you apologize to all your *leads?*" Ripley asked with an emphasis on the word 'leads.'

"No," Kenna replied.

"Why me then?"

"Because I've asked you out multiple times now, and you still haven't officially said no." Kenna shrugged. "Look, will you talk to me if I say everything is off the record? Nothing you say here tonight will go into the story."

"This isn't a date, Kenna."

"No, it's not, but it *can* just be two friends talking, if that's what you need."

"We're not friends, Kenna. We're, at most, acquaintances."

Kenna took a long drink of her Manhattan before she set the glass back down and motioned·to the bartender to bring another. She also pointed at Ripley and nodded to indicate she'd have another one as well. Since Ripley had already broken her rule about one drink, Kenna figured another one wouldn't hurt.

"You're still sitting here, Ripley," Kenna replied. "No one is forcing you to have more than one drink with me tonight. You've held up your end of the deal. You could leave now, and I wouldn't follow you out. I wouldn't ask you for coffee, drinks, or dinner again, and I'd leave you out of the story. So, why don't you start by asking yourself why you're still sitting there?"

***

Ripley hated to admit, but Kenna was right. As the third shot was placed in front of her along with Kenna's new Manhattan, Ripley knew she didn't really want to go. She wanted to stay and talk to this woman. She downed her third shot, pulled Kenna's old Manhattan to her side of the table, and finished it as well. That earned a small laugh from her companion, who tipped her new drink to her own lips. Ripley clasped her hands around the empty glass, save the ice, the orange peel, and cherry.

"I don't know," Ripley admitted. "Honestly, I don't, but I don't want to go."

"Well, that's something, isn't it?" Kenna asked with no sign of that confident smirk.

"I guess."

Ripley started to feel it. She had only been drunk a handful of times, and each of those times, she had been by herself and in her own apartment. She would only sip on drinks when at work functions or the rare party she had been invited to. At dinners with Jessica's family, she would maybe finish one glass of wine. Ripley knew she shouldn't have finished three shots where the sugar hid the flavor of the alcohol, along with basically an entire Manhattan, but she couldn't do anything about that now.

"I know what the news said of what happened. Do you want to tell me what really happened?"

"No," Ripley said and felt the fog of intoxication take over. "Can we talk about something else?"

"What do you want to talk about?" Kenna took a drink and leaned forward.

"Why did you become a reporter?" Ripley asked.

"It's the only thing I've ever wanted to do."

"That's it?" Ripley asked. "That's all I get?"

She knew she wasn't slurring her speech, but she also knew it was coming out a little slower than normal now.

"Ask me a better question, and you might get a better answer."

"Spoken like a true reporter," Ripley said.

"That I am." Kenna smiled and took another drink.

Ripley noticed another shot had been placed in front of her by the bartender. She looked up at the woman and gave her a confused expression.

"From that guy over there." The bartender pointed at a man sitting by himself at the bar and walked off.

"You have a fan," Kenna said and leaned to the side so she could see the man more clearly. "He's not bad."

Ripley turned back to Kenna after giving the man a polite nod.

"He's not my type."

"Who is your type?"

"Normally, no one." Ripley took the shot and downed it. "Am I obligated to go talk to him now?"

Kenna laughed and said, "No." She leaned forward while turning her head to the side to make eye contact with the guy before reaching across the table to clasp Ripley's hand. The man's eyes went wide, and he turned away. "I think he gets it."

Ripley felt the warmth of Kenna's hand along with the warmth from the alcohol she'd imbibed. She wanted to entwine their fingers. She wanted to flip her palm over and show Kenna that she was interested in being more than mere acquaintances, but that wasn't Ripley's style. Instead, she slowly pulled her hand away and used it to lift her water glass to her lips. Despite her thoughts feeling muddled, she knew one of the things she did well at her job was ask kids questions to get them to open up. She wondered if it would translate to her current situation.

"Start at the beginning," she said.

"Beginning of what?" Kenna smirked at her. "Time?"

"Describe the first moment you knew you wanted to be a journalist. What was it like? What do you remember? How did it make you feel? What did you do?"

"Wait a second. I thought *I* was the journalist. You're rapid-firing there." She held up her hands in supplication. "I will answer all of those, but I think you should stick with water and, maybe, go back on your whole coffee-after-five thing. I can see if they have decaf."

"I'm okay."

Kenna squinted at her as if to verify that statement before she replied, "I remember being nine years old."

Kenna told Ripley the story of how she used to interview her stuffed animals. She later interviewed her mom, trying to get the woman to extend her bedtime for another half hour, and when her mother agreed, Kenna said she'd been hooked. She continued to talk about how she worked on the daily announcements in high school and fell in love with being on camera, but the research appealed to her just as much. Ripley listened as intently as she could, but Kenna's mouth was just so nice. Her lips had a slight gloss on them, and it hit the light as they moved. Kenna had licked her lips a few times after taking drinks of her Manhattan. Ripley liked how she did that and found herself staring more than once. She had asked the bartender to refill her water, and she had gulped that down in an attempt to catch up with the alcohol, but it was too late.

"It's getting late," Ripley said as she glanced at the time on her phone.

"Is it?" Kenna asked and turned Ripley's phone to face her. "Not for a Friday night."

"You just touch and take, don't you?" Ripley asked.

"What?" Kenna laughed lightly.

Ripley realized what she'd said probably hadn't come out right.

"You took my phone, you took my bag, you-"

"You took my drink," Kenna interjected. "Turnabout and all that."

47

"What?" It was Ripley's turn to question.

"Never mind." Kenna laughed. "It's not even nine yet, but if you want to go, you're free. Just let me drive you."

"Oh." Ripley realized something. "I cannot drive."

"No, you cannot." Kenna laughed again. "I'll take you home, okay?"

"You got me drunk." She squinted across the table at Kenna.

"No, I absolutely did not. You did that to yourself, Rip. Let me pay, and we'll get out of here."

"I can pay."

"I'm sure you can, but I invited you." Kenna stood.

Ripley watched as she made her way to the bar and passed her credit card to the bartender. Once they were paid up, Kenna returned, reached for Ripley's bag, slung it over her own shoulder, and then reached for Ripley's hand.

"You are carrying my bag," Ripley said after a moment.

"Better than you doing it right now. I don't want you to break your laptop."

They made their way out of the bar, and Ripley noticed Kenna was still holding on to her hand. Their fingers weren't entwined, but neither of them let go until they walked the half block to Kenna's car. Kenna opened the door for Ripley, who climbed into the passenger's seat and immediately placed her head back against the headrest. Kenna placed her bag in the back seat and climbed in next to her.

"Where are we going?" Ripley asked.

"To wherever you live, Ripley." Kenna laughed and turned the ignition. "Are you too far gone to give me directions?"

"Turn left, right, right, left, and right."

Kenna laughed more and reached over into Ripley's front jeans pocket, where Ripley had stuffed her phone before leaving the bar.

"Is your address programmed in?"

"Hey, you can't-"

"Just getting your phone." Kenna smiled at her. "I'm going to use it to get you home, okay?"

"Password is my mom's birthday. You probably know when that is, since you researched me."

Ripley's eyes closed, and Kenna took Ripley's hand. Ripley's eyes opened again at the contact, but before she could smile, she watched Kenna take her index finger and place it to the phone to unlock it with her fingerprint.

"You need to get the facial recognition one; much easier when you're like this."

"I'm never like this," Ripley said.

CHAPTER 7

RIPLEY wasn't lying when she said she rarely drank. She had a very low tolerance. So much so that she'd fallen asleep on the short drive to her apartment. Kenna had been lucky in that there were only four units in this two-story apartment building, and Ripley's name was on the outside buzzer. Ripley, herself, was resting against Kenna's side as Kenna searched Ripley's bag for the woman's keys.

"Victory," she nearly shouted as she pulled out a keyring with car keys and two other keys attached and held it in front of Ripley's face. "Rip, which one?"

"Number fourteen," Ripley said with her head hung low.

"Yes, I know; you're in unit fourteen."

"No, the key says it." Ripley used her right hand to snatch the keys from Kenna. "Here."

Ripley held up one key from the bunch, and sure enough, the number fourteen was etched into the metal.

"Okay, I got it."

Kenna took the key and unlocked the outer door before ushering Ripley inside. She quickly saw the number fourteen on the second door on the left and took Ripley's hand. She pulled the woman along and used the same key again to unlock it. Ripley immediately walked through the door, leaving Kenna alone in the hallway.

"I haven't cleaned," she said.

Kenna smiled for a second, shook her head, and made

her way inside the apartment, assuming that comment meant Ripley was inviting her inside. What she saw was a sparsely decorated, decent-sized apartment. The television on top of a small table was covered up by a shirt or a sweater. There was a coffee table, a sofa, and not much else in the living room. The dining area had a small square table with files all over it, and the kitchen was mostly out of view. Kenna walked in a little farther inside and could see a door leading to a bedroom, one leading to a bathroom, and likely, a closet. The living room wasn't filthy, but the treadmill in the corner did have a sports bra hanging off it and what looked like yoga pants on the floor next to it. Ripley rushed from item to item and picked each up in turn before moving into the bedroom. She emerged with nothing in hand but looked worse for wear.

"Are you okay?" Kenna took the ten steps to get to Ripley, who looked a little pale and possibly dizzy as she leaned into the doorframe of her bedroom.

"I wasn't expecting company," Ripley said.

"I guess that means you're not on Tinder." Kenna laughed at her own joke. "If you're that concerned about a few pieces of clothing, you probably don't bring over women for one-night stands often, huh?"

Ripley gave her a look that told her she had no idea what Kenna was talking about.

"I don't do that," she replied.

"Bad joke."

"I'm going to go to sleep," Ripley said and hooked a thumb into her bedroom.

"How about you drink some water first? Take some ibuprofen or something?"

"I'll be okay, Kenna."

"I feel bad, Ripley. I didn't mean for you to have a massive hangover tomorrow."

Ripley took a step backward and faltered. Kenna's arms were on her hips in an instant.

"I'm fine," Ripley said softly.

"Okay. Get in bed," Kenna ordered. "I'll get you water and scavenge in your medicine cabinet. Come on."

Kenna gave Ripley a gentle shove toward her bed, and the woman didn't seem to have the energy to argue. Ripley stood at the side of her bed before she sat down on the edge. Kenna knelt in front of her and removed both of her shoes, which were adorable ballet flats in beige that bordered on light-pink and went well with her beige slacks, her blazer, and the soft pink blouse beneath. Kenna moved the shoes over to the small dresser in the corner so that Ripley wouldn't trip over them in the morning, and then went to the bathroom.

The bathroom contents were sparse as well. There was next to nothing on the counter. One cup, likely for rinsing after brushing her teeth, rested next to an electric toothbrush in its charger. Kenna turned to the bathtub. The shower curtain was open, and she could see Ripley's body wash, a razor, shampoo, conditioner, and that was it. She didn't want to be nosy and go through the cabinet beneath the counter, but as she thought about her own bathroom and how crowded it was even with two sinks at her disposal, her curiosity got the better of her. Ripley had to have at least a few things tucked out of view. Kenna also needed to find something for her to take to, hopefully, prevent a hangover. Ripley had no medicine cabinet hidden behind a mirror.

Kenna bent and opened the singular cabinet. Inside, she found some backup toilet paper, backup shampoo, conditioner, and just a few medications. One was for allergies, and she wondered if Ripley normally took that before bed or in the morning. She pulled it out just in case. Besides a couple of cleaning products pushed toward the back, that was about all the cabinet held. Luckily, Ripley had some painkillers that should help the impending hangover. Kenna pulled that bottle out, grabbed the cup, filled it with water, and returned to the bedroom, where she found Ripley trying to slide her pants down her legs while still lying in bed.

"Hold on," Kenna said.

"I'm tired," Ripley replied with an adorably soft voice.

Kenna smiled as she placed the cup on the bedside table, opened the bottle, and took out a few capsules. She set the bottle down, lifted Ripley's head, and passed her the cup of water. She then put the pills in Ripley's free hand and kept her own on the back of Ripley's head while she took the pills and passed the cup back. Kenna placed it back on the table and lowered Ripley's head back on the pillow.

Kenna moved to the foot of the bed, where she pulled Ripley's slacks off her legs, carefully avoiding taking a peep at the near half-naked woman on the bed in front of her. She folded the pants and placed them on the dresser. When she turned back, she saw Ripley was now trying to shrug off her blazer. Before Kenna could stop them, her eyes moved to her legs, that were now bare. God, Ripley had nice legs. Kenna cleared her throat, moved back to Ripley's side, and took the blazer off. Ripley's hands went to the buttons of her shirt next, and Kenna about lost her damn mind. Ripley clearly had no inhibitions when drunk and was about to strip in front of her.

"Hey, hold on there, Rip," Kenna said. "Where are your sleep clothes?"

"Drawer," Ripley replied while maneuvering the second button free.

Kenna moved to the dresser, opened the top drawer, and realized that was Ripley's underwear drawer. She resisted the urge to look through it but did notice at least one lacy, pink pair. She bit her lower lip so hard, she thought she might draw blood. She turned back to Ripley moments later with a pair of shorts and a t-shirt in hand. She averted her gaze as Ripley was now clad only in her bra and panties. Kenna tossed the shorts onto the bed and moved back around to Ripley's side.

"You put those on." She handed Ripley the shirt. "And this. I'm going into your kitchen to get you a large glass of water. When I get back in here, you better be clothed."

"Okay," Ripley replied halfheartedly.

Kenna shook her head and smiled before she left for the kitchen. She continued to shake her head as she filled a glass with water. How had she ended up at Ripley Fox's apartment late on a Friday night? How was she taking care of the drunk woman? How was Ripley half-naked? How was Kenna in the kitchen when Ripley was half-naked? She silently scolded herself. She wasn't the type of woman who would take advantage like that, but she'd had fun with Ripley.

Once they'd gotten over that initial awkwardness, things had gone well. They'd dropped the topic of Kenna's story and didn't speak again about the fire. Kenna had talked about how she had gotten into journalism. She had talked about Bella and the rest of her family. They had also shared a few laughs, and Kenna had enjoyed seeing Ripley smile. That was it. No pressure. They hadn't even gotten to Ripley's work, what had brought the woman to it, or what made her so good at it. Kenna had only gone to Ripley's office to convince Ripley's boss to allow her to do the story.

As she turned off the faucet, Kenna felt a little bad about that. She had shown up when she had known Ripley would be out of the office. She had specifically gone there with the intent of getting Jessica to wrangle her employee into doing the story and even brought up Christopher Marshall as a reason their department needed good publicity. Once Ripley had shown up, though, Kenna knew she'd be in trouble. That was an interesting concept. She had never cared before what a subject would think about her doing something like that. Tonight, for some reason, Kenna cared about what Ripley thought, despite the fact that, initially, she had decided not to tell the woman she'd intended on doing the story about her until she'd seen her standing next to Jessica at the office.

"Do you have everything you need?" Kenna asked when she set the glass on the table. "I put some more ibuprofen here for tomorrow morning. Oh, do you need these now?" She held up the allergy pills she'd found earlier.

"I take those in the morning." Ripley opened her eyes, squinted them at the bottle, and closed her eyes again.

"I'll put them back," Kenna replied.

"Are you staying?" Ripley asked just as Kenna had turned to go back to the bathroom.

"Here?" Kenna questioned as she turned back to Ripley, who was still lying down but had opened her eyes to meet Kenna's.

"You can, if you want. It's late," Ripley replied with a softness in her glance that had Kenna reconsidering her stance on taking advantage of her.

"I'm going to go. I'm only about ten minutes away from here. I'll be okay."

Ripley's lips, that had been in a straight line, formed into a small frown as she said, "Okay."

Kenna moved toward the bed and sat on the edge of it next to Ripley. She turned to her and smiled down at the woman with the still magically straight dark hair that was now fanned over the pillow. Her eyes were heavy. Her expression was sad.

"Do you want me to stay?" Kenna asked.

"You don't want to stay," Ripley replied.

"I never said that."

"Why are we always talking around each other?" Ripley asked.

"I don't know. I guess that's our thing." Kenna smiled down at her.

"I don't have a lot of friends," Ripley said after a moment. "None, really."

"And that's what I am? A friend?" Kenna asked with a hint of disappointment unhidden in her tone.

"Better than a nuisance," Ripley smirked up at her.

"You are way too drunk to be using big words like that," Kenna replied.

"I'm starting to come out of it."

"Then, I should go if you're okay," Kenna said.

"Kenna, please stay," Ripley replied with her hand moving to Kenna's bicep. "I could use a friend tonight. There's a reason I don't drink a lot."

As Kenna took Ripley in, she saw that a bit of fear had taken over her expression.

"I can sleep on the couch," Kenna replied. "Do you have an extra blanket or something?"

"Can you sleep in here?" Ripley asked. "Just in case."

"In case of what?" Kenna asked.

"You can borrow something to wear – just grab whatever you want. I only have my toothbrush in there, but the head is changeable, and I have extras in the cabinet," she explained.

"You just scolded me for us talking around each other." Kenna lifted an eyebrow at her, but Ripley's expression didn't change from serious. "I'll change in the bathroom and come back in, okay?"

"Thank you."

When Kenna stood and headed to the bathroom, she looked back once to see Ripley lying on top of her blanket, watching her as she went. Ripley looked so small. Kenna smiled softly at her, made her way into the bathroom, and placed both of her hands on the counter. This was definitely not how she'd planned to spend her night.

CHAPTER 8

RIPLEY'S thoughts still weren't clear, but she did remember asking Kenna to stay the night, which would explain the body lying next to her and the soft sounds of that body breathing. That would also explain the arm that was on Ripley's stomach, rubbing circles over her shirt, and the eyes staring down at her as she opened her own.

"Are you okay?" Kenna asked her, still with sleep in her eyes.

"Why?" Ripley asked.

"You're sweating. And you made some sounds a minute ago," Kenna replied.

How did this woman still look so put-together in the morning? Her hair was slightly ruffled but not much more than a light breeze would cause. Kenna had, apparently, washed her face the night before because it was void of makeup, but she was still gorgeous with those blue eyes of hers and light hair. Her face showed her concern. Her hand still moved on Ripley's stomach as she waited for Ripley to reply.

"Sorry."

"You did that a few times throughout the night. I'd hear you and wake up. I didn't know what to do at first, but I rubbed your back for a minute, and you stopped. So, I thought I'd do that this time as well, but you were on your back, so I had to settle for your stomach. Sorry."

Kenna pulled her hand back and rested it on her side with her head on her elbow.

"I should apologize to you."

"You already did." Kenna smiled at her. "What's going on?"

"I'm used to only waking myself up." Ripley tried to play it off by giving Kenna a shrug.

"Tell me," Kenna said with a little more force in her tone than she'd been using.

"Tell you what?"

"Rip, tell me what's going on. I think I know, but I'd like to hear it from you."

"Off the record?" Ripley asked with a lifted eyebrow.

"I held you for, like, half the night. Do you really need to ask me that?" Kenna questioned.

"I've never known a reporter before, Kenna. I don't know how any of this works," Ripley argued.

Kenna shook her head from side to side and moved to get out of the bed. She was wearing Ripley's old university t-shirt with a pair of her old sweats, and she looked both sexy and adorable. Ripley had to remind herself that they were having a discussion about something important. She met Kenna's serious eyes with her own.

"That's bullshit, and you know it. I told you last night I'd leave you out of the story. I brought you home. I made sure you were safe, Ripley. I stayed the night for you. Do you honestly think I did all that just so I could get a pull-quote?" Kenna asked.

Ripley knew she had been off-base, and she could tell by Kenna's expression that she was disappointed at Ripley's questions. Ripley wanted to hang her head because Kenna was right. This woman had been nothing but kind to her last night and had even stayed over because Ripley had asked her to. Kenna also hadn't brought up the story or the fire again after Ripley had requested a reprieve. Ripley owed her better than this.

"I'm sorry." Ripley sat as she rolled on her side. "I probably don't look great right now. I'm used to waking up alone, and I would exercise, shower, and then get ready for the day. Can we postpone any deep conversation until after all that? I can take you to breakfast."

Kenna's demeanor changed from tense and angry to a little less tense and slightly less angry, but Ripley would take that. Kenna turned to the dresser where she'd left both her own and Ripley's clothing the night before. She grabbed her stuff and turned back toward the bed.

"I'll make you another deal. You do all that, and I'll run home and change. I'll pick you up in an hour, and we'll drive to your car so you can pick it up and head to breakfast."

***

"You slept over?" Bella asked.

"Nothing happened," Kenna began. "She was drunk, and I took her home."

Kenna was sitting outside the PV Bistro, which was one of the most popular breakfast destinations in the city. Kenna knew the owner well and always got seated right away, no matter how busy they were. Ripley was parking, and they'd be heading inside momentarily, but Bella had called, and Kenna needed to fill her sister in on the recent events.

"How many times have you slept in the same bed with a story subject, Ken?"

"None. Still none. She's not the subject of the story I'm writing anymore."

"You're backing down? You never back down."

"I'm not backing down; I'm choosing to pursue a friendship with someone I think I might like to be friends with instead of pissing her off by running with the story."

Bella chuckled, and Kenna wasn't sure how to take that. She watched Ripley climb out of her car and glance in her direction. She held up one finger to indicate she'd be just a moment.

"Ken, are you sure you know what you're doing here?"

"I've got to go, Bell. I'm about to have breakfast."

She hung up the phone before her sister could reply, climbed out of her car, and headed toward Ripley. They walked into the restaurant together. It was jam-packed, like it typically was on a Saturday morning. The few seats in the lobby were filled, and it was standing room only at this point. Kenna waited her turn while a family in front of them was added to the waitlist. When Kenna and Ripley stood in front of the podium, the owner of the small restaurant met Kenna with a smile.

"Ken, didn't expect you in today," her cousin, Danielle, said.

"I was hoping you could squeeze us in. Party of two." Kenna held up two fingers.

Danielle was two years older than Bella, which meant Kenna and her hadn't been close when they were growing up, despite Kenna's family's overall closeness. As an adult, though, Kenna considered Danielle to be one of her closest friends.

"Let me get something cleared off for you," Danielle replied and walked off, leaving the podium in the hands of one of the hostesses.

"Ex-girlfriend?" Ripley asked so quietly, Kenna almost didn't hear it over the sounds of the people awaiting their tables.

"What?"

"Is she an ex?" Ripley repeated.

"Oh, no. Danielle's my cousin." Kenna smiled at Ripley. "She owns the place."

Danielle returned before Ripley could say anything else, and she led them to their table, which was right in the middle of the room. Kenna wasn't exactly happy with the table selection, but everything else was taken. They'd have to deal with it. She only hoped it wouldn't prevent Ripley from opening up to her.

They ordered coffee and their food. Then, the awkwardness set in. Kenna didn't know how to start. She didn't want to be the one to bring up what Ripley had said she would tell her, so she just sat with her hands clasped together on the table and waited. Ripley didn't appear to be in a hurry, either. She looked around at the people at the other tables, played with the silverware, and twirled the straw in her water glass. Once their coffee had been placed in front of them and they'd each added the appropriate accoutrements, Kenna wondered if they'd go through the entire meal in silence.

"I have nightmares," Ripley said suddenly after what had felt like an eternity.

"Because of that night?" Kenna asked.

"I was just old enough to really remember everything, and it's still stuck in there." Ripley pressed a finger to her temple. "It gets worse this time of year: the anniversary is coming up. I can't believe it's been twenty years."

"That's why you wanted me to stay last night?" Kenna took a sip of her still scalding coffee and winced at the burning sensation on her tongue.

"I told you I don't drink much; that's the reason," Ripley explained. "When I was finally old enough to drink, I thought the alcohol might make the nightmares go away. I wasn't an alcoholic or anything, but if they got worse, I'd try to make them go away by drinking them away. I learned my lesson the hard way: alcohol seems to make them worse."

"I'm sorry, Ripley. I shouldn't have-"

"It wasn't your fault. I know myself; I shouldn't have kept drinking like that." Ripley took a sip of her coffee. "That was why I asked you to stay. I worried it might get bad. And I shouldn't have asked you that; we just met. I shouldn't be putting you through all this."

"I wanted to stay," Kenna said with an open expression on her face. "I wanted to stay for other reasons, though, if I'm being completely honest."

"If I ask if the story was one of the other reasons, you can't get mad at me, because if I ask if it was for personal reasons, like you actually like me and want to spend more time with me, that makes me sound a little narcissistic," Ripley delivered with a shy smile.

"I do like you," Kenna told her and smiled back. "And it's the only reason I've agreed not to pursue telling your story. I'll stick with the puff piece on social work, and it'll play okay, but it won't be nearly as good as talking about what happened to you and your family, Ripley." Kenna paused. "I'm more than willing to do that if it means we can talk about other things."

"Other things?"

"Like how you got half-naked with me in the room last night." Kenna lifted an eyebrow.

"I was trying to forget that, actually." Ripley blushed red.

"I'm not," Kenna replied. "Trust me; I'm kind of hoping I remember that forever."

"I told you before: I don't have a lot of friends. I'm pretty used to being on my own," Ripley said.

"Why is that, though? I haven't spent all that much time with you, but I like you so far."

"I think you know," Ripley replied.

"Do you want to talk about it?" Kenna asked as the waiter approached with their meals, and Ripley looked around the crowded room. "It doesn't have to be here," Kenna added.

"What do you know?" Ripley asked. "You probably know more than me."

"I doubt that," Kenna replied and picked up her fork.

"No, seriously. I don't know much beyond what I experienced," Ripley said. "I was only eight, and there was no one left to take care of me, so I ended up in the system. No one there knew any details; they just knew I was an orphan. It wasn't until I aged out at eighteen and went to college on a scholarship that I tracked down a couple of the police officers that investigated what happened that night, but the case had gone cold by then. They knew it was arson, but they hadn't caught anyone."

"And you didn't have any ideas?"

"I was just a kid. The only adults I knew were family members and teachers. I had two older brothers, and I was the kid sister who wasn't allowed to hang out with them or their friends. I had a couple of friends myself, but I'm pretty sure my third-grade classmates were ruled out right away." Ripley smiled a little. "I didn't even know the fire was set on purpose until I met with those officers. It was a lot to take in, and I don't like thinking about it." She shook her head from side to side as she snapped into a strip of crispy bacon.

"God, we are such polar opposites." Kenna chuckled and salted her eggs. "Had that happened to me, I never would have let it go. I'd need to know what happened, and I'd have to hold that person responsible."

"They don't know who that person is. I'm not a cop, and I'm no arson investigator. I just don't see the point in making my life all about this one terrible thing that happened to me. I've worked so hard, Kenna." Ripley lowered her fork to her plate. "I put myself through college; I put myself through grad school. Now, I'm just hoping to pay off those student loans, and I want to pursue a Ph. D. in Child Development. I spend my time trying to help kids find homes and families that will love and support them."

"That's honorable, Ripley. And I think that's amazing. I just know myself: I'd have to know," Kenna replied.

"Is our relationship going to be about this?" Ripley asked. "I had fun last night, and it had nothing to do with what happened to me when I was eight years old, Kenna. If we're going to be spending time together, I don't want it to be because you pity me, and I don't want it to be all about the fire."

"I had fun with you, too," Kenna said. She took a long drink of her coffee before she added, "Can we go out? Like, on a date? Like, a date where I pick you up, and we talk about our hopes, dreams, and aspirations, and how we both ended up where we did? No pressure. Just two women getting to know one another to see if there's something there. I feel like there might be. I don't know how you feel. You're probably annoyed with me about eighty percent of the time, but I had to ask."

CHAPTER 9

RIPLEY stared into Kenna's blue eyes as they stared back at her, likely waiting for a response after putting all her cards on the table. Kenna took another drink of her coffee, and Ripley kind of liked her like this: she appeared to be at least slightly nervous. Ripley wondered if anyone else ever made this woman nervous.

"It's actually about ninety-five percent," Ripley said with a wink.

Kenna rolled her eyes, placed her coffee mug back on the table, and leaned forward, clasping her hands together over her plate.

"Is that other five percent at least something positive that might get you to agree to go out with me?" Kenna asked.

"How did you know?"

"How did I know what?" Kenna asked.

"That I was gay? You just knew," Ripley said.

"I didn't *just* know." Kenna leaned back and resumed eating. "You never said otherwise. I asked you out within about a minute of meeting you, I asked you out again later, and I just did it again. At no time have you said anything about being straight or not into women."

"And you are…" Ripley wasn't sure how to ask. She also wasn't sure why she really needed to know. "Never mind."

"I'm gay. It's exclusively women for me, if that's what you're asking. Now that you know that, will you finally agree to go out with me already?" Kenna gave her an exasperated expression, which caused Ripley to nod. "Finally. God, you play hard to get. I'll pick you up at seven."

"Tonight?" Ripley asked, surprised.

"Unless you have something else going on."

"I don't, but-"

"Have I told you I like that honesty? Most women would make something up. You don't, though, do you?"

"No, I don't. I guess it comes from a long history in the system," Ripley replied.

"How so?"

"When I first became a foster kid, I was too busy grieving. I bounced from home to home while they tried to see if there was a family member to take me. Eventually, I figured out that wasn't going to happen. Then, it was all about trying to get adopted into a decent family and getting out of the system. When I was in the houses with lots of kids, it was insanity all the time. I discovered that if I was calm, just stuck to myself, and did well in school, I was left alone. I would eat only what was offered, and I was always honest with my foster parents. If they wanted to know who'd spilled soda on their carpet or something, I'd tell them if I knew. I didn't want to take the blame myself because it could mean they'd dump me somewhere else."

"So, you were a narc?" Kenna chuckled at her.

"It's pretty much every kid for themselves. And I was still moved around a lot, so I'm not really sure how much good it did me, but I was left to my own devices a lot because I was always on my best behavior. That enabled me to study more and earn my scholarship, which was my only chance at going to college."

"I want to hear more about all of this when I pick you up tonight," Kenna said.

"We can wait until next weekend. I'm sure you have something else you'd—"

"Ripley, I have no plans tonight. I'm going to my nephew's wrestling match this afternoon, but I'm free after that."

"It's just that the anniversary is in three days... I tend to stick to myself a lot this time of year. I'll probably even work from home for most of the week so that my mood doesn't impact anyone else."

Kenna gave her a soft smile and leaned in again.

"We can always go out next week if that's important to you. I don't know, and I could be wrong here, but I think it might be good for you to get out a little; spend some time with me. We'll get to know one another. If nothing else happens, at least it could help you take your mind off it for a while."

Ripley thought about that for a moment. She had dated, but rarely and never around the anniversary of the fire. She'd always thought it was important to have her solitude this time of year. It was her way of remembering them. The reality was, though, that she always had her solitude. She was a loner and had been ever since that night. She always remembered her family and what happened. That would never go away. Maybe she could try something different this year.

"Okay," she replied.

***

"You're going on a date with her?" Bella asked while watching Brady attempt to pin his opponent to the mat. "Go, Brady!"

"Never underestimate a mother's ability to multi-task," Kenna replied, chuckling.

"That is motherhood."

"Yes, I'm going out with her," Kenna said. "Tonight. I need to leave after this match, actually, to make it back in time and get ready."

"You're ditching your adorable nephew and long-suffering sister for a date?" Bella asked her playfully.

"I just watched my adorable nephew wrestle three other tiny wrestlers; I think I've done my aunt's duties for the day. It's kind of strange, Bell. I just left her a few hours ago, but I'm really looking forward to seeing her again already. I like her a lot."

"And this isn't just because of her history and how you got involved with her, to begin with?"

"No."

"Because you've done that in the past." Bella turned to her a little.

"I have not."

"Not with women, Ken. You did that story about those rugby players and got really into it for a while. Then, when you figured out that state senator was corrupt, you spent nearly six months trying to find all the other corrupt politicians. You didn't let it go until the station told you to move on or they'd start picking your stories for you again," Bella explained.

"You think I won't be able to just let the story go even if it means I could lose her," Kenna asked.

"Lose her? You just met her, Ken. You haven't even gone on a date with the woman yet."

"You know what I mean," Kenna said.

"Just be careful. I know you. I love you to death, but you are like a dog with a bone. If you really like this woman and want to see what could happen, I'm all for that. Just don't make it about what happened to her back then or your need to talk about it on the news today."

As Kenna readied herself for her first official date with Ripley a few hours later, she considered Bella's words. Bella was older and definitely wiser. She was also happy and completely settled with her life. She had the family she'd always wanted, the career she had always wanted, and a good group of friends she spent time with nearly every week. Kenna was still working on a lot in her life, and she looked up to her sister. She took her advice seriously. If Bella told her to be careful, she would be careful with Ripley.

She buzzed Ripley's door a few minutes early. Ripley buzzed her in immediately. Kenna didn't have to knock on her apartment door because Ripley was waiting just outside it. She was dressed casually, in jeans and a white shirt with a gray cardigan over it that she had left unbuttoned. Kenna smiled at her as she passed her a bouquet of multi-colored freesias.

"You should probably put these in water before we go," Kenna said.

"Thank you. You didn't have to do that," Ripley replied and took the flowers. "Sorry, we can go in. I'm just anxious. I think I've forgotten how to do this."

Ripley turned and unlocked her door. They entered. Kenna closed the door behind them while Ripley made her way to the kitchen.

"I thought we'd make it easy on ourselves and do something completely normal tonight. I think we could use a little normal," Kenna said.

She heard the water running and cabinets opening. A few moments later, Ripley emerged with the flowers in a vase, placed them on the coffee table in the living room, and stared at them for a moment with a smile on her face.

"These are freesias, right?"

"That they are."

"Did you get these on purpose?" Ripley asked as she made her way back toward Kenna and the door.

"You mean, did I accidentally buy you flowers?"

Ripley laughed and replied, "Did you just pick a random bouquet at the grocery store, or did you purposely pick freesias?"

"No, Ripley," Kenna said and opened the door for them. "I know exactly what kind of flowers those are. I went to a florist earlier and picked them out."

Ripley nodded with a smaller but shy smile, and Kenna knew she had accomplished what she'd hoped she would. Freesias meant trust. That was what she wanted Ripley to know more than anything, given how they'd met: Ripley could trust her.

"One of the women at work had them in her wedding

bouquet, and I overheard her talking about it a few months ago," Ripley said. "Wait. What did you mean when you said we're doing something normal tonight?"

"Dinner and a movie." Kenna ushered her outside and to her waiting car. "I thought we'd keep it simple, too."

"That sounds nice," Ripley replied, and they drove in silence to their destination.

Kenna hoped it would be okay. She'd worked really hard to make this a great first date for the two of them, and she wanted the evening to go well. She wanted Ripley to know that she could open up to her, that Kenna would be there for her, and that she wanted her. Kenna knew it now: she wanted Ripley. Ripley was her opposite; that was true. But Kenna was ready to see if they could find a way to make that work for them.

"I hope this is okay," Kenna said when she parked her car.

"What is this?" Ripley looked around at the outside.

"This is my place. My condo is on the fifth floor," Kenna said.

"Your place?"

"We could go to a movie theater and not talk for two hours, and we could go to dinner at some fancy restaurant. I thought it might be nice to just do something here instead. We can find a movie to watch online, I can put it up on the TV, and since there's no one else around, we can pause it to go to the bathroom. We can talk as much or as little as we want. Since it's in my living room, we can also eat dinner while we watch. I made chili. I hope that's okay, too."

"You made chili?" Ripley asked.

"My dad's recipe."

"When did you have time to do this?" Ripley turned in her seat to ask.

"I've had a busy day," Kenna shrugged.

"Why did you pick me up? I could have just driven over."

"I thought about that, but I told you I'd pick you up. I

wanted to do the whole flowers-at-the-front-door thing."

"Kenna, that's sweet," Ripley replied.

"So, you're still in?" she asked hopefully.

"I'm still in." Ripley chuckled a little.

"Good." Kenna nodded and turned off the car. "Let's go then."

They made their way up to Kenna's condo, which was a two-bedroom. One of those bedrooms had been converted into her home office, but it did have a pull-out sofa lining one of the walls, for guests. It was particularly handy whenever Bella's kids wanted to stay the night at their aunt's, but other than that, it hardly got any use. She hadn't had time in her day to tidy up, but she was a pretty clean person. Her place looked okay by her standards, and she hoped Ripley would agree. Her living room was decorated with a very soft purple on the walls and a light tan couch with purple accent pillows, and her tables were all a dark mahogany to provide depth. Kenna liked her home. When she'd purchased it two years prior, she'd made sure to include enough money in her overall budget beforehand to turn the house into a home. It wasn't the place she would live in forever, but she wasn't ready for a yard to mow and other responsibilities that her condo association handled for her.

"Your place is nice, Kenna," Ripley said.

"Thank you. Have a seat. I know wine doesn't usually go with chili, but I have red, white, and I also have beer."

"I think I'll skip the alcohol tonight," Ripley replied as she stood awkwardly in Kenna's living room.

"Right," Kenna silently scolded herself. "Iced tea or water?"

"Water is fine."

"I have sparkling."

"Do you have an entire restaurant back there?" Ripley asked as she sat down on the couch.

"My sister buys it and leaves it here for herself." Kenna laughed. "I think I also have a couple cans of soda from when her kids visited. I don't usually drink that stuff, but I can check."

"Regular old tap water is fine."

"I'll be right back. Make yourself comfortable." Kenna turned to head to the kitchen but remembered something. "I'm a bad host. I should offer you the tour."

"Why don't we eat first and get the movie started? We can do the tour later."

Kenna nodded at her. She then moved into her kitchen and let out a deep breath. Again, she was nervous. Why was she so nervous?

"Get it together, Crawford," she mumbled to herself.

She'd kept the chili warm in her slow cooker, which had been a gift from her mother. She'd told her Christmas morning, when she gave it to her, that Kenna could use that to make home-cooked meals for her family one day. Kenna had rolled her eyes. The slow cooker was being used for the first time tonight. She hadn't had time to make cornbread from scratch but knew a store variety that was pretty good. When she'd bought her chili ingredients, she had picked up a box and mixed it together quickly. It had been kept warm in the microwave while she'd been picking up Ripley. She turned the microwave on for another fifteen seconds to heat it through while she spooned her favorite thing that her father cooked into two overly large bowls. She filled two glasses with water, pulled the cornbread out, and left it in the basket.

"Can I help with anything?" Ripley asked, standing in the doorway of her kitchen.

"Yeah, actually. Can you carry our drinks?" Kenna asked.

They worked together to get everything onto the coffee table before Kenna picked up the remote, turned the TV on, and switched it to her streaming device. She glanced over at Ripley then. The brunette had her hair down but back behind her ears, and Kenna smiled as she took in the other woman's slightly nervous demeanor. Ripley stared at the TV screen while holding on to a bowl in her lap. Kenna's bowl was on the table.

"What are we watching?"

"I thought we could search for something together," Kenna said. "You can get comfortable. Take your shoes off if you want."

Ripley kicked off the flats she'd worn. They landed on the floor in front of the couch, and Ripley settled in more by crossing her legs under her body and resting the bowl in her lap again. Kenna had a hard time taking her eyes off her, but she returned them to the TV to try to find something for them to watch.

"I'm not much into scary movies," Ripley offered while spooning her chili.

"Neither am I. How about something in the romantic comedy category?" Kenna asked.

They searched for a few minutes before settling on one neither of them had seen. Kenna started it up, and they ate in relative silence. Ripley complimented her cooking while Kenna sampled the cornbread to make sure it tasted okay before Ripley took a piece. The movie was a third of the way through when Kenna stood to take their dishes to the kitchen sink. When she returned, Ripley was still in her spot on the sofa. She had paused the movie for Kenna and smiled when she returned, pressing play.

Kenna sat back in her spot. As she turned her head toward Ripley, she tried to figure out what to do next. They had hardly spoken since this date had begun, and Kenna was never one to run out of words. She made her living off words. She decided to scoot sideways a few inches, and her arm went over the back of the couch. She watched Ripley smile.

"That's your move?" Ripley asked without looking away from the TV.

"It's one of them," Kenna replied.

Ripley laughed a little but moved closer to Kenna. Kenna's hand moved to Ripley's shoulder to encourage her closer. Once Ripley's head was resting on her shoulder, Kenna knew this was right. She had no real reason to know that, but she did anyway. Ripley snuggled a little closer every few minutes until her arm was wrapped around Kenna's stomach. Kenna's heart was racing. She knew Ripley could probably feel it, but the woman hadn't said anything. Kenna decided not to be embarrassed by her body's reaction to a beautiful woman wrapping herself around her.

"That wasn't bad," Ripley said as the credits rolled.

"My cuddling or the movie?" Kenna replied and was promptly smacked lightly on her stomach.

"The movie." Ripley laughed.

"Want to watch another one?" Kenna asked. "I'll let you pick this time."

"I was thinking about that, actually." Ripley pulled away to face her. "You don't live all that far from Brinkley's," she said.

"The ice cream place? Yeah, it's around the corner."

"What if we walk there and I buy dessert? They're open late on weekends."

"You want to go for a walk?"

"We haven't really talked yet." Ripley shrugged. "I think we should, and it's very comfortable just lying on this couch with you. I don't know how much talking is going to happen if we put on another movie."

"Can I hold your hand while we walk?" Kenna asked.

Ripley slid her feet into her shoes, but Kenna could make out the smile she tried to hide. She had no problem walking to Brinkley's with this woman, sharing dessert with her, and coming back here to repeat the past two hours with another movie and more of that physical closeness on the couch.

***

"You did not do that?" Ripley asked Kenna as they walked back to the apartment with ice cream cones in hand.

"I did. There was a wrong, and I needed to right it," Kenna replied. "Trade."

They'd each gotten their favorite flavor of ice cream, but they had been taking turns passing them back and forth so they could each enjoy both. The night was a sticky one, thanks to the high humidity. The cold from the ice cream was a welcomed change. Ripley hoped her hair still looked okay. She had been pressed into Kenna's side earlier, and now they were walking outside where the heat sometimes wreaked havoc on her long locks.

"She was your principal," Ripley said as she licked a rogue bit of ice cream off her hand.

Ripley's other hand was clasped in Kenna's, and, despite it being the first time they had done that, it felt surprisingly natural. Kenna squeezed her hand a little to indicate they should turn right. Ripley had lost track of where they were on their trip home. She'd been enjoying their conversation. Now that the whole topic of her history had been discussed and left behind, they could laugh more; they could just enjoy each other's company. Ripley knew that the fire would come back into their conversation at some point. It was such a big part of who she was as a person; she had always known that if she'd gotten serious with a woman, she'd have to be willing to open up all the way to her, and she had yet to feel the pull to do so. She couldn't believe that the one person she'd even entertained the notion with was a reporter of all things.

"She promised us we'd have pizza on Tuesdays, and she reneged on that promise," Kenna began. "I found the video interview footage, aired it during announcements for everyone to see, and next semester, we had pizza on Tuesdays."

Ripley laughed at her date, finding Kenna's tenaciousness adorable now that it wasn't aimed in her direction.

"Unbelievable," she said when her laughter died down. "Trade."

They traded their cones back.

"We've done most embarrassing stories, favorite stuff, and worst first date. I'm happy, by the way, you didn't include this one in that," Kenna said and squeezed Ripley's hand again. "Let's do first dates overall."

"Like, my very first date?" Ripley asked, turned to Kenna to check, and turned back to the sidewalk after Kenna nodded. "Oh, that is actually a little embarrassing, too."

"How so?"

"Because I didn't have my first date until I was a junior in college," Ripley admitted.

Kenna stopped walking with that comment, and Ripley stopped, too, by default, turning toward her. They were still linked by one hand while their other hands held their ice cream cones. Kenna smiled at her, and in an instant, all Ripley's thoughts of being embarrassed by that statement disappeared. Kenna lifted her cone between them and promptly tapped Ripley on the nose with it.

"Tell me," Kenna said as she tried to hold back her laughter.

"I'm not telling you anything now," Ripley replied while laughing and wiping at the cold ice cream.

"Come on." Kenna started then walking again.

"I told you before, I tried not to cause trouble when I was a foster kid. That included dating. I had a foster sister once who ran off with her boyfriend, who was also in the system. When it didn't work out, they wouldn't let her back in our house, and it was a good house. Those are sometimes hard to come by. I didn't want to risk losing my spot."

"Did you know back then that you were gay?"

"I'd figured that part out, yeah. I guess that added to my complications. It's one thing trying to date as a kid in the system. I knew it would be a whole other thing if I tried to date another girl," Ripley explained. "So, I didn't. Then, I got to school and spent the whole first year just trying to keep up with classes and make a few friends. I was on scholarship; I couldn't mess around. I had to keep a B-average, or I'd lose it. It wasn't until my junior year that I finally thought I had a handle on things. My roommate convinced me to go to a party with her. I did, and I met someone."

"Someone you went on a date with later?" Kenna asked with lightness in her tone.

"Yes, but only a few," Ripley told her. "It didn't go anywhere."

"Why not?"

"She asked about my family. When I told her just the basics, I saw the reaction on her face. It kind of told me all I needed to know. In a way, it was actually good that you knew ahead of time. It meant I didn't have to see your reaction to the story. We might have not been here if I had to see that," Ripley shared.

"She didn't deserve you then," Kenna said, and Ripley scoffed. "What?" Kenna asked. "You think because you had this thing happen to you, you don't deserve someone who can appreciate what you went through?"

"It's not about that," Ripley began. "I didn't exactly turn out to be a well-adjusted adult."

"What are you talking about?"

"I have no friends outside of work, and you're the first person I've dated in over a year, Kenna. I'm in therapy once a week, and I still have nightmares. I'm a twenty-eight-year-old woman who has nightmares at least once a week; more than that this time of year."

"None of us know how we'd react to what happened to you. It would be easy for me to say I would have handled it differently, but that would've been a lie, and it certainly wouldn't be fair. If anyone judges you for putting yourself through school and for being one of the best social workers out there, helping kids – that's their loss. As for the friends thing, I don't have all that many of them, either. My sister is my best friend. I have a few cousins I hang out with, but maybe only one or two other people I spend time with. It's not all that regularly, either, since we're all busy. And I'm pretty sure that therapy for adults is actually now a sign of being well-adjusted."

Ripley laughed lightly as they approached Kenna's building.

"Thank you for walking with me." Ripley changed the subject.

"I'd like to do more than just walk with you, Ripley." Kenna tossed the small remainder of her ice cream cone into the trash can by the sidewalk. "I'd like to watch another movie with you; I'd like you to stay over tonight; I'd like to get breakfast with you tomorrow; and I'd definitely like to go out with you again."

Ripley tossed the remainder of her own ice cream into the trash and replied, "It's been a long time, Kenna."

"Since you've been with someone?"

"Yes," Ripley answered and felt that all too familiar blush creep up her neck and hit her cheeks.

They were standing under a streetlight. There was no way Kenna couldn't see her embarrassment. Kenna placed her hands on both of Ripley's cheeks and used her thumbs to stroke the skin gently, as if attempting to wipe away her blush.

"Stay with me tonight," she asked. "We don't have to do anything."

"I told you I'm not good company this time-"

"You've been great company so far, and I had no problem last night," Kenna interrupted her. "I know if you don't want to stay, you'll tell me, because you've been honest so far. But if you do want to stay, please just stay, Ripley. You don't have to warn me about anything."

Ripley moved her hands to Kenna's hips and pulled the woman toward her. Kenna's hands remained on her cheeks at first but then moved as Ripley wrapped her own arms around Kenna's waist and pulled her closer for a hug. Kenna's arms went around her neck. Ripley wasn't sure if Kenna had been expecting or hoping for a kiss and was, therefore, disappointed, but Ripley needed a hug. It didn't seem as if Kenna was disappointed, though. Kenna's head rested securely on Ripley's shoulder, and she pulled Ripley in tighter. Her fingers were toying with strands of Ripley's hair. They stood that way for several minutes, under the light illuminating the front of Kenna's building, until Ripley finally pulled away. Kenna stared at her with those gorgeous, made-for-TV eyes. Ripley smiled, leaned in, and gave Kenna a gentle peck on the lips.

"I'm picking the movie," Ripley stated. "But can we watch it in the bedroom?"

"Sure. Yeah," Kenna replied, a little taken aback.

Ripley smirked at her, and they made their way back inside.

CHAPTER 10

KENNA was happy. She was still nervous, which she had been trying to shake off since first meeting Ripley, but she was happy. They were in her bedroom. She had changed into something comfortable and loaned Ripley clothes so that she could do the same. They were on her bed, and Ripley was resting with her back against Kenna's front, between Kenna's legs. They were watching their second movie of the night. Kenna had taken a few liberties over the course of the past hour and a half. She had kissed Ripley's temples, her cheeks, and her neck a few times while pulling her closer into her body. Her arms were under Ripley's shirt – which was actually one of Kenna's shirts – resting on her stomach. Every now and then, she would draw shapes with her fingertips, and she'd hear Ripley's breathing pick up and halt before picking up again. Kenna would stop then and smile. Ripley had found opportunities to touch her, too. Her fingers played with Kenna's arms on her stomach. Her hand would slide up and down Kenna's calf and rest on her knee. A few times, she'd wrapped her arm around the back of Kenna's neck and rested it there, encouraging Kenna even closer. *This was what it was supposed to be like*, Kenna reasoned.

When their movie ended, Kenna went to move, only to discover that Ripley had fallen asleep. She didn't want to move her, but she also knew they couldn't fall asleep like this. As she was about to rub Ripley's stomach to coax her awake, the woman in front of her began to mumble something under her breath. She also moved slightly. Her hand twitched. Then, she muttered something else. Her arms over Kenna's tightened, and Kenna held on to her.

"Ripley?" she whispered into Ripley's ear. "Hey, I'm here."

Ripley moved again, but this time, it was a slight jump forward. It was enough to pull her out of Kenna's arms and wake her up. She didn't turn around to face Kenna; she just hunched over and shook her head slowly. She appeared to be trying to catch her breath, and Kenna sat there, waiting. She didn't want to push Ripley or try to pull anything out of her. She waited because whatever Ripley was going through needed time to process.

"Sorry," Ripley said softly after a moment.

"Why?" Kenna moved toward her slightly. She wasn't sure if she should touch her, but she wanted to. "You don't have to apologize. Do you want to tell me what happened, though?"

"Not really," Ripley replied.

Then, something remarkable happened: Ripley leaned back. She didn't even look to see that Kenna was there to support her; she leaned back into her again, expecting Kenna to just be there. And Kenna *was* there. She wrapped her arms around Ripley's neck and kissed her just behind the earlobe.

"How about we just go to sleep?" Kenna suggested after a moment and didn't get a response right away.

When Ripley's breathing returned to normal, she said, "I'm afraid to go to sleep."

"What do you see?" Kenna risked.

"Things I didn't even see that night," Ripley said. "Like my parents or my brothers burning; none of that happened. I was in my bedroom alone that night. The only person I saw was the fireman that saved me."

"I think you have to try to remember that then. I'm no therapist, but it seems like that's something you should try to remember: you didn't see that."

"But it did happen. They died."

"Maybe they slept through it. I've interviewed a fire chief and a few families that were victims of that batch of fires that happened in a row recently. I'm not an expert or anything, but sometimes, the smoke inhalation at least knocks people out. They don't feel the rest."

"I hope that's what happened." Ripley nodded slowly. "Sometimes, I actually dream about them, though. I'll see Ethan, who was thirteen when it happened, playing soccer. He was so good; he scored in nearly every game. I'll see Ethan playing in the swimming pool with all his friends, and I'll see Benji, who was eleven when it happened, playing his favorite video game, screaming at the screen when he lost. Sometimes, I see my mom mowing the lawn since my dad hated that chore. He'd just cook instead. I can see him sitting in the living room, watching TV or at his desk, probably paying bills or doing some other adult activity. I love those nights. It's like I'm with them again."

"Tell me more about them," Kenna said. "Let's get more comfortable first, and then I want to hear all about them."

They settled in for the night under the blanket. Kenna lay on her back, and Ripley immediately moved into her and rested her head on Kenna's chest. They stayed that way for the next hour while Ripley told Kenna stories of her family. Kenna shared a few of her growing-up stories, too, but she was happy to just listen to Ripley talk. She guessed she was the first person Ripley had told most of these stories to, outside of a therapist's office. Maybe she hadn't even told them in there. Kenna thought about that as Ripley began to slow down her speech, and her breathing slowed into that pace that told Kenna she was about to fall asleep. Kenna loved her family. She talked about them all the time. Ripley hadn't been able to do that, and Kenna wanted more than anything to be that person for her.

***

When Ripley woke up the next morning, it was in Kenna's bed. It was also after a night of restful sleep. As she rolled onto her back, needing to change positions after a being pressed against Kenna for hours, she wondered if sharing some stories with the woman had helped her to avoid the nightmares. She hadn't dreamed either, though. She hadn't seen her father stop watching the game so that she could change the channel to her favorite cartoon. She hadn't seen Ethan give her the rest of his cookie when he thought no one else was looking; or Benji, trying to teach her how to play soccer in their backyard. Ripley missed it, but she also didn't.

"Morning," Kenna said and leaned over to kiss her on the forehead.

"Good morning," Ripley replied.

"How'd you sleep?" Kenna asked as she stared down at her.

"Better than I have in a while."

Kenna's smile spread wide. Ripley had to smile up at her.

"I'm thinking about making you breakfast. I have eggs, I can make you toast, I also have some bacon, and I think I have pancake mix somewhere – pick your poison."

"Bacon sounds nice," Ripley replied. "With pancakes on the side."

"Pancakes on the side of your bacon? Sounds like my kind of woman." Kenna leaned down and kissed her forehead again.

Ripley knew then that Kenna was trying to take things slow for her. She had kissed Ripley all over the place last night, but not on the lips, even after Ripley had kissed her briefly there outside. Kenna had touched her but hadn't taken it far and had stilled her hands just when Ripley would start to react. Kenna slid off the bed and stretched, and Ripley liked the sight of her in the morning. Her blonde hair was mussed, she had no makeup on, and she wore a pair of comfortable shorts with a black t-shirt.

Kenna made her way to the bathroom first, and Ripley stayed in her position until Kenna emerged, gave her a smile, and then moved to the kitchen. Ripley entered the bathroom next. She'd used an extra toothbrush last night. Kenna had told her she had bought it specifically for her when she'd gone shopping yesterday. She'd been hopeful Ripley would stay over. It was one of the cutest things that had happened between them last night. Kenna's face had been a little concerned when she had admitted that part of the reason why she'd wanted to pick Ripley up had been because she wanted her to stay the night. As Ripley finished up in the bathroom, she couldn't help but smile. Kenna was amazing. Ripley didn't know where things would go with them after today, but she knew what she wanted to do right now, so she went into the kitchen where she found Kenna standing in front of the stove, reading the back of the pancake mix box.

"How many do you think you'll eat?" Kenna asked without looking up. "I think I'll make like six, just in case."

"Kenna?" Ripley asked.

"Yeah?" Kenna looked over at her.

Ripley moved to her, took the box, and set it on the stovetop. She then moved into Kenna's space, and Kenna hadn't been expecting it. Her expression of surprise told Ripley that much. She reached for Kenna's hips, pulled them completely against her own, wrapped her arms around Kenna's neck, and pressed their lips together.

Kenna responded immediately; her arms went around Ripley's waist and under the back of her shirt. Ripley wasted no time. She pushed a little with her hips until Kenna took the hint and stepped backward. Now, Kenna was against the wall; her mouth was hot, and Ripley wanted more. She slid her tongue inside Kenna's mouth and earned a moan as her reward. Kenna's hands were sliding all over her back now, seemingly unable to find a destination they'd be satisfied with. Ripley parted their mouths for a moment and stared into Kenna's now dark eyes.

"Do you want it off?" she asked of Kenna.

"Yes," Kenna whispered.

Ripley pulled at the shirt Kenna had loaned her up, until it was over her head. She tossed it to the floor and watched Kenna's eyes drift down to her bare chest. Kenna's hands slid around Ripley's body to rest just under her breasts before she cupped them fully, closed her eyes as if in reverence, and then opened them again. They were another shade darker now.

Ripley kissed her again, allowing their tongues to slide around and play while Kenna massaged her breasts. Kenna took both nipples in between her thumb and forefinger, gave them a light pull to test the waters, and when Ripley moaned, she pulled a little harder. Ripley's hands went under Kenna's shirt; and Ripley was never like this: she had never been the instigator. She had never been so turned on she couldn't wait to get a woman's clothes off. That was what she was now, though. She grasped Kenna's breasts as she moved her mouth to right next to Kenna's ear.

"Off," she whispered.

Kenna lifted her arms into the air, and Ripley slid Kenna's shirt over her head and tossed it to the floor. Her eyes took in Kenna's breasts and her toned stomach. She watched Kenna's chest rise and fall, and then she looked back up to Kenna's nearly swollen lips before she took Kenna's bottom one between her teeth. Kenna whimpered a little, and her arms reached around to Ripley's ass. She squeezed it as Ripley kissed her again. One of Ripley's arms went to the wall next to Kenna's head, and the other rested on Kenna's abs. When she rubbed the skin and felt the muscles beneath, Ripley nearly growled at how good it felt to be touching Kenna like this. Her lips met Kenna's neck, and she kissed, sucked, and licked Kenna's skin while her hand drifted lower. She finally rested it at the waistband of Kenna's shorts, allowing Kenna to tell her to stop. Kenna didn't tell her to stop, though.

Ripley's hand slid not only inside Kenna's shorts but into her panties as well. She felt soft curls between Kenna's thighs and moved her hand lower. Kenna's head went back against the wall when Ripley cupped her completely, and Ripley moaned as she dragged one finger through Kenna's wetness. Kenna was wet for her. Ripley had gotten this woman so turned on, it had manifested physically in the slick heat between her legs. Ripley kissed her; she slid her tongue against Kenna's as her hand moved around inside Kenna's panties.

"Ripley," Kenna breathed out. "There."

Ripley pulled back a little and allowed herself to smirk. Kenna's eyes were closed, her head was back, and she was begging Ripley to touch her there. Ripley moved two fingers on either side of Kenna's clit, squeezed, and then watched Kenna's expression. Kenna squinted her eyes, her mouth opened, and her hands on Ripley's ass released. Ripley leaned back in, took Kenna's earlobe between her teeth, moved her free hand to Kenna's nipple, and began stroking her deliberately between her legs. Kenna's breathing picked up; her hips began moving; Kenna's hands went to the back of Ripley's neck to encourage her closer, and Ripley loved every second of it.

Kenna's hands then slid down the back of her body, gripped Ripley's shorts, and started to tug them down. Ripley knew what she wanted, but she was too occupied to oblige. Kenna was moaning into her ear, and it sounded so good. She flicked her clit a few more times before lowering her fingers and sliding two of them inside Kenna.

Kenna gasped at the sensation, and Ripley gasped, too. Kenna was soft, warm, and wet. Ripley moved inside her slowly as she pressed their breasts together. She reveled in the feel of Kenna, backed against the wall, allowing Ripley to take her like this because this was the way Ripley needed this to happen. Ripley tugged on Kenna's shorts this time until she had them at the woman's thighs. She lowered her body to kneel in front of Kenna, pulled the shorts down entirely, and let them rest at Kenna's ankles. She then felt Kenna kicking them off as she stared at Kenna's sex, with her fingers moving in and out. She gulped at the sight in front of her before she lowered her head, placed her free hand on Kenna's breast again, and took Kenna with her mouth.

She slid her tongue between Kenna's folds and stroked Kenna's clit up and down while her fingers curled inside her. Kenna's hand found the back of her head, and as Ripley continued to move faster, she earned a few moans and heard her name spring from Kenna's mouth a few times. She sucked Kenna fully into her mouth, reveling in the taste of her, and her fingers moved faster. Kenna tugged on her hair, and it hurt, but Ripley kept going. She stroked Kenna with her tongue while her fingers matched her rhythm. Way too soon, Kenna's walls collapsed around her fingers, and Ripley heard – just barely due to the squeeze of Kenna's thighs – the sounds of Kenna's climax. Ripley slowed her strokes, waited for Kenna's grip on her head to loosen, and then kissed Kenna's clit once more before she looked up at the woman she had just dismantled. She stood, allowing Kenna to practically collapse into her arms, and she held on to her tightly, slowly stroking Kenna's back with her fingertips while Kenna was fully recovering.

"Oh, my God!" Kenna mumbled into Ripley's shoulder.

"Are you okay?" Ripley asked and laughed a little.

"I did not see that coming," Kenna replied. "Poor choice of words," she added, and they both laughed against the other's skin.

"Should I apologize for interrupting breakfast?" Ripley asked.

"No way." Kenna lifted her head and met Ripley's eyes. "I thought you'd want to wait. I was trying to take things slow; but that was anything other than slow."

"Are you complaining?" Ripley lifted an eyebrow.

"Take those off." Kenna gripped the shorts that were still, despite her prior efforts, on Ripley's body.

***

THE FIRE

Kenna had ordered Ripley to take her shorts off, but she didn't wait for the woman to do it. She tugged at them until they fell to Ripley's ankles, and Ripley kicked them off. Kenna moved back into her and pressed their naked bodies together fully for the first time. She grasped Ripley's hips, gave her a light shove backward, and kissed her as they stumbled into the dining room off the kitchen. Kenna had Ripley up against the dining room table in an instant. She moved her hands to Ripley's sides and lifted up, which was Ripley's indication to climb on top of the table.

"On this?" Ripley asked.

"It's solid wood," Kenna replied.

Ripley followed the instruction and sat atop the table. Kenna spread her legs and moved between them. She said nothing as she leaned in and kissed Ripley. Ripley's hands were on the back of her neck, pulling her in closer. Kenna moved until her body was pressed to Ripley's center. She gave a few short thrusts of her hips into Ripley's body, earning a gasp with each one, and used her hands to push lightly on Ripley's shoulders. She then watched as Ripley lay back onto the table, taking in the beautiful woman in front of her. Ripley was nude, lying on her dining room table, waiting for Kenna to touch her. Her eyes showed desire. Her chest heaved. She wanted Kenna. And Kenna, more than anything right now, wanted her.

Kenna ran her hands down Ripley's torso, then moved them back up, cupped Ripley's breasts, and played with her nipples before she replaced one hand with her lips. She leaned over the table to take it into her mouth. Ripley gasped almost soundlessly while Kenna sucked on her one nipple and twisted the other. Kenna gave the other nipple the same treatment before she kissed down the middle of Ripley's stomach. She wanted to wait. She wanted to make Ripley earn her pleasure with sounds and hip movements, but Kenna couldn't wait.

With Ripley open before her, she knelt in front of her, pulled her to the very edge of the table, and took her. She slid her tongue into the wetness, slid it back down, and entered her. Ripley moaned loudly then. Kenna moved her tongue in and out for a few strokes before moving it back up, gripping the outside of Ripley's thighs, and sucking her clit hard into her mouth. It didn't take long for Ripley's hips to thrust up each time Kenna stroked her with her tongue. She sucked again. She flicked Ripley's clit side to side and then moved her tongue back down to slide inside her. She pulled out and licked until Ripley came in her mouth. She waited until the tremors subsided before she stood up fully, took both of Ripley's hands, and pulled Ripley up into her body. She held Ripley there until she'd just about recovered from her climax.

Then, Kenna turned Ripley around in place and pushed her down softly with a hand in the middle of her back. Ripley gave in and lowered her body onto the table. Kenna stood behind her and spread Ripley's legs with two hands between Ripley's thighs. She took two fingers and stroked her clit from behind. Ripley's arms instantly unfolded and reached for the other edge of the table. She held on as Kenna continued to stroke with one hand while her other hand moved to Ripley's ass and further down. She slid it between Ripley's legs and thrust two fingers inside.

"Wow!" Ripley exclaimed.

Kenna wanted to smirk, but she couldn't. Ripley was letting her touch her like this; she was allowing Kenna to fuck her from behind after having allowed Kenna to taste her. Kenna stroked Ripley's clit and kept thrusting inside her, loving the feel of this woman against her fingers. When Ripley came, Kenna watched her knuckles whiten as they gripped the table. Kenna leaned down and kissed Ripley's back over and over, until Ripley's hand moved from the edge of the table to between her own legs to halt Kenna's strokes. Kenna stood up, allowing Ripley to do the same. Ripley turned slowly in her arms, glanced at her with hazy eyes, and hugged her.

CHAPTER 11

KENNA stared down at Ripley while her fingers continued to plunge inside and then pull out of her. Ripley's eyes were open in admiration as Kenna moved her eyes to Ripley's breasts. She lowered her mouth to one and sucked it. Ripley came for the seventh time that morning as Kenna hit a particularly wonderful spot inside. She then gripped Kenna's arm as Kenna attempted to stroke her clit to make her come yet again.

"I need a break," Ripley said as she tried to get her breathing back to normal.

"Breaks? There's no such thing," Kenna replied as she moved to kiss Ripley's lips.

They'd made their way to the bedroom following their first time in the kitchen. She'd had Kenna nearly as many times as Kenna had had her now, but she wanted her more. She wanted Kenna again, and again. As Kenna collapsed onto the bed next to her, Ripley could only stare up at the ceiling in amazement. She'd never come like that before. Hell, she wasn't even sure she'd had a real orgasm with another woman before Kenna.

"Kenna, that…" Ripley rolled onto her side and lost the words she was about to say.

Kenna smiled at her, ran a hand through Ripley's now messy hair, and said, "Now, I think I will make us breakfast. We can eat and then do that all over again."

Ripley smiled at her, placed her hand on her neck, and kissed her.

"I'd like that, but I can't stay much longer. I have a home visit today that I need to prep for," Ripley said.

"It's Sunday," Kenna reminded her.

"I know. We do surprise visits. I sometimes do mine on Sundays because no one expects government employees to work on Sundays."

"So, you chose sex over breakfast?" Kenna lifted an eyebrow. "You chose wisely."

"I agree," Ripley said.

"Do you have time for a shower? I'll take you home after if you let me join. If not, you're walking," she joked and winked at Ripley.

Ripley laughed and replied, "I have time for a shower with you."

***

Kenna said goodbye to Ripley with a long kiss at her front door. She'd insisted on walking her all the way inside, kissing her on her doorstep, and then walking backward toward the outer door. That had earned a laugh from Ripley, which only made Kenna melt inside. They hadn't made any official plans, but Ripley had already texted Kenna that she wanted to see her again. Kenna wanted to see her, too. She would have been happy with Ripley staying the night again or inviting her to stay at Ripley's place, but she understood; Ripley had to work. She also had an important anniversary coming up.

"Wait. You slept with her?" Bella said loudly. "Shit."

"What?"

"The kids may or may not have heard that," Bella replied.

"Bell! They know you're on the phone with me."

"They better not know what that means yet. And if they do, I'm blaming their father." Bella seemed to move from a loud location to a quieter one. "Okay. You slept with her on the first date?"

"It does happen. Not everyone is a prude like you."

"Please, I know several guys that can attest to my lack of prudishness," Bella returned. "Do not tell my husband."

"Bell, focus on me, please. I had sex with Ripley, and it was amazing,"

"That good?"

"More than *that good*. We spent all morning in bed, but it's not just that. Last night, we just watched a movie and talked. We walked to get ice cream and talked. We then lay in bed and talked. It was nice."

"She sounds different than the others," Bella said.

"She is different."

"When are you seeing her again?"

"I don't know. Soon, I hope."

"No plans yet?"

"We've texted about it, but we'll find a time when she's done working for the day. I asked her to call me later. Is that desperate?"

"You really have never been in this situation, have you?" Bella asked.

"No, I haven't." Kenna rolled her eyes at her sister. "That is not my fault, though."

"I guess not. You can't help it if women fawn all over you, I guess." Bella paused for a second. "It's not desperate, Ken; it's sweet. You seem sweet with her, based on what you've told me, and I think that's great."

"I do, too. I like how I am when I'm with her. It's not all about the story, or the lead, or finding answers. It's just about being with her. I like just being with her."

"Do not let Mom hear you say that. She'll start planning your wedding and buying onesies for your imaginary children."

"God, I'm keeping her away from Mom for as long as I can. I don't need Mom freaking her out."

"When can *I* meet her?" Bella asked.

"Are you going to tell her a bunch of lies about me?"

"Probably," Bella replied and laughed at her own joke.

"Then, you can meet her right after Mom."

"Who's going to talk you up then? Someone has to tell her how awesome you are, Ken. Just spending time with you is only going to give her a glimpse at your annoying side."

"Don't you have children to parent right about now?" Kenna asked.

"Seriously, I'd love to meet her. We can keep it casual; just the three of us. Leave the husband and kids out of it for now."

"I'll ask her but, Bell, she doesn't have family. I don't know how she'll feel about just jumping into meeting mine."

"Maybe we're actually exactly what she needs."

Kenna hung up on her sister, dropped her phone on her desk, and returned to her laptop to begin lining up everything she'd need to get the story about the Pleasant Valley social workers going. She also wanted to pick out at least two small pieces to work on simultaneously, and if she had time, pick out her next big feature piece. Normally, she had no trouble focusing on her work. In fact, over-focusing was a problem for her. She often forgot to eat and worked well into the night without realizing she needed to sleep. Today, though, she found it difficult to focus. She could only think of Ripley Fox. Ripley, who'd had her up against the wall in her kitchen, sliding her hand inside Kenna's panties just to touch her as quickly as she could. Ripley, who'd splayed herself over Kenna's table. Ripley, who'd showered with her a couple of hours later, gave Kenna one more orgasm with her mouth, and then allowed Kenna to soap her skin.

She picked up her phone again to text Ripley. She wanted the woman to know that she couldn't stop thinking about her, and she also hoped that by being as honest as possible with her and not doing that usual beginning-of-a-relationship bullshit people normally did, that they might have a real chance. Kenna didn't want to wait three days before calling her. She didn't want to pretend like she was busy and couldn't see Ripley again until the weekend. She wanted to see her tonight. As she was about to type her message, her phone rang instead. For an instant, Kenna hoped it was Ripley, but the name on the screen read Malcolm. Surprised he'd be calling her at all, but especially on a Sunday afternoon, she answered.

"Mal, what's up?"

"Hey, I know you told me to cool it on that social worker thing, but Shannon got a hold of what I'd given you. She asked me to dig more."

"Shannon asked you to dig?"

Shannon was her producer. She rarely got involved this early in any of Kenna's stories outside of giving her approval to follow one. She'd been one of Kenna's biggest supporters; a total asset to Kenna and her ambition to eventually get out of Pleasant Valley and possibly into an anchor position on a reputable network one day.

"She did. And I did," Malcolm replied. "Normally, I wouldn't bother you on a Sunday like this, but I didn't want her to surprise you with it tomorrow when you get to the office."

"Surprise me with what? Did you find something?"

Kenna's reporter instincts kicked in. She opened the notes application on her computer, put her phone on speaker, and readied her hands above the keys.

"The fire was arson; we know that. But I got my hands on the arson report and the police report. Don't ask me how."

"You've got to give me more than that, Mal."

"I just emailed it all to you. The hard copies will be on Shannon's desk tomorrow since she's the one who asked." Mal paused. "The police report has suspects listed, and it also has the transcripts of the interviews. Ultimately, they dismissed everyone, but I don't know... I feel like they missed something."

"Like what?"

"I worked homicide for twenty years before I went out on my own; I can't answer that question. All I can tell you is that there's something in my gut telling me that whoever did this is in that file, but we're missing something."

"You think the person who killed Ripley's family is in that file?" Kenna asked him.

"Read it, and you tell me if I'm crazy," he replied.

Kenna had already opened her email. The files he'd attached were currently downloading.

"Thanks, Mal."

"I hate to tell you, but I don't think Shannon's going to give you a choice here. I haven't told her because I knew you'd be pissed, but if she sniffs this out, she'll run it with or without you. You know how she is."

"She's like me; I know." Kenna bit her bottom lip. "Thanks for the heads-up on this."

"No problem. I plan to keep at it on the side when I can; this case has piqued my curiosity. That doesn't happen all that often."

"I've got to go, Mal. I'll talk to you later."

Kenna hung up. Her eyes glued to her computer screen as she opened the first file, which was the official arson report. The arson investigator was a woman named Bethany Wilkes. Kenna stopped for a moment to respect a woman in a traditionally male-dominated field. The report outlined that kerosene had been used as an accelerant. It had been placed upstairs first. In fact, the investigator believed the fire had started in Ethan and Benji's bedroom. The accelerant was then placed in the hallway before the arsonist moved downstairs and out the front door. It was enough kerosene to nearly cover the floor in the boys' bedroom and leak into the hallway and under the door of Ripley's parents' room, which was directly across the hall. The report said that the upstairs actually went up in flames nearly entirely before the fire truly began to cover the downstairs, which brought the house down. The young girl's room had been spared for last due to its placement near the outside of the house. The grandmother likely died of smoke inhalation before the fire even reached her.

"God, Ripley…"

Kenna clutched at her mouth, thinking about how Ripley had survived that. She thought back to Ripley's nightmares and wondered if Ripley had even seen this report. Did she know that at least her grandmother was spared a painful death? Maybe Kenna could find the autopsy reports on the rest of her family and find that more had died the same way. Maybe that could help alleviate some of Ripley's pain. Kenna then shook her head because she couldn't; she'd told Ripley there would be no story. While just reading these documents wasn't technically wrong, it also wasn't very right. Still, Kenna had to know more. If Malcolm thought something was here, she wanted to know it.

CHAPTER 12

RIPLEY had gone a full three days without seeing Kenna. It had been annoying that their schedules hadn't lined up to allow them to spend any time together. They'd talked on the phone, and they had texted, but Kenna had spent time in the editing bay helping a cub reporter edit a piece each night after completing her own work. She'd offered to come to Ripley's late one night, but Ripley knew she was exhausted.

She considered waiting until after the anniversary to reach out for another date, but when the night before arrived, she knew she didn't want to spend it alone. That was something so strange and new to Ripley, she almost didn't trust it. It took everything in her to pick up the phone to call Kenna and ask her to come over. Kenna showed up with two pints of ice cream from Brinkley's and food from the PV Bistro.

"You're amazing," Ripley said when she took the bag of food from Kenna.

"I missed you," Kenna said and leaned in to kiss her on the lips.

"I missed you, too," Ripley replied.

She was a little taken aback by Kenna's admission. She had assumed she'd been more into this budding romance than Kenna. Kenna had friends and family that she spent time with; she also probably had an active love life or could have had an active love life. She was smart, talented, and gorgeous. It would be easy for Kenna to find a date for every night of the week.

"I thought we could catch up on our weeks, eat copious amounts of junk food, and go to sleep," Kenna said.

She moved into the apartment, and Ripley followed her into the living room. When Ripley sat on the sofa, Kenna joined her. They opened their food containers and got settled in for what Ripley assumed was their second date. Ripley grabbed them drinks from the kitchen, and Kenna sorted their food. They ate in comfortable silence for the first several minutes before Kenna started filling Ripley in on the help she had offered the other reporter and the details of the story she'd be doing on the social workers of Pleasant Valley. Ripley was grateful that Kenna had yet to bring up the anniversary or even ask Ripley why she'd asked her to come over.

When they finished eating and had placed the remainder of the ice cream in the freezer, Ripley realized she had nothing else planned for them to do. It was still early. Her apartment was sparse. She had a TV, but it wasn't like Kenna's. It wasn't hooked up to the internet, and they couldn't stream from it. Ripley also didn't even have cable. They could watch whatever was on one of the basic channels, or they could stream something from her laptop like two college students.

"Hey, what's wrong?" Kenna leaned into her on the couch.

"I should have gone to your place tonight. I'm starting to realize I still live like I did in the dorm room," Ripley replied.

"You live fine," Kenna said. "I don't need to be entertained, Ripley."

"Good. I don't have anything here to entertain you."

"Oh, I beg to differ," Kenna replied and ran a finger down Ripley's cheek to her neck and down between her breasts. "You are more than entertaining."

"No, I'm not." Ripley laughed before placing her head on Kenna's shoulder.

Kenna wrapped an arm around her, and they just sat there for a few minutes. Ripley enjoyed the silence between them. Neither of them felt the need to fill the space with sound, and there was something comforting about having that with someone, especially someone so new to Ripley's life. Kenna began playing with the strands of Ripley's hair, and Ripley closed her eyes at the sensation. Her skin tingled as Kenna's fingertips drifted from her hair to her neck. Kenna dragged them lower still to Ripley's collarbone. Her fingers moved again to that space between Ripley's breasts. Ripley knew Kenna was silently asking for permission to continue. When Ripley failed to say anything, Kenna used her fingers to undo the top button of Ripley's shirt from work she still hadn't changed out of. When Kenna's fingers undid the second button, Ripley's skin grew hot, and her breathing picked up in speed. Kenna's hand slid inside her shirt and squeezed Ripley's breast through the material of her bra. Ripley's nipple responded and hardened with the contact, and she had yet to look up at Kenna. Ripley could feel Kenna's heart begin to match the speed of her own breaths as Kenna continued to cup and massage her breast.

When Ripley finally looked down at her own clothing, she withheld her smile because she knew Kenna would be able to feel it, and she didn't want the woman to stop anything she was doing. Kenna's arm was around the back of Ripley's neck now, massaging the skin just beneath her hairline. Her other hand was massaging Ripley's other breast. Before Ripley could even stop herself, she spread her legs wide and reached for the third button of her shirt. Once undone, Kenna's hand slid to Ripley's abdomen. It dragged across her skin and caused her to gasp in pleasure. Kenna's hand then moved back up to undo the rest of Ripley's buttons. She spread Ripley's shirt open, and Ripley could feel Kenna's eyes on her. Kenna's hand slid up and down her abdomen. She lowered the strap of Ripley's bra and exposed one of her breasts, taking one of Ripley's hands to place it on top, and encouraging Ripley to massage her own breast.

Ripley massaged her breast as her head tipped back. Kenna leaned in and sucked Ripley's earlobe into her mouth. Kenna's hand then drifted back down, resting on Ripley's knee momentarily, and then moved under Ripley's skirt to her inner thigh. It stilled there as she nibbled at the sensitive flesh of Ripley's ear. Kenna allowed her hand to move closer to Ripley's sex, and she dragged her finger up and down Ripley's clit that was already hard, ready for whatever Kenna was planning. Ripley gasped when she felt Kenna tug at her panties to pull them aside. Then, she felt Kenna's finger sliding against her skin, stroking all the tension out of her body as Ripley continued to massage her own breast.

Hearing Kenna's heated breathing in her ear was nearly enough to throw Ripley over the edge. Kenna's fingers were moving fast and hard, and it wasn't just that Ripley wanted to come; Kenna clearly wanted Ripley to come. So much so that Kenna's other hand gave Ripley's neck a slight push to the side, indicating that she wanted Ripley to lie down on the couch. Ripley didn't want to move, though. She wanted to come. She wrapped her free arm around the back of Kenna's neck, pulling the woman closer while spreading her own legs wider. Kenna took the hint and continued to stroke her.

When Ripley came, Kenna didn't allow her to come down slowly. There was no recovery time. There was Kenna pushing Ripley down onto the couch, removing her own shirt and bra, undoing the button of her black slacks, and spreading Ripley's legs again, sliding Ripley's panties aside once more, and pressing two fingers inside Ripley. Then, there was Ripley grasping one of Kenna's breasts. She slid her other hand between Kenna's legs and inside Kenna's underwear.

Kenna was wet and ready for her. Ripley cupped Kenna's sex and watched Kenna grind into her hand. Kenna's fingers were still inside her, moving her quickly toward another orgasm. When Kenna's thrusts turned less rhythmic and more chaotic, Ripley knew it was because Kenna was close to coming herself. She witnessed Kenna come while still thrusting inside Ripley, and she watched Kenna's eyes close and her head roll back as she slowed her hip movement. Ripley came when Kenna curled her fingers inside her while she watched Kenna come undone on top of her.

Kenna collapsed on top of Ripley moments later. She was breathing rapidly into Ripley's ear. They stayed like that, with Ripley's hand still tucked between Kenna's legs and Kenna's hand now on the inside of Ripley's thigh, for several minutes, until Kenna's phone sounded with a text message and disturbed their remarkable after-sex silence.

"You can get that," Ripley said into Kenna's ear.

"Why would I do that?" Kenna replied. "All I want to do is lie here with you."

"Are you sure?" Ripley asked. "You don't want to, maybe, move this to the bedroom and continue with less clothing?"

"That sounds really good," Kenna replied.

"You'll have to get off me then," Ripley told her and laughed a little.

Kenna grunted but lifted herself up, and Ripley slid her hand out of Kenna's slacks. Ripley wanted to laugh. She'd never had sex on the couch before. She had also never had *this* kind of sex on a couch before: the kind that had to happen because you both needed it to happen; the kind where Ripley couldn't wait to get all their clothes off – they just had to touch one another. Kenna stood and dropped her pants to her ankles. She then kicked them off and stood there only in her black panties. Ripley stood as well and unzipped her skirt, allowing it to fall to the floor. They made their way into the bedroom in silence, with Kenna leading her by the hand.

***

Kenna hadn't gone over to Ripley's for sex. She had gone there because she wanted to see her, she wanted to be near her, to talk to her. She also wanted to hold her. The next day would be a difficult one for Ripley, and Kenna was honored that the woman actually wanted to spend the night before the anniversary with her, when she normally spent it alone.

When they'd entered Ripley's bedroom, Ripley had been all over Kenna. She made Kenna come three times in what seemed like as many minutes. Ripley had knelt on the floor and used her mouth and that exquisite tongue. She'd climbed on top of Kenna and used her fingers to reach not just inside Kenna's body, but into her soul as well. Kenna met those hazel eyes above her and wanted nothing more than to spend the rest of the night making love with this woman. She wanted to hold her through the entire next day until the day after came and another year was behind Ripley.

She had no idea how this could have happened to her. Kenna had so little experience with real love; she wasn't even sure this was what it felt like. If not that, whatever this was, though – it felt good. Ripley was the calm to her storm. Kenna would do whatever it took to keep this thing on track. Unfortunately, her boss had insisted she continue on the trail with Mal to find out if the investigators missed something about the fire. Kenna hated the fact, but she also liked doing this part of her job. She liked spending hours upon hours digging into the documents. She'd even lined up an interview with Bethany Wilkes and a few of the neighbors who witnessed the fire. She hadn't told Ripley about any of this yet, and she knew she'd have to soon, but as Ripley lay on her chest with slow, steady breaths tickling Kenna's skin, she knew she'd wait for as long as she could.

Kenna woke up hours later to a shivering Ripley, who was lying in the fetal position facing away from her. Kenna wrapped her arm around Ripley's naked form and pulled her back into herself. She then wiped damp hair from Ripley's forehead and soothed her with words until Ripley stopped shivering and appeared to calm down. Ripley then woke up again later, and Kenna just pulled her back into herself a second time. She also moved Ripley closer to the middle of the bed. Kenna didn't fall asleep again, but Ripley appeared to. When the woman started sweating, Kenna knew she was having another nightmare. In her sleep, Ripley was trying to slide to the edge of the bed again, but this time, Kenna climbed half on top of her to keep her in place.

"Ripley, you're okay," she whispered. "You're okay. It's okay."

Kenna stayed in that position until her alarm went off the next morning. She moved to turn it off, wishing she wouldn't have set it to begin with, and Ripley woke with a start. She glanced around herself while her hand slid over the sheets as if checking for Kenna, who had moved to the other edge of the bed to deal with her phone.

"You're still here?" Ripley asked when she looked at Kenna, who climbed back in bed.

"Of course, I'm still here."

Kenna moved into Ripley's body, wrapping her arm over Ripley's waist and placing her head on Ripley's chest.

"I had a rough night," Ripley said after a moment. "I'm sorry. I hate that I probably kept you awake."

"You did, but I don't mind." Kenna knew it was the truth. "I actually liked watching over you while you slept."

"And while I woke up? While I nearly sweated through the sheets and shook?" Ripley asked more than told.

"I just held you, Rip. I have no problem holding you," Kenna said.

"I should get up. I have to get my workout in before work," Ripley replied.

"I thought you were working from home today."

"I am, but I work out every morning." Ripley paused. "It helps. Today, I need it more than normal."

"I don't want to put this out there if you think it's crass, but I know of a particularly good workout that involves distracting you from your thoughts and also burns calories," Kenna chanced as she dragged her two fingertips over Ripley's abdomen. Ripley didn't say anything in response, and from Kenna's position on her chest, she couldn't see Ripley's reaction. "Rip, I'm sorry. I didn't–"

"It's okay," Ripley interrupted. "I would love to do that with you. Hell, I'd love to do that with you all day, but today isn't a good day for me. I love that you stayed last night, but I think I need to be alone today. I'm sorry. I thought I could do this. Had I known I'd be freaking out this morning, I wouldn't have asked you to come over."

"What do you mean?" Kenna sat up to face her. "Do you regret last night?"

"No, Kenna," Ripley stated immediately. "I just can't do it today."

"I'm sorry. It was a stupid thing to say. If you really think you need to be alone, I'll go, but I did take today off in case you needed me here."

"You took today off?" Ripley asked.

"If you didn't need me, I was just going to work from home. I just wanted to be here for you if you did," Kenna explained. "This is new. I didn't know what the protocol was, but I get that you want to be alone."

"I didn't know you took the day off," Ripley said and stood up. "I wish you would have told me."

"Why? It wouldn't have changed anything. I didn't intentionally keep it from you, though. I just forgot to mention it."

"I need to work out." Ripley crossed her arms over her bare chest as she stood in front of the bed, naked.

"What's really going on?" Kenna shifted so that she was sitting with her legs hanging over the end of the bed just a few feet away from Ripley.

"Kenna, this is a really hard day for me. I'm normally by myself. I shouldn't have called you last night. I should have known better, that I couldn't do this."

"If you want me to go, I'll go; but please don't say that you shouldn't have called last night. Last night was amazing for me, and I'm not just talking about sex. I'd missed you the past few days. I wanted to see you. I think you wanted that, too."

"I did, Kenna." Ripley's arms tightened over her chest. "I don't want to fight with you."

"No, do it. Fight with me," Kenna replied. "Let's do it. Let's get it all out there. Tell me exactly what you're thinking right now."

"Kenna, please, just go." Ripley turned to her dresser and pulled out some clothes Kenna couldn't see from her position. "I have a routine I need to do. It helps. And I can't do it with you here."

"You did it the other day when you slept over."

"This isn't the other day!" Ripley's voice was louder and firmer than it had been only moments before. "This is *the* day. My entire family was murdered, Kenna. Someone lit our house on fire and killed them all." Ripley paused and slid on a pair of underwear before standing upright and facing Kenna. "Please, just go," she added softly.

"Keep going," Kenna encouraged.

"What? No," Ripley replied and slid her athletic shorts on. "Why are you egging me on like this?"

"Because someone has to. You're angry, but you don't let it out."

"I have a therapist, Kenna; I don't need you."

That last line hurt Kenna in her soul. She knew how Ripley meant it, but that didn't change the way the words hit Kenna like a brick in her chest. She didn't lower her head, though. She didn't stand to gather her clothes. She just sat there on the edge of the bed while Ripley put on a sports bra.

"I don't want to be your therapist, Ripley. I wouldn't mind being someone in your life that cares about you, that supports you, and that you fight with sometimes," she said.

"Why? I am a mess, Kenna. You know that already."

"And I'm still here."

Ripley had a shirt on now, and she had moved several feet away from Kenna. Her arms crossed over her chest again. Kenna stood, still nude, and moved toward her. She lowered Ripley's arms to her sides and wrapped her own around her waist. It took a moment, but Ripley's arms moved around her neck. Then, she pulled Kenna in hard. They stood like that, embracing, for several moments before Ripley started to shudder, and the tears began to fall against Kenna's skin.

Kenna pulled her ever closer. She tightened her arms, rubbed Ripley's back, and let her know without words that she was there. She wouldn't let her go until Ripley was ready. After a while, Kenna moved them back to bed, where she helped Ripley lie down, threw on one of Ripley's t-shirts, and moved to lie next to her while Ripley still cried. Kenna stayed next to her, pressing soft kisses to her cheek and neck. At some point, she also went to the bathroom to retrieve tissues and to get Ripley some water from the kitchen, and when she returned to bed, Ripley still cried. Kenna could only watch the hurt come through in Ripley's tears, and she wished she could do something to take the pain away, to bring back Ripley's family.

When it appeared Ripley was out of tears to cry, Kenna started the shower for her, returning to the bedroom right after to help remove Ripley's clothes. Kenna also pulled her t-shirt off, and they climbed under the water together. She washed Ripley's skin as she kissed her cheeks and eyelids. Ripley said nothing as Kenna cared for her, and Kenna did nothing to break the silence out of fear Ripley would again ask her to go. When they were done in the shower, Kenna toweled the woman off and dressed her back in her shorts and shirt sans the sports bra. Ripley didn't argue. She rolled onto her side and stared off into space. Kenna rubbed her back for a few minutes before she went into the kitchen to see if Ripley had anything she could make for breakfast.

"Hey, Danielle," Kenna said softly into her phone. "I know you don't normally deliver, but I'm in a bit of a situation."

"What's up?" her cousin asked.

"Can you have someone drop off some food for me

about fifteen minutes from the restaurant? I can't leave right now – long story – but I'd owe you big time," Kenna said.

"We're kind of slammed right now, but I can probably step out for a few minutes and bring it to you."

"Really? There's a big tip in it for you," Kenna joked.

"For the food I give you for free? There better be," Danielle joked back. "What do you want, and where am I bringing it?"

After giving Danielle the order, Kenna returned to Ripley's side. She spooned the woman from behind, wishing it was for a different reason than consoling Ripley. About thirty minutes later, there was a buzz from the outer door.

"Who's that?" Ripley spoke for the first time in a while.

"Food. I'll be right back."

Kenna kissed Ripley's shoulder and climbed out of bed. She grabbed the food from her cousin without giving her too many details but informing her that this was not a one-night-stand situation she was trying to wiggle out of by using food. Danielle left it at that and departed. Kenna felt it was important to try to treat today as normally as possible for Ripley. She set the food out on the coffee table, made them coffee in Ripley's kitchen, and moved back into the bedroom.

"Rip, I have breakfast in the living room. I asked Danielle to make what you ordered the other day," Kenna told her as she leaned over the bed and rubbed her back. "Come on, babe."

"I'm not hungry," Ripley replied.

"I am," Kenna said. "So, I'll be eating in the living room. I'd love it if you join me."

Kenna stood, after kissing Ripley on the cheek, and went into the living room.

CHAPTER 13

Ripley didn't move for another several minutes before she finally had to admit that she was hungry. She also had to acknowledge that Kenna was being amazing. Ripley moved slowly into the living room, and Kenna smiled at her when Ripley sat next to her. They ate in relative silence. Once they were both finished, Ripley's head made its way to Kenna's lap, and they just sat like that – with Kenna playing with Ripley's hair and applying soft touches to her skin – for a long time.

When Ripley finally felt like she was a person again, she grabbed her laptop and a few of her hard copy files to get some work done. Kenna had her laptop in her bag by the door. Ripley took her usual spot at the dining room table while Kenna worked in the living room. Ripley guessed she was doing research or communicating via email with her colleagues since Kenna was silent as she worked.

"Are you working on the story for Jessica?" Ripley asked and finally broke the silence between them.

"What?" Kenna snapped out of it and looked away from her computer.

"Your work? Are you working on the story for Jessica?"

"Oh," Kenna said and seemed a little surprised. "That and some other things. I don't usually work on one thing at a time. There's a lot of overlap."

"Can you take a break?" Ripley asked.

"Of course," Kenna said, immediately closing her laptop.

Ripley considered what to say next. For some reason, she hadn't prepared herself for Kenna saying yes. She had been crying most of the morning, and crying was something she was very much accustomed to after a night of difficult nightmares. The part she wasn't accustomed to was crying around someone else. She hated that Kenna had seen her that way, but Kenna had been there. She'd been the one to hold Ripley last night, to assure her she was still there and not leaving. She'd hugged her this morning, when all Ripley wanted to do was to push her away.

Ripley hated that she'd missed out on having parents tell her how to navigate relationships like this. Not a single foster parent ever gave her advice about her love life or lack thereof. Friends were nice in these situations, too, but Ripley didn't really have any. There was something to be said, however, about a parent advising you about a potential or current partner. It was as if their wisdom, coming from being much older and having been through the situation likely more than once, was their secret they shared only with their children. At least, that was Ripley's understanding of it. She had never experienced it herself.

"Can we take a drive?" she asked.

"Where do you want to go?" Kenna asked back.

*   *   *

The drive was relatively short. It was then that Kenna realized Ripley lived only about ten minutes from where this horrible thing had happened to her. Even Ripley's college campus was in town and only another ten minutes away in the opposite direction from her apartment. That meant Ripley had always lived within twenty minutes of her old house. Well, that house wasn't there anymore. What was there was a different house on the same land that was about eighteen years old now. Kenna knew that because she had been researching what had happened after the fire. She had actually been in this neighborhood the other day to introduce herself to a few neighbors and set up interviews.

"This is it," Ripley said, and Kenna had to remind herself to act like she didn't already know that.

"The house?" she asked.

"It's a different house in its place. Mine was burned to the ground," Ripley replied.

They sat in Kenna's car, which was parked on the other side of the street opposite the house. Kenna hesitated to get out of the car. If one of the neighbors she had talked to saw her now, that would be difficult to explain to Ripley. She could lie to her about meeting the neighbors before she had agreed to drop the story, but she didn't want to lie to Ripley. Kenna hated keeping this from her, but as much as she wanted to tell her what Shannon was making her work on, she couldn't do that to Ripley today of all days.

"Do you come back here often?"

"I never come back here," Ripley replied, still with her eyes on the house across the street. "This is the first time I've been back since it happened."

"What?" Kenna turned in her seat to face her. "You live, like, ten minutes away."

"I avoid this street," Ripley confessed. "I actually had a case here once; down the street, technically. When I realized what street it was on, I asked Jessica to give it to someone else."

"Why did you want to come today?" Kenna asked.

Ripley reached for her hand and took it. Kenna looked down at their joined hands and smiled. Ripley finally met her gaze when she looked back up.

"Because I needed to finally do this."

"Do you want to walk around?" Kenna asked. "I can wait here."

"No, this is about all I can handle today."

"I can drive us back to your place when you're ready," Kenna offered. "Or, we can get lunch. It's after two, and you haven't eaten since breakfast."

"I have an idea," Ripley said.

"What's your idea?" Kenna smiled when she noticed Ripley smile for the first time that day.

"Thank you for taking care of me today. You've gone above and beyond, Kenna," Ripley said.

Kenna's smile widened, and she replied, "I care about you. I know this started as some story to me, but I hope you know it's much more than that now."

Kenna gulped then. She really did hope Ripley knew that, because if Shannon kept persisting, the story about Ripley would come out with or without an interview from the subject. That might even play better in Shannon's mind. Kenna could hear Shannon's argument about still going ahead with it even though Ripley didn't want to participate. She'd frame it like Ripley was too traumatized to tell her story even twenty years later. And Kenna knew Shannon was already upset with her as-is for missing the chance to air the story at or around the anniversary date.

"I do know that," Ripley said. "I think I'd like to be alone for a little while, though. I'd like to actually walk home from here and try to get myself out of this funk that always comes over me."

"If that's what you want, it's fine."

"Can I come to your place for dinner? I can bring the food."

"You want to come over tonight?"

"Unless you have plans," Ripley said.

"I don't. And I'd love it if you came over for dinner."

Ripley smiled and asked, "Can I stay?"

"You can absolutely stay over," Kenna answered. "Tonight is probably not the night, but I think we should talk about what we're doing here sooner than later."

"We can talk about it now." Ripley leaned in and kissed Kenna gently on the lips. "I like you, and I like what we're doing. I'd like to do more of it."

"I guess that works for now." Kenna kissed her back.

"Do you need more than that?" Ripley sat back a little but still kept her hand in Kenna's.

"Not yet." Kenna shrugged.

"Not yet?" Ripley's left eyebrow lifted.

"You're sexy when you do that, so don't do that now," Kenna said.

"When I do what?" Ripley laughed.

"Lift that eyebrow." Kenna pointed at it with her free hand. "Stop it."

Ripley's eyebrow-lift intensified, and she smiled with her eyes. It was a beautiful sight.

"You said 'not yet' before. Does that mean you'd like this to turn into something?" Ripley asked as she dropped her eyebrow and a playful smile.

"It already is something, Rip."

***

Ripley walked home deep in thought. She thought about her parents, her brothers, and her grandmother. She thought about that night, replaying it over and over in her head. She thought about watching the fire spread through her bedroom. She thought about the fireman who rescued her from the blaze. As she walked, though, Ripley thought less and less about the fire and how she'd lost her family; thoughts of her various foster homes faded from her mind, and thoughts of Kenna Crawford took over. Kenna stayed. She watched Ripley fall apart, and she stayed. No one had ever stayed before or wanted Ripley to stay with them. When she arrived at Kenna's a few hours later, it was with dinner and a smile on her face she still couldn't believe.

"You seem chipper," Kenna said and leaned in to kiss Ripley on the lips.

Ripley then carried the food to the dining room table she'd been sprawled all over a few days ago.

"You did clean this, right?" she asked.

Kenna laughed and said, "Yes, it's clean."

"This is going to come out wrong, but I honestly don't care." Ripley turned back to face the woman, who still stood by the door that she had just closed. "I want to have sex with you," she added. "Right now."

"What?" Kenna chuckled for a second before she took in Ripley's serious expression. "You're serious?"

"Very serious. I want you. I've thought about you all afternoon, Kenna." Ripley moved into Kenna's space and wrapped her arms around the woman's waist. "I don't want to talk about anything. I just want you to take me into your bedroom and do whatever you want to me."

"That's really not a problem." Kenna gulped. "But what about the food?"

"I ordered salads," Ripley said with a smirk before she leaned in and captured Kenna's lips.

***

They ate those salads several hours later and in bed. Then, Kenna went to draw them a bath while Ripley tossed their trash in the kitchen. Ripley passed Kenna's office on the way back into the bedroom and realized she never did get that tour of Kenna's place. She walked inside and took a look around the room. It was fairly organized and slightly decorated while still using some wall space for functional purposes. Kenna had a bulletin board on one wall and a painting on another. Ripley noticed that Kenna's desk had a pile of papers all over it, which made her think of her own kitchen table covered in files. One piece of paper was on the floor next to Kenna's desk chair. Ripley bent over to pick it up for her and placed it back on Kenna's desk. That was when she noticed it. Then, she noticed something else and something else after that.

"Please, let me explain," Kenna said from behind her.

CHAPTER 14

"THIS says 'arson report' and has my address on it," Ripley stated. "This is a picture of my old house, Kenna." She pointed at a photograph on Kenna's desk. "Kenna, this is the story. You said you weren't doing it."

"I'm not." Kenna walked over to her. "Shannon is."

"Who is Shannon?" Ripley didn't even look at Kenna. She just kept looking down at Kenna's desk. "Why does she care about what happened to me?"

"She's my producer, Ripley. She found out about my pitch and is going to pursue it with or without me."

"Then, why do you have all this here?" Ripley turned to her. "Shouldn't Shannon have all this stuff?"

Kenna lowered her head and realized they were both still naked. They hadn't bothered to put on clothing to eat their dinner in bed.

"Our investigator has found some new information."

"Investigator?"

"The station has one we use for stuff like this. His name is Malcolm, and he found some stuff he wanted to continue looking into. He sent it to me, and I've been looking into it myself. I was going to tell you."

"When?" Ripley asked.

"Not today, Ripley," Kenna stated. "I found out the other day that Shannon was pursuing it, and I spent an hour trying to convince her to just let me do the social work story and forget about you. She didn't listen."

113

"So, you're hoping to get an interview with me before we fall asleep tonight? Or are you hoping for another round of sex to loosen me up more so you can get me to divulge all my secrets?" Ripley asked.

"*I'm* not doing the story. Shannon has someone else on it now." Kenna tried to take Ripley's hands, but Ripley wouldn't unfold them from her chest. "She's my boss. There's nothing I can do."

"Then, why do you have research on your desk, Kenna?"

"Can we just go back into the bedroom and throw on some clothes? The bath is running; I need to turn it off."

"I'm putting on clothes, yes. Then, I'm leaving."

"Ripley, come on," Kenna said.

"Kenna, I asked you not to do this. I asked you about the story," Ripley replied as she moved past Kenna and out of the office.

Kenna followed close behind but veered into the bathroom to turn off what was supposed to be their relaxing bath. She went into the bedroom, where she saw Ripley hastily putting on her bra.

"I didn't do anything, Ripley. Before you and I started this, I asked Malcolm to look into you; that is true. Then, I told him to stop."

"You asked an investigator to look into me? And when did you tell him to stop? Before or after we had sex?"

"Are you kidding me right now?" Kenna's voice grew louder. "Are you really asking me that?"

Ripley had her shirt and underwear on now. She only had to slide her jeans and shoes on, and she'd be out the door. Kenna would lose this chance to explain.

"How am I supposed to know?" Ripley asked.

"Because you know me. I'm not that person. I didn't sleep with you for some story. I slept with you because I like you. If I just wanted a story out of you, do you think I would have held you last night? Do you think I would have wiped sweat from your forehead? That I would have whispered

114

that everything will be okay? Ripley, I told Mal to stop before you and I even went to that bar. I told him to stop before I stayed at your place and slept next to you for the first time. The only thing I've done wrong here is not tell you that Shannon is putting someone else on the story."

"Then, why do you have the files?" Ripley questioned. "They're on your desk, Kenna. They're at your house."

Her pants were on now. She slid her shoes onto her feet and looked around, likely for her phone or purse.

"I am a reporter," Kenna began. "It's part of me. I research. I dig. I need to know."

"Well, I don't!" Ripley yelled, and it was the loudest Kenna had ever heard her speak. "I don't need to know! I don't need to relive it for you or for some news story!"

"I should have told you. I'm sorry."

"I'm going home."

"Ripley, don't just leave."

Ripley was past her and heading toward Kenna's front door. Kenna grabbed at the shirt Ripley had stripped off her when she had first arrived and slid it on so that she was at least half-clothed.

"Of course, I'm leaving. I just found out my girl-" Ripley stopped herself when she reached the front door. "You've been researching me. You've read reports on what happened to me and to my family."

Kenna knew Ripley was about to say the word 'girlfriend.' And the fact that she'd stopped made Kenna worry that this was over. She had messed up.

"Please, stay. Sit down, and we'll talk about this."

"We're not talking. We're fighting."

"Then fight!" Kenna yelled.

"I don't want to fight." Ripley turned back to her to say. "I want to go home."

"You don't just leave when things get hard, Ripley."

"Maybe I do."

"Ripley, I am asking you to please stay," Kenna said softly. "Stay and fight with me. Stay and fight because it matters." Kenna let out a deep breath. "Because I matter to you."

Ripley turned back to the door, opened it, and closed it behind her.

***

"Jessica, can I talk to you?" Ripley asked. "In private?"

"Sure." The woman pointed at one of the available conference rooms, and they walked there together.

Ripley entered second and closed the door behind them. Jessica sat down in the chair facing the window outside, and Ripley sat facing her.

"I know you met with Kenna Crawford about doing a story for Channel 8."

"I did," Jessica replied.

"I don't think it's a good idea, Jess. I'm really worried they're planning something."

"She promised me the good PR, Rip."

Ripley wanted to make a comment about how Kenna had promised her things, too, but this wasn't the time or the place.

"Her boss wants to turn the story. I'm worried Kenna, even if she has good intentions, isn't the person with the final say about what's going out there."

"You think her boss might take whatever she does and turn it into something that works against us?" Jessica asked as she leaned forward in her seat.

"I don't know, and that's what worries me," Ripley said.

"What are you basing this on?" Jessica asked.

"I guess it's a gut feeling," Ripley answered.

"Because she tried to make it about you first?"

Ripley took a deep breath and said, "Because I don't know her boss, Jess."

"How about this? I'll ask Kenna for a meeting with her boss to see what all this is about. We'll get an agreement on what can air and what's off the record before anything begins. That way, we're protected."

"Oh, I guess that could work," Ripley said and tried to appear nonchalant. She'd been hoping to persuade Jessica to not do the story at all. "Are you sure this is worth it?"

"I trust your gut, Rip. You have great instincts. It's one of the things that makes you so good at your job. I'll talk to the boss and see what's going on. If the station is trying to railroad us, I'll stop it before it starts. Is that good?" Jessica placed both palms flat on the table and pushed her chair back, indicating that she was done with the meeting.

Ripley just nodded in response. Jessica nodded back confidently and left the room. Ripley was left sitting in her chair as she felt the vibration of her phone in her pocket for at least the tenth time that day. Kenna had called her three times after Ripley left her condo. She had also texted a bunch of times. Ripley hadn't known how to respond. She'd just gone to work the next day after waking up to more texts and a few voicemails.

This morning though, she'd woken up to nothing. Maybe Kenna had given up. Maybe she would just move on and find some other story to pursue and another woman to sleep with, while Ripley just went to work and focused on the kids she helped. That was what Ripley was good at: helping kids. She wasn't good at this adult relationship stuff. It was probably for the best. That was what she'd tried to convince herself of for the past two days, until she saw Kenna standing on the steps of her office building, holding a cup of coffee in her hand.

CHAPTER 15

KENNA had called. She'd texted. She'd left many voicemails. Ripley hadn't replied to any of her attempts, though. The way Kenna viewed it, today might be her last shot. It was Friday afternoon. She got a decaf for Ripley, a regular coffee for herself, and was now standing outside the municipal building, waiting for Ripley to go home for the weekend. She knew the woman was there because her car was still in the lot. She also knew the coffees in her hands were now cold because it was after six, and there was still no sign of Ripley. Finally, Ripley appeared. She noticed Kenna right away, and while Kenna smiled at her hopefully, Ripley closed her eyes in aggravation before taking a few steps toward her.

"Kenna, why are you here?"

"Because you won't return any of my messages," Kenna told her and held out Ripley's coffee. "This is cold now, but I got it for you."

"I don't want your coffee, Kenna," Ripley replied.

"Fine." Kenna tossed it in the trash can along with her own untouched cup. "Did you at least read my texts or listen to my voicemails?"

"Yes," Ripley replied. "But it doesn't change anything, Kenna. I'm still mad at you."

"Then, be mad. Just talk to me. Fight with me if you want to, but don't disappear," Kenna tried.

Ripley stood next to her on the bottom step but looked at the parking lot across the street and not at Kenna. Kenna moved in front of her, effectively forcing Ripley to meet her eye.

"I don't get mad, Kenna – at least, not with stuff involving me or what happened. I get mad because kids don't have loving homes to go home to each night. I don't get mad about what happened to me because it doesn't do me any good. It happened. There's nothing I can do to bring them back."

"This isn't about that, Ripley. This is about you being upset with me for not telling you I was still working on the fire. You have every right to be upset with me about that. Every right," Kenna repeated. "But if this is going to work between us, you have to be willing to fight with me when I do something stupid or when you're angry with me."

"Isn't this over?" Ripley asked.

"It just started," Kenna said. "I don't want it to be over. I will do whatever you need me to, Ripley. I promise, I'm not doing a story on you. While I can't control what the station does, I promise I tried to stop Shannon."

"What is it exactly that you seem to need to know about what happened? Why all the reports?"

"Because I want to know who did this to you. Someone did this to your family, and they've gotten away with it. You may not want to know, but I do, because that person deserves to be locked away for the rest of their lives, Ripley. They hurt you. I don't want anyone to hurt you," Kenna said and knew it was true. "I don't ever want to hurt you again."

"I don't want you to hurt me, either," Ripley replied. "I've been hurt enough, Kenna."

"Can we try again?"

"Can you stop working on finding out what happened?" Ripley asked.

"This is part of me, Ripley: this need to know, the drive to uncover; it's a big part of me. I can't just turn it off."

"I'm not asking you to turn it off. I'm asking you to back away from the fire."

"Can I just show you what I've done so far? What I've found out with Mal?"

"Kenna, I–"

"Please," Kenna interrupted. "Come over tonight. I'll show you what we have, and if you really want me to stop after that, I will."

"If I tell you to stop after you show me whatever it is you're working on, you'll stop?" Ripley checked.

"I promise. I'll even give you all the hard copies, and you can delete the digital stuff yourself," Kenna offered.

Ripley stared at her with those gorgeous hazel eyes. Kenna waited for what felt like several minutes for her to respond.

Finally, Ripley nodded and said, "I'll drive myself there."

Kenna smiled wide and motioned for Ripley to walk ahead of her. They walked to the parking lot without another word before Ripley climbed into her car first, and Kenna had to walk a little bit farther to where she had parked, a few rows over. Ripley beat her to the condo, but not by much. She was now standing outside her car, waiting, with her messenger bag across her chest. She was playing with the strap again. As soon as Kenna approached her, she took the bag from her shoulder and put it over her own. Ripley blushed a little and gave her a small smile before they went inside the building.

"Mal found something interesting," Kenna began when she sat on the sofa inside her office next to Ripley. She held out a file for Ripley to take, which she did. "Did you know anyone named Patrick Wilkes?"

"I don't think so. Why?" Ripley asked and rifled through the file.

"He was the same age as your brother, Ethan. They were in the same class at school."

"Patty? Right, I remember him. He and Ethan were

friends. He used to come over to the house sometimes."

"Was he there that night?" Kenna asked.

"I don't think so. Why?" Ripley glanced up at Kenna.

"Would you mind walking me through that night? Before the fire? I promise, I will never ask you to do this again, Rip." Kenna placed her hand on Ripley's thigh.

Ripley looked back down at the file first, and then back up at Kenna with knitted eyebrows.

"I don't remember that much."

"Just whatever you do remember."

"I think it was really hot that day. I don't know. Maybe that's just the heat from the fire invading my memory. I know Benji had three of his friends over. They played soccer in the backyard. We had one of those goal things. I tried to play, too, but he told me they had even numbers." Ripley smiled at the memory. "My mom made us chicken nuggets for dinner, and my dad was in his office. I remember that because my mom made me take him a plate because he didn't come out for dinner. He did that sometimes." She paused and squinted as if by doing so, the memories would come back to her. "Ethan spent most of the evening in his room. I remember walking by it when mom made me wash up for dinner. He was on the phone." Ripley glanced over at Kenna. "We didn't have cell phones then. He was on the landline. I remember he saw me, stood up, and closed the door so I couldn't hear."

"Was he talking to a girl or something?" Kenna smiled.

"I don't know, but I don't think so. He sounded upset, though. I don't remember him having a girlfriend, and he wouldn't have told me anyway; I was his kid sister." Ripley paused again. "That's about it. I went to bed before the boys. I think they stayed downstairs and watched TV with my mom, but I don't know."

"And you didn't hear anyone come into the house?" Kenna asked.

"No, I was asleep."

"What do you remember about Patrick?"

"Not much. He and Ethan hung out sometimes, but Ethan and I were in different schools. I was at Scott Elementary, and he was in Junior High."

"Patrick had been to your house, though?"

"A few times at least, I'm sure," Ripley replied. "Why are you asking about Patrick?"

"He was new in town, right?" Kenna didn't answer her question.

"I don't know. Maybe."

"His family moved here the year before the fire."

"If you know that, why did you ask me?" Ripley asked.

"Look at this." Kenna pointed at a page in the file Ripley still held. "Mal found this. Patrick and his mom moved here from Blessings, Montana, when he was twelve. He had a record as a juvenile. It was sealed, but Mal somehow found it." Ripley looked at her with a concerned expression, so Kenna added, "I don't ask. It's better that way."

"What was it for?"

"He started fires, Ripley." Kenna pointed to the charge that was outlined on one of the pages. "He started two garbage can fires on the main street in town and got off with warnings. Then, he started one in the woods behind his neighbor's house. One of the trees caught fire and fell over. According to the report, it caused major structural damage to their house. His mom had to pay for the damages, and he did time in juvenile hall. They moved here after he got out."

"You think a thirteen-year-old boy started the fire that killed my family?" Ripley closed the file in her hands. "Kenna, it's one thing to light cans on fire. He would have intentionally lit my house on fire, knowing people were inside. He killed them, Kenna."

"It happens, Ripley. People escalate. I checked into it, and there were two other fires before that one. One was just outside a bookstore and started in a trash can. The other was inside a hardware store. There were things stolen from there, too, Rip. Whoever did it, stole bolt cutters, some duct tape, and kerosene."

"Kerosene?" Ripley asked softly.

"I'm sorry." Kenna rubbed Ripley's back. "Patrick went to live with his dad after the fire. Did you hear about the fires recently? There were three of them around town."

"I guess, yeah."

"Patrick moved back about seven months ago. He works at that hardware store now," Kenna explained.

"How do you know this? How did you even begin to think about Patrick, Kenna?"

"Malcolm found the arson report by the fire department's investigator. He remembered seeing a name that sounded familiar from one of the interviews done on the scene. Patrick was there, Ripley. He was, for some reason, down the street when it happened, according to the report. He gave a statement to the police that he was walking home from your house after hanging out with Ethan, and he told them he hadn't seen anything."

"What about his record from the other town?" Ripley asked, her voice growing stronger.

"It was sealed, remember? No one outside of his mom knew about his past," Kenna told her. "That's not the worst part, though. Patrick's mother is the arson investigator. Her name is Bethany Wilkes. She's still the city's only arson investigator."

"You think his mother covered it up for him?"

"I talked to her yesterday. I tried to make it about the new fires. I wanted to see how she'd respond. She gave me the standard line that she couldn't comment about an open investigation, and I asked if she thought they had any connection to some old fires I'd dug up in my research. She clammed up for a second before she gave the same speech. Since it was arson, and people were killed, it's still an open investigation, too, even though it's cold."

"You talked to her?" Ripley asked, lifting both eyebrows in surprise.

"I wanted to meet her face to face. I wanted to see how

she'd react, and it was exactly what I thought it would be."

"Why would he do it? He and Ethan were friends." Ripley let go of more than tossed the file to the floor. "Why would he do this?"

"I don't know. Maybe Ethan was talking to Patrick on the phone that night. You said he sounded like he was fighting with someone. Maybe it was Patrick, and it ticked him off."

"Enough to kill my whole family?" Ripley shouted and stood.

"I don't know," Kenna answered honestly. "People like Patrick aren't like you and me. They think differently."

Ripley looked around Kenna's office for a moment. Then, she sat back down next to her on the couch. Kenna wrapped an arm around the back of it but didn't touch her.

"What happens now?" Ripley asked.

CHAPTER 16

RIPLEY reviewed the file again. Then, she looked at the arson investigator's report. She reviewed every other document Kenna had on her desk with the exception of the autopsy reports; there was no way she'd ever be able to review those. Kenna had gone into the kitchen to make them sandwiches for dinner, leaving Ripley alone in her office. She returned, dropped a plate on the desk next to Ripley, and moved to the office couch after kissing Ripley on the top of the head. Ripley continued to read while she took bites out of her sandwich. Kenna was typing away on her laptop. They worked independently and silently until Kenna stood, approached the desk, and wrapped her arms around Ripley's neck.

"It's getting late. Let's go to bed," she said and kissed Ripley's cheek.

"What if Malcolm calls?" Ripley asked.

"He won't be calling tonight, babe." Kenna rubbed Ripley's shoulders. "He's going to wait until tomorrow to call his old captain at the precinct to see about getting the investigation started again. Why don't we try to get some sleep? If you want, I can call Mal tomorrow to check in."

"Okay," Ripley replied.

It was well after midnight at this point. After Ripley had agreed that they should pursue this further, Kenna had called Malcolm. He had decided that going about this the right way was important if it was going to go to trial. He knew his old captain would be interested in solving this very old case. They made the plan that he'd call him tomorrow morning and get a meeting on the books to review what Malcolm had discovered. After her initial shock had worn off, Ripley dove into Kenna's research.

"I might not be able to sleep after looking at all this," Ripley replied as she looked up to meet Kenna's eyes.

"We can stay up and talk if you want," Kenna offered before kissing her forehead.

They made their way to the bedroom, where Kenna again let Ripley borrow clothes to sleep in. As Ripley changed, Kenna watched her. Ripley could feel Kenna's eyes on her. She turned around and met Kenna's blue stare.

"You're worried about me, aren't you?" Ripley asked.

"I don't want to hurt you. I already have once. I guess I'm worried that if nothing happens with this or even if something does, it's going to come back to me letting you down."

"Kenna, you haven't let me down," Ripley said. "You've been amazing. You've taken care of me. You've managed to make me laugh, which isn't easy. I'll admit, I'm still not a hundred percent happy that you didn't tell me about all this when you first found out about it, but I guess I can understand why you didn't."

Ripley sat in Kenna's lap, straddling her thighs and placing her arms around Kenna's neck. Kenna's own hand moved around Ripley's lower back and rubbed up and down over her shirt.

"I want this to end well. If he's responsible, I want him to pay for what he did to you and your family, Rip."

"Let's not talk about it now. We've spent the whole night on it already,"

"Deal," Kenna agreed.

Ripley leaned down to kiss her. They hadn't shared a proper kiss since before all this came up, and Ripley wanted to kiss Kenna. She'd missed her so much.

"Hey, thank you." Ripley separated their lips but kept them only millimeters away from Kenna's.

"For what? Am I that good of a kisser?" Kenna smiled.

"Yes." Ripley chuckled and kissed her lips again. "But you're also stubborn, and you didn't let me hide. You kept pushing until I talked to you."

"I don't want you to hide." Kenna kissed her again. "Not from this, not from me, or from anything else."

Ripley captured her lips again, placing both of her hands on Kenna's cheeks. One of the things Ripley liked so much about this woman she was straddling was that she always seemed to know what Ripley needed. Kenna's lips moved in pace with her own. Ripley moved slowly and deliberately at first, but Kenna's hands under her shirt turned her on; she had no choice but to intensify their kiss. One of her favorite things about Kenna, though, was that she communicated so much silently. Instead of asking Ripley if she could touch her, or breaking their kiss to interrupt it with any words at all, Kenna just placed one hand on Ripley's stomach, sliding her thumb along the waistband of the shorts Ripley was borrowing.

Kenna didn't ask if they should just go to sleep instead, given that it had been a difficult day for Ripley. She didn't suggest they talk more about what had happened or try to plan what will happen. She just kissed Ripley's neck while her hand slid between Ripley's legs and cupped her. Kenna's fingers played in Ripley's already gathering wetness until they found her clit, and she stroked Ripley with one hand while holding her lower back with the other. Kenna slid inside her while Ripley ground down into her hand, rocking her hips into Kenna's stomach. Ripley pulled her shirt over her head, and Kenna's lips immediately found a nipple and sucked it into her mouth. Ripley loved this. She loved Kenna touching her in this way, without words, and reaching deep inside Ripley physically and emotionally to coax pleasure from her. Kenna's teeth pulled at Ripley's nipple, and she let it go with a pop. Ripley pushed Kenna's shoulders down, causing Kenna to flop onto the bed with a smirk on her face. Her free hand started tugging at Ripley's shorts on one side. Ripley pulled them down as far as they could go while Kenna was still inside her, stroking, rubbing, and curling in just the right way. Ripley's hips rode Kenna's fingers faster and harder, and her hands moved to either side of Kenna's head, allowing Kenna to thrust up and into her. Ripley wanted her clit to come, so she pushed harder into Kenna's palm. Kenna's hips moved up and into her, matching her pace and desire. Ripley's orgasm took form with a particularly hard thrust deep inside, and it moved higher when Kenna pulled out and thrust back into Ripley even harder. What took her over the edge, though, was Kenna's fingers curling inside her and rubbing her. Ripley couldn't believe this woman wanted her. As she came, she said Kenna's name into Kenna's ear, and she took a hand and slid it under Kenna's shirt, craving her skin. She kissed Kenna hard as her orgasm continued to roll through her. When she finally started to come down, Ripley leaned up, put her hand on Kenna's wrist, and slid Kenna's hand out of her body.

Ripley stood, removed her shorts and underwear before reaching for Kenna's. Once she had them off, and Kenna had removed her own shirt, Ripley straddled Kenna again. She had never done what she was about to do, but she wanted to do it now. Kenna's hands were on Ripley's hips as she waited to see what Ripley would do next. Ripley could feel her own wetness on Kenna's fingers as she held her. Kenna's eyes were glued to Ripley's, and they were darker than ever before. They followed Ripley's hand as she slid it down her own neck, between her breasts, over her stomach, and between her legs. Ripley watched Kenna watch her. Kenna's hands gripped her hips harder as Ripley spread her lower lips with one hand to allow Kenna to see. Kenna lifted her head as much as she could in her position and stared as Ripley's other hand covered her sex. Ripley cupped herself as Kenna gulped, met her eyes quickly in approval, and lowered them back to Ripley's center.

Ripley moved her hips against her own hand, allowing the pressure of it to guide her slowly toward another climax.

She bit her lower lip as she removed her palm and used one finger to stroke her hard, swollen clit. Kenna let out a deep breath and a near gasp as Ripley showed her how she liked to be touched, even though Kenna already knew how, because she always made Ripley come when she touched her. One of Kenna's hands slid closer to Ripley's sex but stilled on her inner thigh. Ripley flicked her clit as she moved her hips a little faster now. She watched as Kenna struggled to see everything she was doing from her position. Ripley put a finger on either side of her clit and squeezed, and Kenna did gasp at that. Then, she licked her lips, and Ripley couldn't take it anymore.

"Do you want to see more?" she asked, breathless.

"Yes," Kenna answered, just as breathless.

Ripley wasted no time. She slid her center up Kenna's body, spreading her wetness over Kenna's stomach and earning her a small moan from the woman beneath her. Ripley lifted her body enough to move her knees next to Kenna's head, placing her sex directly over Kenna's mouth. She then placed her hands on the bed frame and rolled her hips down an inch or so away from Kenna's face. Kenna's hands both went to her ass, cupped it, and lowered Ripley into her. She then licked at Ripley's clit like she had been waiting to do that all day. And maybe she had. She sucked it, hard and full of need, into her mouth and moaned again. Ripley ground into her more. She knew she wouldn't last long as she sat back up, which allowed one of Kenna's hands to squeeze her breast while the other squeezed her ass. Ripley came into Kenna's mouth, twitching into her orgasm, as Kenna pressed her tongue flat to her clit; she rode it out while Kenna grunted her own pleasure beneath her.

When Ripley finally fell to Kenna's side, she turned her head to see Kenna lick her lips. Ripley took a few deep breaths. Then, she slid her hand between Kenna's legs, felt her unbelievably wet sex, and stroked Kenna until she came, calling Ripley's name.

***

"I've never done that before," Ripley said.

"Which part?" Kenna asked.

Kenna was lying on her stomach while Ripley ran her fingers up and down her back. Kenna had her head resting on her hands, with her arms folded beneath her. Her eyes were closed, and she was enjoying the light touches Ripley provided.

"Touching myself."

"I liked that part," Kenna admitted without opening her eyes. "A lot."

"I wasn't sure if I…" Ripley faded.

"Ripley, you are beautiful." Kenna opened her eyes. "And sexy as hell when you take what you want like that. I loved watching you. And it was really hard, not touching you myself, but it was worth it. We can do that again whenever you want."

"Yeah?" Ripley smiled.

"Can I ask you something?" Kenna rolled onto her side to face her.

"Of course." Ripley squinted her eyes in concern.

"When I was in my twenties, I wasn't exactly the relationship type," Kenna began as she twirled a strand of Ripley's mussed hair between two fingers. "I'm in my thirties now, and I still haven't been able to get it right."

"Get what right?" Ripley asked and placed her hand on Kenna's hip.

"The girlfriend thing," Kenna answered. "I've had them – short-term things, mostly, that did not end well – but I've never had a long-term relationship; and I think I want one with you, Ripley."

"You think?" Ripley lifted one side of her mouth into a sideways smile.

"Okay, I know." Kenna smiled at her. "I would like us to give this a try."

"Us?"

"Yes. I want to be with you," Kenna said. "And I hope you want to be with me."

"Kenna, I've never been with anyone like that. You know that, right? Relationships in general, I don't have the best track record with."

"Then, we're in this together." Kenna shrugged with one shoulder. "When I first met you, I asked you out, Ripley. I knew it then, and I was right. This works. You and I, we work."

"Even though you're frustrating all the time," Ripley said playfully while sliding her thumb along Kenna's skin.

"And even though you don't return my calls when I beg for your forgiveness," Kenna returned and moved on top of Ripley. "Babe, just face it: you like me." She smiled down at Ripley before kissing her jaw. "And I like you."

Ripley kissed Kenna's lips, tasting herself on them from their earlier activities.

"I'm afraid, Kenna," she admitted in a soft voice.

"Of me?" Kenna asked, staring into concerned, hazel eyes.

"Of everything." Ripley paused as she wrapped her arms around Kenna's neck. "I'm scared of what happens next with Patrick Wilkes. I don't want to have to testify at a trial and relive that. I relive it almost every night already." Ripley closed her eyes for a moment. "I'm scared of not being good enough for you." She shrugged. "I've never done anything like that; at least, not anything that's real. Kenna, the only thing I've ever been good at is my work. I have an album on my phone filled with pictures of some of the kids I've helped, and it's probably my most important possession. It gets me through the day sometimes. I have no friends outside of work, and I still have a lot of student loan debt that I'll likely never be able to pay off and afford that Ph. D that I want."

"Instead of looking at what you don't have yet or what you can't afford, why don't you look back at all you've accomplished?" Kenna suggested as she still hovered over her. "When you look at pictures of those kids, what do you see?"

"Them."

"Ripley, what do you see?"

"How strong some of them are. How happy some of them are that we managed to find them a good home."

"Babe, you can see all that, but you should also see how *you* did those things. You helped make them strong. You worked to find them that home that's making them happy. I know you're scared, but please try to remember everything you've accomplished." Kenna kissed Ripley. "If it makes you feel any better, I'm afraid of this, too. You can ask Bella; I have never done this before. I have no idea how I'll be as a girlfriend."

"You're doing pretty good so far." Ripley brought Kenna down closer. "Can I meet her?"

"Bella?"

"Is it too soon?"

"No, she's been asking about you since the beginning. She asked again the other night. She's a nurse. When she has the late shift, I usually go over to her house, and we have a late dinner. I didn't last time because I was with you." She kissed Ripley's nose. "I can set something up if you want."

"Is she going to like me?"

"If she doesn't, I'll kill her." Kenna kissed Ripley's forehead as Ripley laughed against her. "She'll love you." Kenna looked into Ripley's eyes. "Do you think you can sleep now?"

"I think so," Ripley replied. "But can you come down here and kiss me again? I think it might help."

CHAPTER 17

"So, you're introducing us now?" Bella asked Kenna.

"Are you going to ask me a question like that every time I bring her up?" Kenna asked back.

"Maybe. Maybe it'll stop once you two get married. I don't know. Maybe it'll turn into something about kids then."

"Oh, God," Kenna muttered. "Kids."

"Are you all right there?" Bella lifted an eyebrow at her.

"She probably wants kids, right? I mean, she literally works with them every day. She loves kids. She probably wants them one day."

Bella placed her hand on top of Kenna's on the table.

"Ken, calm down. You've been with her for, like, two days. I doubt she's expecting you two to have a kid next week," Bella reasoned. "But that *is* something you two should probably talk about if this gets serious."

"It is serious, Bell. We're together now. She's my girlfriend."

"Ken, people can have boyfriends and girlfriends, but it doesn't mean it's full-on serious."

"I want serious with her," Kenna replied.

"You've never had serious with anyone."

"I know," Kenna said. "And I want it with her."

"Well, all right then." Bella winked at her. "Where is

this woman? I need to meet the person who managed to get my kid sister to settle down. Mom is going to love her."

"Mom isn't meeting her until after I propose." Kenna rolled her eyes at her sister.

"Damn, Ken. Talking proposals already? Maybe you *should* talk about kids tonight," Bella joked and removed her hand from Kenna's. "I think your girl's here." She nodded in the direction of the door to the restaurant. Kenna smiled at the sight of Ripley standing there, looking around the restaurant. "You really do like her. I can tell already."

"I'll be right back," Kenna said and stood quickly, leaving her napkin that had been in her lap, on the table.

Her smile continued and grew even wider as she approached the woman. Ripley dressed up for this dinner, and it was adorable. Her hands were clasped together in front of her, and she looked nervous but also gorgeous. She had worn black heels with a black pencil skirt and a gray silk blouse. Her hair was down as usual, and she had put on a little makeup.

"Hi. Sorry, I'm late. I couldn't find a parking spot," Ripley said when Kenna kissed her on the cheek.

"You're not late. Bell and I were early," Kenna replied. "You look beautiful, by the way."

"I do?"

"You do." Kenna smiled at her. "I felt like I should say that first because I also wanted to say that you look sexy; I-can't-wait-to-get-you-home-later level of sexy."

Ripley laughed at her and took Kenna's hand.

"Take me to meet your sister, and do not say any of that in front of her," Ripley said. "You look hot, too," she added in a whisper as they approached the table.

"Ripley, this is Bella. Bella, this is my girlfriend, Ripley," Kenna introduced.

"Nice to meet you, Ripley." Bella stood to shake her hand and sat back down once finished.

"You too. Kenna talks about you all the time," Ripley offered.

Kenna pulled out Ripley's chair. Ripley sat, and Kenna pushed the chair back in before sitting down herself. Bella watched the whole thing and gave her sister a knowing glance.

"Ripley is an interesting name. Where did it come from?" Bella asked.

"Oh, I don't know, I guess." Ripley glanced at Kenna. "I never asked."

"Way to bring a conversation down there, Bell." Kenna glared at her sister.

"It's not her fault." Ripley placed her hand on the back of Kenna's neck and toyed with the little hairs there.

Kenna wondered if this touch was replacing Ripley's normal nervous touch with her messenger bag strap. It didn't matter either way. It felt really good to be sitting across from her sister with her beautiful girlfriend who was touching her so intimately; in a way, claiming her in the restaurant for all to see.

"I'm sorry," Bella said.

"It's really okay," Ripley told her. "Honestly, I don't know where my name came from. I guess it could have been a family name. It also could have just been something my parents picked out from a book."

"Either way, it's nice."

"Thank you," Ripley replied. "Kenna says you're a nurse?"

"I am. Pediatrics." Bella took a drink of her water.

Kenna listened to their conversation go back and forth for the next forty-five minutes. She participated when necessary, made sure to touch Ripley's thigh under the table when it appeared the woman was nervous, and just let them get to know one another when it was clear they didn't need her to join in. When Ripley excused herself to go to the bathroom after they'd paid the check, Kenna took the opportunity to ask Bella what she thought.

"She's great, Kenna."

"Yeah?"

"You're crazy about her, aren't you? I can tell. She's crazy about you, too. I can see that clear as day."

"She is?" Kenna asked as she glanced in the direction of the bathroom to make sure Ripley wouldn't overhear. "I do really like her."

"Oh, please. You're in love with that girl. Anyone can see it."

"Bell!" Kenna whisper-shouted at her.

"I'm right, aren't I?"

"It's been a couple of weeks."

"Kenna, there's no rule about falling in love. It's different for everyone. You know that. People fall in love after years of knowing each other. Others, it's at first sight. Maybe that's how it was for you."

"I did ask her out the day I met her." Kenna shrugged.

"Well, there you go." Bella finished the water in her glass. "I'm happy for you, Ken. She seems *right* for you. Also, she's coming. We should change the subject," she said the last part rapidly, and as Ripley approached, she added, "Hi, Ripley. Ready to go?"

"Yes, thanks."

Kenna stood and took Ripley's hand. They said goodbye to Bella in the parking lot before Kenna walked Ripley to her car. She had driven with Bella specifically so that Ripley could take them both back to Kenna's place after dinner.

"Did I pass?" Ripley asked after she pulled the car out of the parking lot.

"What? The sister test?" Kenna teased.

"Yes, the sister test. I've never taken one before. How did I do?"

"Passed with flying colors, overachiever." Kenna slid her thumb along the side of Ripley's neck. "You're staying over tonight, right?"

"I thought that's what we planned." Ripley glanced at her for a moment before returning her eyes to the road.

"I just wanted to make sure."

136

Kenna continued stroking Ripley's skin in that way until they pulled up in front of her condo. Then, she helped Ripley with both her messenger bag and the overnight bag Ripley had packed. When they got inside the condo, Kenna walked them silently into the bathroom, where she drew them a bath, helped Ripley get out of her clothes, and slid in behind her into the hot water as it continued to fill the tub. As Kenna wrapped her arms around Ripley, she knew her sister was right: she was in love.

***

The flames swarmed around her. Her toes were sizzling in pain. Ripley couldn't cry. She couldn't scream. She knew so little about death. Her mom had tried to explain it to her once. She'd talked about heaven. Ripley didn't understand heaven, though. She only understood the pain in this moment.

"Babe?" Ripley heard a voice but didn't recognize it. "Babe." The voice came again. It wasn't her mom's or her dad's. It didn't sound like her grandma, Ethan, or Benji. "Ripley." The voice said her name. Ripley watched the flames crawl over her legs and meet her knees. "Ripley?"

Ripley woke with a start. She was on the floor of Kenna's bedroom, and the blankets were half around her legs. She must have fallen out of the bed. Then, she felt a hand on her back and realized she was sweating through her shirt.

"Kenna?"

"Hey, you rolled out of bed. Let's get you back to sleep," Kenna said.

"I saw it again," Ripley told her as Kenna picked her up off the floor. "My parents burning. I saw Ethan, too."

"I'm sorry." Kenna held her and pulled Ripley closer to her.

She, apparently, didn't care that Ripley was clammy, gross, and exhausted from not having a solid night of sleep in the past few weeks.

"It's okay. I'm here. Let's go back to sleep, okay?" Kenna added.

"Okay," Ripley agreed.

She slid under the blankets Kenna fixed for her, and Kenna climbed in next to her, wrapping a warm arm around Ripley's waist and pulling Ripley back into herself. Ripley reveled in the feeling of Kenna's strength. She needed it now, it appeared, more than ever. As Kenna whispered sweet words in her ear, Ripley knew. She knew she'd finally fallen in love for the first time.

CHAPTER 18

"MISS Fox, thank you for taking the time to come in today," Captain Thorne said.

"Marty, you've known me for years. You called me Rip, like, three days ago," Ripley replied.

"Well, these are different circumstances, aren't they?" he asked. "Normally, we're colleagues. Today, you're here as a witness and a victim to a crime."

Ripley hated that word. She'd heard it first right after the fire. Adults threw it around her, thinking she either didn't hear them or didn't understand the meaning. She understood, though. This was the first time she'd had it directed toward her as an adult, and while she didn't like how it felt back then, she certainly didn't like it now.

"Kenna's investigator gave you everything you need. What do you need from me?" she asked him.

The two of them were sitting in his precinct office. Ripley had been in there many times over the years to pick up children that were either in the system already or needed to be placed. She had known Marty to be a great cop and a good man; and his wife, Helen, was a wonderful woman whom Ripley had met years ago at a Christmas party. Of all the cops in Pleasant Valley, Ripley trusted Marty the most. Still, sitting alone in his office, talking about what happened all those years ago, was difficult. He'd known her as Ripley Fox, a social worker. Now, he had a first-row seat into the life of Ripley Fox, an orphan and a foster kid.

"I have your statement from the morning after the fire. I was hoping to review it with you," he said.

He held a file folder in both hands as he looked at her with concerned brown eyes. Ripley turned her head slightly to see Kenna sitting in a black plastic chair in the makeshift station waiting area. She'd come with her for moral support, but Ripley had asked her to do this part alone.

"I reread it the other day. There's nothing I have to add to it. I'm sorry, but I haven't had any new memories pop up over the years, Marty," she replied honestly. "If anything, I've had a lot of stuff that didn't happen enter my brain over the years."

"How so?" he asked and dropped the file on his desk.

"It's just stuff I've talked to my therapist about. It's nothing that gets me any closer to helping you find the person responsible."

"Are you sure? Sometimes, we think our memories lie to us or don't make sense, but they really do. Have you considered that they might actually be real?"

"I went to bed that night," Ripley explained. "Before the fire started. I didn't see anyone in my family after I fell asleep. I only woke to the fire, and I saw the fireman after that. Then, I was on the street. The only thing I see in my nightmares, Marty, is the members of my family burning alive. I don't think that will help you."

He sighed and said, "I'm sorry, Rip. This stuff Mal brought us is going to reopen the investigation. Technically, it was never closed, but this is big. Patrick Wilkes is now a person of interest. But between you and me, he's the main and only suspect in a series of fires in Pleasant Valley and the murder of your five family members. We're going to bring him in for an interview tomorrow, and I've also had an unmarked car on him since Mal called me. He hasn't done anything out of the ordinary, but there also haven't been any fires in Pleasant Valley since he's been covered. That doesn't exactly bode well for him, though."

"What happens after you talk to him?" she asked.

"We'll bring the details to the DA to see what he wants to do about it. There wasn't any physical evidence left at the scene, but that's common with arsons. I doubt we'll be able to get him to confess after all these years."

"What about his mom? The investigator?"

"That's a double-edged sword. All her work, related to these fires and probably everything else, is going to be questioned. That might work for this case, but it could harm others."

"I understand," Ripley replied, clasping her hands together in her lap.

"Her career is over. My guess is the DA is going to want to press charges once he sees all the circumstantial evidence. We're still investigating one of the new fires. There was a fingerprint, and if it matches his, we have a good shot at arson. Plus, there's a pattern. In all these new fires, kerosene was the accelerant."

"What do I do?" Ripley asked.

"If you don't have anything to add to your statement, nothing. I'll call you once we know how we're proceeding. If it gets to trial, you'll likely be called as a witness. If he's found guilty at sentencing, you'll be asked if you want to give a victim impact statement."

"I don't want to do either of those thing," Ripley said. "Marty, if Patrick Wilkes did this thing, I want him to be locked away. I certainly don't want him to do this to anyone else, but I don't want to testify about that night; I don't want to relive it. And I definitely don't want to stand in front of people and make a statement."

"Okay. Let's just take it one step at a time. We don't know it'll get that far."

"Fine," she replied. "I can do that, I guess." Ripley let out a deep sigh. "I should get going. Kenna and I came here on our lunch break."

"I'll call you." He stood and shook her hand as she stood in front of his desk. "We'll get him, Rip."

***

Kenna stood as Ripley emerged from the office. The woman seemed okay when she smiled in her direction. Kenna reached out her hand for Ripley to take, which she did.

"How are you?"

"Fine," Ripley told her. "He's going to bring Patrick in tomorrow. There's an officer watching him now."

"Rip, I asked how you are. We can talk about the case part later," Kenna said.

She let go of Ripley's hand to place both of her own on Ripley's hips instead.

"I'm okay," Ripley offered. "I guess this is all still a shock to me. I never would have thought of Patty Wilkes. I didn't even know his last name until you told me."

"I don't think the cops thought of him, either," Kenna said and kissed her cheeks. "He was a kid. I doubt they considered anyone that young. Let's go. I should get back to the station. Dinner tonight?"

"I'm excited to meet your nephews," Ripley said with a smile as they made their way out of the station. "I hope they like me."

"They'll love you." Kenna almost added that they'd love her like Kenna did, but she didn't. "You're amazing."

"I don't feel amazing, but when you say it, I believe you," Ripley replied.

Kenna did believe it. She believed that Ripley was amazing. And not only because Ripley had overcome and worked hard for so much, but because of how she was with people. Kenna had gotten the chance to watch Ripley with siblings that needed an immediate emergency placement after their foster parents decided to move away from Pleasant Valley. It had been just that morning.

Kenna had gone to pick Ripley up in order to drive to the station together, and she happened to listen as Ripley spoke to the two young children with such kindness and patience. She gave them both a snack from the vending machine, which they gobbled up. One of them was all smiles, but the other took some coaxing. Kenna watched in utter amazement as Ripley, with a few words, got the young girl to open up to her. Both children left the building with their actual caseworker and with smiles on their faces.

Kenna dropped Ripley back at work before returning to the station. She'd been at her desk for about an hour before Shannon sat in the empty chair next to her.

"Yes, Shannon?" Kenna asked without looking away from her computer.

"Where are we with Ripley Fox?"

"I told you I'm not working that," Kenna replied and turned toward her. "I've asked you, like, a hundred times to leave it alone."

"I have never seen you turn down a good story, Crawford. Want to tell me why you don't want this when it's gold? This could be carried by Dateline or 20/20 if we do it right."

"She doesn't want to be on the news or either of those shows, Shannon." Kenna crossed her arms over her chest.

"Since when has that stopped you? Honestly, you're my best reporter. You dig until there's nothing left to find, and then you still find something," Shannon argued.

"I'm dating her, Shannon. We're together."

"You're what?" Shannon leaned forward in her borrowed chair.

"Ripley and I are a couple."

"You fell for a story?" Shannon lifted an eyebrow.

"I *fell* for Ripley," Kenna corrected. "I *met* her because of the story."

"I'm going to put on my friend hat for a moment and remove my boss one." Shannon paused and then smiled widely. "I'm happy for you, Kenna." The woman paused again, and her smile disappeared. "Boss hat back on. I'm going to have to give this to Mandy, and she's going to pester Ripley until she agrees to do an interview."

"Shannon, I am asking you to let this one go. I have

been an asset to you and this station for a long time. I am asking you to leave my girlfriend alone. She's a private person, and she's been through enough."

"If you were doing the story, I doubt it will feel like she's being pestered," Shannon proposed. "It's not just me asking; Clark got wind of the story."

"He's obsessed with the crime beat; that makes sense."

"He's also my boss, Kenna. He's in charge. If you don't do this, you know he's just going to give it to Mandy or someone else. He heard from Mal, and he knows about the suspect."

Kenna leaned back in her chair, still with her arms crossed over her chest. She squinted at Shannon as she considered her options.

"They can run it without her. They don't need Ripley's face or her story."

"Maybe not, but Clark wants it, and it would make for a better story," Shannon said.

"What do I have to do to keep you guys from hounding her? Honestly, I'll do anything."

"I can't think of anything, Kenna. I'm sorry. If she really wants us to leave her alone, you might have to go the restraining-order route. You know how reporters are." Shannon stood and shrugged.

Kenna leaned back in her chair. She sighed again at the thought of Mandy following Ripley out of the building and asking her questions with a microphone shoved into Ripley's face. Kenna knew Ripley wouldn't sit down to give an on-camera interview. She would likely rush past Mandy silently or issue a "no comment" as she moved away. Kenna didn't want that for her, but she also didn't see a way to avoid it. That would be especially true if Patrick Wilkes were arrested.

CHAPTER 19

"AUNT Kenna, will you watch us practice?" Brady asked her.

"Practice wrestling?" Kenna asked him back. "Aren't you, like, twice his size?" She rubbed the top of Brady's head, mussing his hair.

"In the basement," Brady replied. "Cody wants to wrestle like me."

"I do not," Cody, his younger brother by two years, disagreed. "I want to play football."

"When you're much older, right?" Kenna questioned her youngest nephew.

"No. Now." Cody gave her a confused look. "So I can be really good when I get older. Duh."

"Yeah, Aunt Kenna. Duh." Bella sat on the couch on the other side of her youngest son.

"I could maybe watch you practice," Ripley suggested from her seat on Kenna's other side.

Cody was so small, the four of them could fit on the couch together, while Brady stood in front of them with his wrestling headgear in his hands.

"Really? Cool. Can we go now, Mom?" Brady asked.

"Be kind to your younger brother, please." Bella mussed Cody's hair as Cody stood to go play with his brother. "Are you sure?" Bella asked Ripley.

"I'm sure."

Ripley squeezed Kenna's thigh, stood, and followed the two boys to the basement door.

"She's great, Ken."

"I know," Kenna said. "I think I'm going to go with her. Those two can be a lot."

"Hey," Bella said playfully.

"I love them like they're my own, you know that." Kenna stood and straightened the t-shirt she'd worn to dinner.

"Speaking of… Did you talk about that with her yet?"

"What? Kids?" Kenna asked. "God, no. Bell, I just got the girl to agree to be my girlfriend."

"I know. I know." Bella stood, approached her, and slapped Kenna's shoulder. "The boys love her."

"Bell, she lost her entire family. I have no idea how she would feel about having one of her own. I'm not asking her any questions dealing with long-term stuff until I have at least some idea."

***

Ripley had gone back up the stairs to get Cody's headgear, which was, apparently, in the living room. With the door to the basement open, though, she could make out part of Kenna and Bella's conversation. She wasn't normally an eavesdropper, but she couldn't stop herself when the subject of long-term relationship stuff came up.

"It should matter what you want, too," Bella said.

"Of course, it should. I'm not bringing up anything, though, until I at least have an indication if a family is what she wants. You know I've always gone either way on that. If my wife wants a family, we'll have a family. If she wants it to be just us, it can be just us. I just want her."

"The wife?" Bella asked.

"Ripley," Kenna replied.

Ripley still stood in the doorway, just out of view from the sisters, thankfully. She smiled for an instant, got terrified the next, and smiled again at the thought of little Kennas running around the house, interviewing their stuffed animals. She grew scared again when she thought about being a mother herself. She only had a few years with her mom to learn what a mother does for and with her children. None of her foster mothers ever compared. Some were terrible, others were adequate, and more than most just left her alone completely. Ripley had no one to guide her. If she had a child of her own and needed advice, she couldn't call her mom for help. She couldn't call her grandmother, either. She couldn't even call her dad or her older brothers or their wives because they would never have them. Hell, could she have one? Kenna had said she wanted a wife. She'd gone even further to say that she wanted Ripley.

"Well, hey," Kenna greeted her when she noticed Ripley was there. "Did they scare you away already?"

"No, I just needed to grab some headgear."

"I don't think we have any in your size," Kenna said, gripped Ripley's waist, and pulled her into herself.

"Cody's headgear." Ripley laughed. "You're cute, though."

"We can watch them play for twenty minutes, and then it's their bedtime. You and I can leave while Bell puts them to bed." Kenna pecked her lips.

They grabbed what they needed and both headed downstairs. There was a small wrestling mat on the floor, and the two boys wrestled. Brady attempted to teach Cody a few moves. Even Kenna fake-wrestled Brady for a few minutes, allowing him to pin her to the mat while Cody called the match a victory for Brady. Ripley smiled and laughed through the whole thing. When it was time for the boys to head up to get some sleep, they hugged Kenna first before moving to her. Each offered her a long hug and smiles, and Ripley couldn't believe how amazing that felt. Then, Bella hugged her goodnight after thanking her for coming. Ripley had been hugged by a lot of children since she'd become a social worker, and she loved each hug she received from all those other children, but these three hugs meant more to her. These hugs felt like they were coming from family.

When they fell into bed that night at Kenna's, Ripley moved over to the middle of Kenna's queen-sized bed and wrapped her arms around her, pulling Kenna in. She'd yet to be the big spoon when they cuddled like this, and she wanted to be the one to hold Kenna tonight.

"Everything okay?" Kenna asked her.

"Everything is more than okay." Ripley kissed her behind the ear. "You're going to make an amazing mom someday, Ken."

Kenna's body tensed for a moment, and Ripley kissed the same spot again.

"Oh, I don't know."

"Yes, you do," Ripley replied. "That's what you want, isn't it? A family?"

"Where is this coming from?" Kenna laughed a little. "My tiny terrors for nephews don't exactly make me want to have two of my own."

"Yes, they do," Ripley stated confidently.

Kenna rolled over in her arms, and Ripley moved back just enough to be able to read Kenna's face.

"I've always said I could do with or without children."

"But what you really meant is that you do want them but don't want to admit it, in case it doesn't happen," Ripley said.

"How did you—"

"You talk about those boys non-stop, Kenna. You have a million pictures of them on your phone, and you're constantly going to their games and matches, babysitting when your sister and brother-in-law need a night out. Plus, I've seen you with them now. You look at them, and I can tell that, sometimes, you're trying to think about what your kids would look like. You and Bella look so similar; it's kind of hard not to do that, I imagine."

"I didn't want to get my hopes up," Kenna said softly.

"My career has always come first. That meant I played around a lot but didn't settle down. I could potentially anchor in a major city if I wanted, and I have a reel of my recent stuff all put together; I just have to send it out. If I did that, I'd be starting over somewhere else; and I'm already thirty-two. I guess I just didn't want to voice what I wanted because I want a lot of things."

"You have a reel put together?" Ripley asked, changing the subject.

"I did it before I met you," Kenna said and placed a hand on Ripley's cheek. "And before you ask, I haven't sent it anywhere."

"Will you?"

"I don't know." Kenna slid her thumb along Ripley's cheekbone. "Things have very suddenly shifted for me. I haven't expected it, but now, the last thing I'm thinking about is my reel and my prospects."

"But you still want that?"

"I'd like to leave Pleasant Valley someday, but that doesn't have to be soon. Ripley, you showed up, and my priorities have changed. My career is at the bottom of the list for the first time ever." Kenna scooted closer to her. "Nearly every night before you, I'd either be on my computer, doing research on the next big story, or I was with Bella and the kids. Now, the furthest thing from my mind is finding a new story."

"Yeah?" Ripley asked softly.

"Ripley, I realize now that I need more than just reporting. I need someone in my life. I need a partner. I would love to have a thriving career, but I want someone to come home to. Maybe a couple of little ones around, too, but the woman is what I want more than anything."

"Are you worried I won't want kids because of what happened to me?" Ripley asked, and Kenna only nodded in response while she continued to stroke Ripley's cheek. "For years after I got out of the system, I *knew* I wouldn't have kids. That was more about me than the system or the fire,"

Ripley explained. "I was such a recluse in my early twenties, I honestly didn't think I'd meet anyone who'd want kids with me; and I knew I wouldn't want to be a single parent."

"And now?" Kenna asked.

"A few years ago, one of the little girls I placed asked me if I would adopt her," Ripley revealed. "Her name was Alex. Her mother had overdosed on heroin, and there was no father on her birth certificate. She was only six and had no other family. She'd been in a home and had run away. Luckily, she'd been found unharmed, but we had to move her because the family had four other fosters and hadn't even noticed that a six-year-old girl had run away from their home. I knelt in front of her, and she asked me to be her mommy." Ripley's eyes welled up with tears. "I couldn't back then. There was no way. I'm not even registered as a foster parent because I knew I couldn't be responsible for a child."

"What happened to her?"

"She got adopted by a good family, and her mom still sends me updates every month or so." Ripley sniffled a little. "But after that happened, I started to rethink things, I guess. I knew financially, I wasn't ready to have a child. I was single, which isn't a deal-breaker for some women, but it is for me." She felt a tear hit her skin, but Kenna's thumb swiped it away. "Kenna, I don't know. That's a very scary thought for me. Having a child is such a commitment. I've seen so many people screw it up in my line of work; I don't know how to *not* do that."

"No one knows how to not screw up a child, Rip. I'd argue that every parent messes up their kid a little, but while my mom is a little obsessive and overbearing, I love her to death. She's my biggest fan. She records every single damn story I do and has a collection of DVDs and files. She loves me and Bella more than life, and my father is the same way. I think you'd agree that's the most important thing. You love your children, and you do your best to provide for them, to make sure they are safe and happy. I think you allow them to make mistakes and work for things so they understand how important the hard work is. You teach them right from wrong, to be kind to people, and to understand that the differences we all have are good things. That's all any parent can do."

Ripley stared into those kind blue eyes as Kenna spoke, thinking everything she had ever wanted might be possible with this woman. She allowed another few tears to fall while feeling Kenna wiping them away as they did. Ripley leaned in and pressed her forehead to Kenna's.

"If we get there, Kenna, I am open to the idea." She exhaled. "I mean, if we get to the point where we're taking those steps together, I think I might like to talk about that with you."

"Really?" Kenna smiled widely, and Ripley felt it in her bones. "You'd be okay with a couple little Ripleys or a few little Kennas running around a house?"

"Only if you're there running around with them," Ripley replied and kissed her.

CHAPTER 20

"PATRICK Wilkes, the thirty-three-year-old man and the son of a fire investigator Bethany Wilkes, has been arrested and charged with three counts of arson and five counts of felony murder in the house fire that cost the lives of five members of the Fox family over twenty years ago. Wilkes has been arraigned this afternoon. His bail was denied. Wilkes has pled not guilty. His mother was at his side in the courtroom today. Also, in the room, was Ripley Fox, the only survivor of the fateful fire that night. Ripley was only eight years old when her entire family was killed in the fire believed to be started by Wilkes. Police have not commented on the case or on the involvement of Bethany Wilkes," Mandy Sneed said into her microphone on the steps of the courthouse.

Ripley exited the building with Kenna, and Mandy launched herself and her microphone in Ripley's direction.

"Miss Fox, how are you feeling? Can you comment on why the police have arrested Patrick Wilkes? Did you know Wilkes? Why do you think he would have done this? How has it been, seeing the man that possibly murdered your family in court? What do you think about his mother investigating the fires he may have caused?"

"Mandy, stop!" Kenna yelled at the woman and moved between her and Ripley. "Leave her alone."

"Kenna? What are you doing here?" Mandy asked,

quickly turned back to her cameraman, and nodded for him to stop rolling. "I'm on this story."

"Ripley is my girlfriend," Kenna answered and squeezed Ripley's hand that she'd been holding since they walked up the stairs into the courthouse. "Why don't you wait in the car?" she said to Ripley.

There were two more cameras and reporters standing nearby, but after Kenna climbed in front of her, they backed off and allowed Ripley to move past them without a single word.

"Kenna, I'm just doing my job."

"I know, Mandy. But she's been through a lot, and you just rapid-fired about a hundred questions at the woman. You might want to soften your approach."

"If I do that, can I get an exclusive, or are you getting all the exclusives with Ripley Fox?" Mandy asked it playfully, and maybe that was what pissed Kenna off the most.

"Don't come near her again," Kenna warned. "If I have to, I'll ask the police to get a protection order. And they'll give it to her because they work with Ripley, and they love her."

"She can't handle a few questions? They're softballs, Kenna. What's the problem?"

"No comment," Kenna said the two words she hated most as a reporter.

***

Ripley sat in the passenger's seat of Kenna's car, wondering how she'd gotten here. She was twenty-eight years old and had her first real girlfriend. They'd been together for over a month now, and she still hadn't screwed it up. Work was going okay. In fact, Ripley was up for a promotion, with Jessica getting promoted as well. The story about social workers in Pleasant Valley had already been put together by Kenna and would be airing soon. It also had no mention of Ripley and was all good PR for Jessica and everyone who worked tirelessly to protect these kids.

Then, there was Patrick Wilkes. He had been interviewed, let go, then interviewed again; he hired an attorney who stonewalled the police at first, then agreed to cooperate and give a statement about that night, and then failed to show up for that meeting and denied ever agreeing to it, to begin with. Bethany Wilkes had been relieved of duty and was under investigation. Ripley worried for a few days that Bethany would be the one punished while Patrick would somehow go free. The fingerprint results had come back to Wilkes, but that had only tied him physically to one fire. His attorney had also found a way to explain how the print had ended up there.

It was an endless back-and-forth. Ripley found it difficult to keep up with all of it. Kenna had done much better with it. That was her dogged reporter side, and Ripley was starting to like it now that Kenna was in her corner. Kenna had followed up with Marty, talked to Malcolm, and even met with the ADA, who was working the case. Ripley would be forever grateful to Kenna for how she'd helped her regardless of whether or not their relationship worked long-term.

"Are you okay?" Kenna asked as soon as she got into the car.

"I'm okay," Ripley answered.

"I'm sorry about Mandy. I've tried to get Shannon—"

"I know, Ken. It's okay." She patted Kenna's thigh. "It's not your fault."

"It feels like it is, though. Shannon and Clark wouldn't have even known about this if it wasn't for me."

"Yeah, but I wouldn't have known you then, Ken."

Ripley smiled as Kenna glanced over and smiled back. Kenna put the car in drive and took them to her place. They'd been spending a lot of time there recently. It was bigger, Kenna's research was there, and it gave them each enough space to work when they needed to. That was one of Ripley's favorite things to do with Kenna, outside of the obvious. Kenna could sit at her desk and work while Ripley sat on the couch in her office and did the same.

"What do you want to do tonight?" Kenna asked. "I was thinking about ordering in while we pick out a movie."

Ripley looked at Kenna, who was changing out of her blazer and into a t-shirt. Her slacks had already been replaced with shorts, and her long, soft legs were already on display.

"Come here." Ripley opened her arms as she sat on the end of the bed. She had already changed into a shirt and shorts. When Kenna straddled her, Ripley placed her face between Kenna's breasts, with the shirt being the only thing between her and Kenna's skin. "You are the only person that has ever protected me, Kenna Crawford." She looked up to meet Kenna's eyes, and Kenna had already wrapped her arms around Ripley's neck. "You're the only person that has ever made me feel truly safe. You're the only one that's ever made me feel special."

"You *are* special," Kenna stated.

"Kenna, I love you," Ripley replied and lifted the hem of Kenna's shirt. She didn't see Kenna's initial reaction to her words with the shirt covering the woman's face after it was removed and tossed to the floor by Ripley. "I love you."

Kenna's eyes were smiling down at her. Her lips had yet to move, but her eyes were smiling. Ripley could only hope that was a good thing. She had no context beyond what she'd seen on TV and in movies or read in books on how soon you should tell someone you love them. For all she knew, this was way too soon. All she did know, though, was that she felt it. She loved Kenna.

"I love you, too," Kenna finally said.

She leaned down and kissed Ripley softly. Ripley enjoyed the warmth of Kenna's lips every time they kissed, but she enjoyed it more now in particular. They'd just said they loved each other for the first time, and Ripley had never said that to anyone before. As she kissed Kenna, she realized that she hadn't said those three words since the last time her mom had tucked her into bed. That meant she hadn't uttered those words in over twenty years.

Ripley moved her lips to Kenna's neck. She didn't fully know why it was so important to her, but it was. She wanted tonight to be about Kenna. The whole day had been about Ripley: they'd spent much of it in the police station before the courthouse; and it felt to her like so much of their relationship had just been surrounded by this thing that happened to her so long ago. Ripley wanted Kenna to know how much she meant to her, how much she loved her. She kissed back up to Kenna's lips, and Kenna started tugging at Ripley's shirt. Ripley allowed her to pull it off before she reconnected their lips.

"Tell me what you want," Ripley said between kisses.

"You," Kenna breathed into her mouth.

"What do you want me to do to you?" Ripley kissed her neck. "Tell me, Kenna. I'd do anything for you."

"Let me fuck you," Kenna said.

"I want this to be about you."

"It will be," Kenna replied and held both of Ripley's cheeks in her hands. "There's one thing we haven't done. Well, there's probably a lot more than one thing, but one thing we've talked about."

"Oh," Ripley said.

"It's okay if—"

"Get it out," Ripley interrupted her.

Kenna didn't say anything else. She just climbed off Ripley's body, moved to her bedside table, and pulled open the bottom drawer. Ripley slid onto the bed, removing all clothing in the process. She lay on her back and watched as Kenna slid on a pair of black boy shorts. Within a few minutes, Kenna had it attached properly and was lying next to Ripley on the bed, sliding her fingers over her skin.

Ripley's eyes lowered to what was now between Kenna's legs. She gulped at the idea of that fitting inside her. She'd never used one with any of her sexual partners, and while she'd used a vibrator before, she had never slid one of those inside her when she was alone. Kenna's eyes followed her eyes. She took one of Ripley's hands and placed it on the skin-toned matching dildo between her legs.

"It's still me inside you," she whispered into Ripley's ear. "When it slides in, that's me touching you. That's me showing you how much I love you. It's still me," she said.

Ripley didn't reply, but she did move her hand. She kissed Kenna until Kenna moved on top of her, and Ripley felt it there where Kenna would normally lower her hips down to create contact. Kenna's lips were on her neck, between her breasts, and then taking a nipple into her mouth. Ripley was already turned on, but feeling Kenna suck on her nipple while reaching down between them both to feel how wet Ripley was, nearly brought her to orgasm before they'd done anything.

Kenna slid two fingers inside her without preamble. She moved them slowly. She curled them slightly, buried them even deeper inside Ripley, and pulled them out. Her mouth was still attached to Ripley's nipple when Ripley lifted her head enough to watch Kenna coat the dildo with the wetness from her fingers before she gripped it with her hand and slid it inside Ripley, little by little. Ripley gasped at the first contact. She tried her best to relax as it slid fully inside her. Kenna placed both of her hands on either side of Ripley's head, stared down into Ripley's eyes with her blue ones, and gave her an expression that told Ripley she was asking for permission. Ripley gripped Kenna's ass and pushed it down.

Kenna started slow hip rolls down and into her, and, God, that felt good. That felt shockingly good. Kenna's breasts were bouncing as they continued to bump into her own with each thrust. Ripley kept her eyes open to attempt to take all this in. Kenna was now thrusting faster, and Ripley took in the woman's face. Kenna was incredibly turned on. She wanted this. She really wanted this. Kenna kissed her in time with a particularly hard thrust that Ripley knew she'd feel later. When Kenna moved her hips faster,

Ripley could tell she was still holding back. Having Kenna on top of her like this, inside her, made her feel invincible every time they made love. That was what they'd been doing, too. They'd been making love. Ever since their first time together, it hadn't been just sex. It had always been more.

"Kenna?" Ripley said softly, and Kenna lifted her head up to look down on her in concern. "Babe, fuck me."

Kenna smirked that unbelievably sexy smirk, and with that, Ripley watched her let go. She drove down into her harder than before, causing Ripley to spread her legs wider for her. Kenna grabbed at Ripley's hip and slid her hand down the back of Ripley's thigh, lifting it up. Before Ripley knew it, Kenna had her leg over her shoulder while she continued to thrust inside. Ripley moaned while Kenna grunted. It was the sexiest thing Ripley had ever seen; had ever been a part of. God, this felt good. Ripley tingled inside. This sensation spread down her legs and up her torso to her arms and fingertips. Once it hit the tips of her toes, Ripley burst inside. She screamed out as she came. Kenna continued to move inside her at her fevered pace, causing Ripley to hold on to Kenna's hip with one hand to keep her driving, bringing her ever higher. She used her other hand to lower Kenna's mouth to her nipple again, and Kenna sucked it between her lips as she pushed into Ripley deeper and deeper.

Ripley's orgasm dissipated but hadn't fully gone when Kenna lifted herself up into a kneeling position, pulling out of Ripley at the same time. Without words, she grasped Ripley's hips, gave her another of those smirks, and rolled Ripley over to her stomach. Then, she pressed her front solidly to Ripley's back. Ripley was breathing hard. She could feel the dildo, wet with her own arousal, on her ass as Kenna moved the tip back to her entrance.

"Can I do it again?" she asked.

"Yes," Ripley replied before gripping the sheets.

Kenna slid back inside her with ease as Ripley moved

on all fours. Kenna gripped her hips and started slow, but soon, she was pumping into Ripley from behind, taking Ripley over the edge again. She yelled Kenna's name just as Kenna reached around her and stroked her clit hard and fast. Ripley came a third time. When Kenna pulled out of her and rolled over onto her side of the bed, Ripley remained on her stomach, sans any energy to move.

"This night was supposed to be me showing you how much I love you and giving you the best sex of your life," Ripley muttered as she turned her head toward Kenna. "How did I just end up getting three mind-blowing orgasms?"

Kenna smiled as she turned her head to Ripley and replied, "Oh, babe. You did just give me the best sex of my life." She ran a hand along Ripley's sweaty back. "You have no idea what you just did to me."

"Well, I didn't give you an orgasm," Ripley said with a smile.

"The night's still young," Kenna suggested.

Ripley rolled onto her side. She glanced down at the shorts Kenna still wore and the dildo sticking up between her legs, and she met Kenna's eyes as she slid her hand under the shorts to stroke her.

"Oh, wow," Ripley whispered when she felt Kenna's wetness with her fingers. "You're so..."

"Because of you."

Ripley stroked Kenna slowly while Kenna's hips lifted on their own. Kenna's eyes closed, but her mouth was open as she luxuriated in Ripley's touch. Ripley couldn't believe she had made this woman this wet. Without stroking Kenna any faster, Kenna came at her fingertips. Ripley slid inside her with ease, and she brought Kenna to another orgasm before she straddled Kenna's thighs and slid the dildo inside herself again. She wasn't sure if she could come again, but the look on Kenna's face told her that this turned Kenna on so much, she was willing to try.

CHAPTER 21

"I AM so exhausted, and it's your fault," Ripley whispered to Kenna. "We got, like, an hour of sleep."

"I'm ready to go all night again," Kenna replied with a smirk.

"I bet you are." Ripley kissed her cheek. "Are you ready?"

"Let's go."

Since declaring their feelings for one another, they'd spent every night of the past week at Kenna's, with Ripley only returning to her own apartment to get new clothes. She'd even done laundry at Kenna's place. They'd been up late nearly every night, exploring one another's body. It was as if the three words they'd both confessed to holding back, initially, connected them together more, and that resonated physically. They hadn't been able to keep their hands off one another. Kenna hadn't ever experienced something as wonderful as Ripley's ability to let go with her.

Ripley had admitted to not ever being able to fully let go with someone in bed. She'd always held something back. She had never told the other person what turned her on or what she wanted. When Kenna had initially brought up the strap-on idea, Ripley told her right away that she'd never used one and wasn't sure she'd wanted to. Then, Kenna explained that it was fine, but that if Ripley changed her mind, Kenna would love to be with her like that. Kenna wanted to be with Ripley in every way imaginable, and after this past week, they were well on their way.

They made their way into the police station and didn't bother checking in before heading straight to the conference room they were told to meet in. When they arrived, Marty was already present. The ADA and another attorney, who would act as second chair if it went to trial, were also in the room.

"Stay with me this time," Ripley said and tugged on Kenna's hand.

Kenna smiled softly and nodded. She loved that Ripley was asking her to go in this time. They'd spent nearly every free moment they had together these days. The case against Patrick Wilkes, unfortunately, was part of their story, and it always would be. Today, they had to at least deal with a meeting about that before they could go home and enjoy their evening.

They sat down next to one another in the same old plastic chairs that were in the waiting area. The ADA greeted them each in turn and introduced his colleague. Kenna shook the hands of all three men. Ripley had introduced Kenna as her girlfriend, and at first, one of the men had given her a glance that, to Kenna, read that he wasn't sure she should be in the meeting, but Ripley just took her hand on the skinny armrest of her chair.

"Patrick Wilkes isn't talking. He hasn't budged on his story that he had nothing to do with it, despite the evidence we have," the ADA began.

"What does that mean for the case?" Kenna asked and looked at Ripley, thinking maybe she shouldn't be asking questions given the context of their situation, but Ripley gave her a soft smile. "What exactly is the evidence? I thought there was no physical evidence tying him to the Fox Fire."

"The Fox Fire?" Ripley looked at her. "Is that what people are calling it?"

The news about the arrest in the cold case had made

its way through Pleasant Valley. Now, there were at least five networks outside the courthouse, police station, DCFS building where Ripley worked, and even a few followed her home to her apartment. While Kenna knew Ripley wanted to spend time with her at her condo, she also knew that at least part of the reason Ripley had basically been living with her was because of the interest in her case, in her, and in her family's tragic story.

"It's true; it's all circumstantial. We do have the kerosene, and that goes to pattern. We still have to get that admitted along with the other fires since that is the crux of our case. The fingerprint that matches is key to that. If we can get the pattern in, we get the fingerprint. The fingerprint gets us the conviction," the ADA explained.

"His mother isn't going to testify against her son, but we're going to call her to the stand anyway, assuming he doesn't plead out. Just having her up there, hammering her with questions she likely won't answer, will play well for us with the jury," the ADA's colleague said.

"So, she hasn't admitted to covering for her son?" Kenna asked. "For allowing him to get away with murder?"

"She hasn't admitted to anything." Marty shrugged and leaned back in his chair. "I looked into that small town he moved to with his father after the fire. They had two small fires about six months after he moved there. No real damage. No deaths. Then, he went away to a military school for three years. No reported fires there, but he likely didn't have much of an opportunity. He did, however, have an extensive disciplinary record and was kicked out at seventeen. His father took him back in but died shortly after. It seems like Patrick was living on his own in his father's house until he moved back here."

"Were there any fires reported in town?" Kenna questioned.

"That's the thing..." Marty leaned forward again. "Oddly enough, there weren't. But there was a total of thirty-seven fire-related incidents in the surrounding towns.

I checked within a fifty-mile radius. I bet if we went wider, we'd find more. As far as I can tell, Wilkes was responsible for three barn fires, the deaths of around twenty-five animals, random garbage can fires, a few stores he nearly destroyed, and at least two more deaths."

"Two more?" Ripley finally spoke up.

"If I'm right, he burned a house while an elderly woman slept. She didn't make it, and a firefighter was lost trying to get her out of there."

"Oh, my God." Ripley held tight to Kenna's hand.

"He's our guy, Rip. I know it in my gut. Patrick Wilkes did this. I only wish we would have figured this out years ago."

"Wilkes was a kid. No one would have seen that coming," the ADA said. "We have two options on this: life without parole or death penalty. Wilkes isn't talking, and he's not likely to take a plea. Even if I offered him one, it would only be to take the death penalty off the table. That's not necessarily going to be enough of an incentive for him to plead guilty and avoid a trial."

"Death penalty?" Ripley asked.

"We're trying him on five counts of felony murder. That's a death penalty case," the colleague said. "Are you anti-death-penalty?"

"I don't know." Ripley looked over at Kenna. "I've never really needed to make an official stance on it."

"What happens if you do offer him the deal and he takes it?" Kenna joined in.

"We'd file the paperwork, and he'd be convicted and sent away."

"And if he doesn't?" Ripley asked.

"We'd go to trial."

"Offer him the deal," Ripley said.

"We will, but he probably won't take it. I can't see a guy like this – who won't admit to anything, especially given the circumstances – taking the deal. The deal comes with allocution. He'd have to tell the court truthfully what he did." The ADA stood and began pacing back and forth in the small room. "I have to offer the deal because it could potentially save taxpayers the cost of a trial. I don't normally include my personal opinions in my work, but if anyone deserves death penalty, it's Patrick Wilkes. He'll turn the deal down, we'll go to trial, and I'll try to get the jury to see that."

Kenna stared at Ripley, who said nothing. She sat and listened as the three men in the room tried to fill her in on the case. They talked to her about how she might have to testify, and Kenna squeezed her hand at that. She knew Ripley had relived that night far too many times already and didn't want to have to do it again. Kenna didn't want that for her, either.

"What can she offer if she testifies? She didn't see Wilkes in the house. She was asleep when the fire broke out," Kenna said when Ripley said nothing.

"She's the heart of the case," the ADA explained. "We need her to show the jury what was lost that night. Ripley lost her grandmother, her parents, and her brothers all in one day because of what Wilkes did. They need to hear that from her."

Ripley squeezed her hand tightly but still didn't say anything.

"What if she doesn't want to testify?" Kenna checked.

"We could subpoena her," the colleague Kenna was really starting not to like said. "We'd like to avoid that, obviously."

"You'd subpoena the victim?" Kenna asked.

"We need her story, Miss Crawford," the ADA added. "It's important to the case."

"If you subpoena my girlfriend to testify when she doesn't want to, I will splatter your faces all over Channel 8 news. I will make Pleasant Valley hate you for putting her through this again when there's absolutely nothing to be gained from this. She doesn't remember anything. She didn't see Wilkes there. All she knows is that she woke up to her bedroom on fire and lost her entire family. Do not put her on that stand unless you're ready to deal with the repercussions of the entire city losing faith in you people doing your jobs. You're supposed to serve and protect." She pointed with her free hand to Marty. "And you're supposed to support the Constitution and punish criminals." Kenna pointed to the ADA, leaving the colleague out of her attack.

"Kenna, we won't do that to her," Marty said. "I promise. I won't let these two subpoena her to testify." He looked at Ripley. "Rip, I know this is hard for you. We don't need to make any decisions today. You can take your time. If I were you, though, I'd want this man locked up. You could help do that by telling the jury and the judge what you do remember of that night. If you choose not to, though, you won't be subpoenaed. Right, gentlemen?" He looked toward the other two men in the room.

"We don't need to make any decisions today," the ADA repeated Marty's words while avoiding the answer to the question.

'Typical lawyer,' Kenna thought. She moved to stand, pulling Ripley up with her. Ripley had, apparently, lost her voice. Kenna would be her voice whenever she needed it.

CHAPTER 22

RIPLEY was lying on her side in Kenna's bed. Her eyes were closed as she attempted to sleep, but sleep wouldn't come. She had been trying for the past several hours. Kenna was sound asleep beside her. When they had climbed into bed, Kenna had snuggled her close. They hadn't spoken much since the meeting. Ripley needed time to process everything that was happening and would be happening with the case.

Kenna had rolled over when she had fallen asleep. Ripley missed her touch but didn't know how to ask for it. She didn't want to wake Kenna. She'd had a long week as well. She had somehow been fending off reporters who were interested in the case and in Ripley specifically. Ripley rolled over to face Kenna, who looked adorable when she slept. Her mouth was typically always half-open, and her nose sometimes scrunched up for a moment or two before returning to normal. Kenna was determined to be Ripley's protector, and Ripley kind of hated that she needed one, but she had never been one to stand up for herself. She had always had a hard time talking about the things that were hard to talk about. There were exactly two people in the world that knew the whole story of that night. One was her current therapist; the third she'd had since starting therapy and the only one she'd been able to open up to fully. The other one was Kenna, her girlfriend, who charmed her from moment one and continued to show Ripley just how much she cared about her.

"Kenna?" Ripley whispered. "Kenna, honey?" Ripley leaned in closer and kissed Kenna's cute nose.

"If you are waking me up to have sex, I'm in." Kenna opened her eyes and smirked immediately.

If Ripley weren't already so exhausted, she would have been all over the gorgeous creature she shared a life with now. That was it for Ripley. That was the defining thing that made what was happening between them so unbelievably different from anyone Ripley had ever been with: Kenna shared Ripley's entire life. She knew everything. Over the course of their time together, Ripley had spilled all her dark secrets, her embarrassing moments, and everything she hoped for in her life. Kenna had done the same, and while there would have to be some conversations later where their ideas of the future might conflict, Ripley was in this. She was willing to have those conversations with this woman.

"Will you come to therapy with me?" Ripley whispered.

Kenna's smirk disappeared immediately, and her face showed concern now. Her arm wrapped around Ripley's waist, and she pulled her in even closer.

"Are you okay?" she asked.

"I'm okay. I just couldn't sleep. I was thinking about my next appointment, and I was hoping you'd come with me. I think it might help to have you there. It's Monday afternoon, though. I don't know if you're free."

"I'll make myself free," Kenna replied. "If you want me there, I'm there, Rip."

"Are you sure? It's just going to be me talking about my problems," Ripley replied. "That's not exactly sexy."

"You are exactly sexy to me no matter the context." Kenna kissed her gently on the lips.

"You say that now." Ripley rolled onto her back.

"And I'll say it again later. Do you think you'll be able

to sleep now?" Kenna asked, resting her head on her elbow.

"I don't know. Maybe. I keep closing my eyes to try, and I see them."

Kenna ran a hand over Ripley's stomach under her shirt and asked, "Dream or nightmare?"

Ripley had explained to Kenna how she sometimes had pleasant dreams, and other times, really terrifying nightmares. A few times now, they'd woken next to one another with Kenna asking this same question.

"Both." Ripley turned her face to the ceiling. "I'll see them there. We're at the dinner table, and we're laughing. Then, I'm in my bed. They're standing in front of me, and they're…" Ripley stopped talking when Kenna stilled her hand. "It's not pretty. It's vivid, though, and that's the problem."

"You're really tense, babe," Kenna offered as she felt the muscles of Ripley's stomach. "You need to relax."

"How can I relax when my entire life is coming back to haunt me?" Ripley asked and turned her head to Kenna.

"Your life isn't coming back to haunt you, honey." Kenna slid on top of her. "It's just time to finally put it all behind you." She leaned down and kissed Ripley's lips. "Do you want a massage? A hot bath or a shower?"

"It's, like, three in the morning, Kenna."

"Just answer the question." Kenna smiled.

"Sometimes, I forget I'm dating a reporter." Ripley glared up at her playfully.

"That's because I normally dial that back around you." Kenna kissed her again.

"You didn't today," Ripley said. "You let them have it in that meeting."

"That guy was an asshole, acting like it's okay to force you to testify when it's not. If they want to make their case, they can do it without you." Kenna sat up, straddling her now. Her fingers toyed with the hem of the t-shirt Ripley wore, before she began a light caress of the skin beneath. "If you want to be a witness, be a witness, but you didn't do anything wrong. They don't get to make you do anything you don't want to do."

Ripley glanced up at her as Kenna looked down to meet her eyes in the darkness. The only light in the room came from the clock on Kenna's side of the bed, and a small amount streamed through the blinds on the window. It created thin lines of light and dark all along Kenna's torso and in her eyes as well.

"I love you," Ripley delivered as she placed her hand on Kenna's heart.

"I love you, too." Kenna's expression told Ripley that Kenna was wondering where that declaration had come from.

"Can I ask you something?"

"Okay," Kenna replied, sounding hesitant.

"What do I do for you?"

"What?" Kenna shook her head as if trying to understand the question.

"You do so much for me, Ken. You're so good to me. I guess I struggle sometimes, trying to figure out exactly what it is that I do for you."

Kenna lifted Ripley's shirt to reveal her breasts. She placed her hand over Ripley's heart, and Ripley could swear she could see Kenna's blue eyes looking a little on the watery side.

"You gave me this," Kenna finally said after a moment. "You've never given this to anyone before, have you?"

"No," Ripley told her. "You're the first."

"And I'm trying to be the only, Ripley." Kenna paused and leaned back down over her. "You calm me. If only you had any idea what I wanted to say to those guys today…" Kenna raised herself back up and removed her shirt. Then, she lowered herself back down and pressed their bodies together. "I wanted to shred them to pieces, Rip. And I would have, too, but your hand kept me grounded. I wanted to kill Mandy the other day, on those courthouse steps, but knowing you didn't want that, that you just wanted to walk away, helped me keep things civil." Kenna slid her hand between their bodies, cupping Ripley over the thin material of her panties. Ripley gasped at the touch. "Before you, I spent every moment I could working. Outside of Bella and the kids, that was the only thing that mattered to me. I didn't realize how lonely I was, honey. I didn't know how much I was missing until I met you." Kenna slid her hand under the fabric of Ripley's panties and stilled. "We balance each other, Rip."

"Yeah, okay." Ripley suddenly didn't care what they were talking about.

"Tell me you believe that. Tell me you can see what you do for me. Tell me you can see how important you are to me."

"I can," Ripley replied softly as Kenna stroked her.

"Tell me, honey."

"I can see it."

Ripley's hips moved up and into Kenna's hand.

"Do you want me to stop?" Kenna asked as she slid her tongue along Ripley's neck.

"No."

"Then, say it louder." Kenna enter her then.

She curled her fingers once, twice, and pulled out. Ripley wanted more. She wanted Kenna to touch her everywhere.

"I can see it," Ripley said, her voice much more confident this time around.

Kenna slid back inside while her thumb flicked at Ripley's suddenly hard clit that begged for attention. Only a moment earlier, Ripley had been exhausted and sated from the last time they'd made love just that morning.

"Good," Kenna replied.

"I thought you said I calmed you down. You seem pretty keyed up all of a sudden there, Ken." Ripley gripped Kenna's ass through her shorts and gasped when Kenna thrust harder.

"We balance, remember? You calm me down, but I light you up, Ripley." She met Ripley's eyes. "I can get you to say what you want, what you need. Like, right now, for example." She pulled out of Ripley completely. "Tell me what you want."

Kenna's eyes were on fire, and Ripley wondered if her own matched their intensity. Kenna's fingers were sliding up and down her lower lips slowly and with purpose.

"I want your mouth." Ripley slid her own hands out of Kenna's shorts. "I want your tongue all over me, and right when I'm about to come, I want you to stop." She hesitated before saying the next part. "Then I want you to watch me while I touch myself, and I want you to touch yourself while you do." Ripley took a deep breath. "Then, I want you to fuck me with your fingers while you go down on me."

"Anything else?" Kenna asked with an obvious gleam in her eye.

"Yes." Ripley pulled at Kenna's shorts. "Then, I want to fuck you with that strap-on."

Kenna's eyes grew wide, and she asked, "You do?"

"Yes." Ripley continued to push at the shorts covering skin she wanted to be touching.

"You know what I want?" Kenna asked her.

"What?"

"Every single thing you just said."

Ripley knew Kenna was right when she stroked herself while Kenna looked on. Never in her wildest dreams had she pictured this being a possibility for her. She had never told other partners the things she wanted in bed. Kenna did bring that out in her. It was remarkable how good it felt to finally be able to express herself fully with another person; emotionally, mentally, and sexually – this was what Ripley had been missing.

Ripley was lying on her back with her hand between her spread legs now, and Kenna was facing the other way on the bed. She was equally naked and equally spread open for Ripley to see. Kenna had licked and sucked Ripley until Ripley had been about to burst. Ripley hadn't wanted her to stop, but she'd lifted Kenna's head and saw Kenna's dark, craving eyes. Kenna licked her own lips and moved into her current position. As Ripley stroked herself, Kenna reached between her own legs. Ripley came as Kenna's fingers slid inside her own body and disappeared from view. Kenna came while watching Ripley come.

Kenna was kneeling on the floor then. She had her fingers buried inside Ripley now, and there was something about knowing those fingers had just been inside Kenna, had touched her so intimately, that got Ripley even more turned on. Kenna's mouth was on her, too, and she was eager, stroking hard and flat with her tongue. Ripley came on a well-timed thrust inside to a well-timed stroke to her clit. Kenna remained on the floor, kissing Ripley's thighs before licking her clit slowly a few more times. Ripley twitched at the touches.

When she then slid away from Kenna's mouth, closed her legs, and pointed to the juncture between her thighs, Kenna smirked, and Ripley nearly pulled the woman back down on top of herself. That expression on Kenna's face, in combination with Kenna wiping her chin with her hand had Ripley wanting her fingers back inside. She just wanted something else more, though.

Kenna slid the shorts onto Ripley's body for her. Ripley remained in her position, requesting Kenna to climb on top of her first, which Kenna did. Ripley wanted to watch the toy slide inside her girlfriend. She'd never done this to a woman, and she had no idea how to make it feel as good as Kenna had managed to make her feel every time they did this. She just hoped she'd be able to figure it out. Kenna slid down on top of it, causing herself and Ripley both to gasp at the same time. Within seconds, Kenna was moving her hips, which Ripley could only hold on to firmly and watch. Kenna's hands moved to her own nipples, and Ripley could not believe she was this lucky.

"This is you," Kenna said as she started lifting herself up and down. "You're inside me. You make me feel so good." Kenna's hips rolled forward and back again. Then, her hand disappeared between her legs as she stroked herself. "Touch me here." She reached for Ripley's hand and placed it on top of her other one. "Feel it."

Ripley was guided to the base of the dildo as Kenna rose and fell onto it softly, at first, and then harder and faster.

"Oh, God."

"Now, touch me here." Kenna moved Ripley's hand to her clit.

Ripley knew what to do now. She'd learned how Kenna liked to be touched there. She pressed her thumb hard as Kenna began moving her hips faster and faster. Ripley sat up then, holding on to one of Kenna's hips, took a nipple into her mouth, and flicked Kenna's swollen clit.

"So hot," Ripley said when she moved to the other nipple to give it equal attention.

"I'm about to come," Kenna said, stopping to move and grab both of Ripley's cheeks with her hands. "Now, fuck me."

Ripley grabbed Kenna's hips hard and rolled them over. Kenna spread her legs wide. Her flushed skin and darkened eyes gave Ripley the confidence she needed. Ripley's hips started moving down hard and fast, and she held herself up with both hands by Kenna's head. She then kissed Kenna hard, sucked Kenna's tongue into her mouth, and heard Kenna moan loudly as she did.

"Touch your clit again," Ripley instructed before she kissed her again.

Kenna's hand slid between her legs, and Ripley pushed deep inside her. Kenna moaned and said her name. Ripley loved seeing Kenna like this. The woman was usually so well put-together, but she was coming undone beneath Ripley and because of her. Ripley's thrusts grew more fevered. She felt the sweat begin to trickle down her forehead and gather between her breasts. Ripley felt the soreness in her arms as she continued to hold herself up and drive into Kenna, wanting the woman to explode beneath her. Kenna's gasps and moans were coming faster and faster, and Ripley wasn't sure how much longer she'd be able to keep up this pace, but she'd give Kenna everything she could.

"I'm coming! Oh, my God!" Kenna screamed. "Ripley!" she yelled. "Yes, baby! Yes!"

Both of Kenna's hands moved to Ripley's ass, and she slid them under the shorts Ripley had donned, squeezing while she pressed Ripley further into her. Ripley's own clit still pulsed, somehow not completely sated anymore.

"Yes!" Ripley said it without realizing it.

She continued her thrusts as Kenna came, but her own orgasm took over with just the right amount of pressure coming from Kenna pressing her down into herself farther. Ripley came, intensifying her thrusts more for herself than for Kenna, and then fell on top of her.

"That was the hottest fucking thing I have ever seen, done, or been a part of," Kenna announced in between several short breaths. "God, I really fucking love you."

Ripley laughed between short, fast breaths of her own.

"I need a cold shower," she replied.

"Care for company?"

CHAPTER 23

"WHY do you look like death warmed over?" Bella asked Kenna the following morning.

"Thanks, sis." Kenna sipped coffee at Bella's kitchen island. "Shouldn't you be gone already?"

"You didn't answer my question." Bella pointed at her before grabbing her purse.

"I was up late last night."

"Would that have anything to do with the woman out in my backyard, playing with my kids? I can't believe you asked if you could bring your girlfriend to babysit. That's so cute, Ken."

"Don't make fun of me." Kenna pointed back at her. "And yes, Ripley is the reason I was up late last night."

"Everything okay?" Bella asked, her playful tone disappearing.

"Everything's fine."

"Oh. You were up late for the other reason, then." Bella nodded. "Nice."

"Bell, stop it." Kenna laughed at her sister.

"Bella, hi. I actually have a question for you before you go, if that's okay." Ripley had, apparently, reentered the house without them noticing and made her way to the kitchen.

"If it has to do with asking for her hand in marriage, the answer is *absolutely yes*. Take her off my hands because she drives me crazy," Bella replied.

"Bella," Kenna warned.

Ripley laughed, placed her hand on Kenna's back, and said, "Maybe someday. But, for now, I was just wondering if it would be okay if the boys and I play basketball on the court down the street. Brady says he wants to teach me."

All Kenna heard from that was the *maybe someday* part of that statement. Not only had Ripley said that, she'd said it so confidently and seriously.

"Well, I'm leaving." Bella looked toward the staircase. "Assuming my husband is ready to go, that is!" That part was yelled loud enough for anyone in the house to hear.

"I'm ready. I was just loading the luggage." The reply came from near the front door. "Now, I'm waiting for you."

"Then, the decision is on you two. I don't think the boys have a basketball, though. Soccer balls, footballs, baseballs – we have, but, somehow, we are without a basketball."

"I bought them one," Ripley offered. "Cody mentioned they didn't have one last time we were here. Is it okay if I give it to them?"

"She even got them a pump to air the thing up. Totally adorable." Kenna played with Ripley's hair that she'd pulled back into a ponytail.

"Go for it. And thank you two for watching them. We appreciate it. Help yourself to anything in the fridge. There's money for pizza tonight, and we'll be back tomorrow by eleven at the latest."

"Have fun. It's your tenth anniversary; you deserve a night away," Kenna said and wrapped an arm around Ripley.

"Is it really okay that I stay over? I can totally go home."

"Ripley, you are more than welcome in our home. Our boys know about their aunt being gay. I don't think they fully grasp it, but we've never hidden it from them. In fact, I think it will be good for them to actually see her with a good woman. She's never brought anyone near them before. As for sleeping arrangements, Kenna normally crashes in the guest room when she's here, so – feel free to join her."

Ripley looked at Kenna, and Bella added, "Just wash

the sheets for me, if they need it." She winked at Kenna before heading out of the kitchen.

"Aunt Kenna, can we go to the park now?" Cody asked her. "Aunt Ripley said she was asking Mommy."

The little boy asked upon entering the kitchen and tugging on Kenna's jeans, and Kenna met Ripley's surprised expression at the word 'aunt.' Kenna lifted an eyebrow at her and gave her a smile and a kiss on the cheek.

"You're in luck, buddy: your mom just left. Aunt Ripley and I are in charge now, and we say we're going to the park."

***

Ripley played basketball with the boys for about an hour before she needed a break. Kenna had played with them as well, but 'playing' was also a relative term. The boys were a little young to make shots on a real basket. The time they spent playing was actually spent watching them try to heave the ball up toward the net or teaching them how to pass the ball and dribble. Ripley was just as terrible as she remembered. When she finally gave up trying, she returned to the blanket they'd laid out in the grass next to the court. Kenna played for a few more minutes before joining her.

"How are you doing with all this?" Kenna asked her.

"I'm giving up on the professional basketball career," Ripley replied.

Kenna bumped shoulders with her as she laughed.

"I meant the whole Aunt Ripley thing. We didn't tell them to call you that, but they're kids."

Ripley let out a deep sigh as she watched the boys fight over the basketball. She flashed back to her older brothers doing the same thing. Ethan was two years older and could fight off Benji with ease, but Benji was always determined to take down his big brother. She'd watched them fight more times than she could count.

"I would have been called that, you know?"

"What do you mean?"

"I don't know for sure, but as I grew up, I could picture Benji and Ethan doing the same. I asked myself what they would be doing with their lives. At first, it was in high school. Ethan would be on the varsity soccer team and have a cute girlfriend. Benji would be on JV and be great in math class."

"Was he good at math?"

"I have no idea," Ripley said as she laughed and watched Cody wrangle the ball from Brady. "When I got to college, I started thinking about how Ethan might still be playing soccer in school. Maybe he'd be there to learn physical therapy or sports management, and Benji would be pre-med."

"That sounds nice, Ripley."

"When I turned twenty-five, I pictured Ethan as a thirty-year-old man, and it was hard to do."

"Boys change a lot between thirteen and thirty."

Ripley turned to face Kenna and replied, "Not because of that; I don't have any pictures of them."

"What?"

"The fire didn't just take them, Kenna; it took everything. It burned all of our possessions. I don't even have pictures of my family. Not everything was digital back then. Even if it had been, I wouldn't have known how to access it. I was only eight."

"I never thought, Rip. I'm so sorry. I can't believe I didn't know that. Your parents didn't have anything in an email account or stored online somewhere? The internet wasn't what it is today back then, but–"

"I didn't ask." Ripley shrugged. "I never thought to ask, honestly. After being moved around so much, I got used to picturing them in my head. Sometimes, I had the nightmares, and I didn't want to see them because I saw them enough, if you know what I mean."

"Babe, I'm sorry." Kenna rubbed her back.

"I always picture Ethan with two kids and a wife.

They're little girls. Right now, they'd be four and six. I picture Benji with a girlfriend. For some reason, I just can't see him married at thirty-one. On their birthdays, I go to the cemetery. I make six trips there a year: the day of the fire and each birthday."

"You didn't go this year?"

"I did." Ripley gave Kenna a small smile. "When I asked for some alone time. I don't spend long there. It's still hard. They're all buried next to one another. I kind of just sit there silently for a while and play with blades of grass."

"Maybe next time you go, I could go with you." Kenna took her hand. "If not, it's okay."

"Aunt Kenna, Cody won't give me the ball back," Brady yelled over from the court.

"Aunt Ripley was going to show me how to dribble between my legs," Cody fired back.

"I don't know how to do that," Ripley yelled to Cody. "I can barely dribble the ball, period."

"All right, you little liar; let Brady take a shot. Then, we'll go get ice cream," Kenna said.

That seemed to do it. Cody passed Brady the ball, but it was too far to the right. It bounced past Brady, who then let out an exasperated grunt and ran after it in the grass.

"I was three feet from you!" Brady yelled.

"Are you sure you want this with me someday?" Kenna asked Ripley as she chuckled. "Those are my nephews, which means, if we ever have kids, they'll probably be just like them."

Ripley looked over at her, leaned in, and pressed her forehead to Kenna's.

"I love you."

"I love you."

"Oh, and I'm not so sure I'd mind having two just like them." Ripley pointed at the boys, who were now fighting over the ball again. "Ice cream!" she yelled to the boys.

**

"Aunt Kenna?" Cody whispered. "Aunt Ripley?"

Kenna's eyes snapped open at the sound of her nephew at the door to their bedroom. Then, she glanced with one eye still closed at the clock. It was after midnight. She looked over at Ripley, who seemed to still be asleep.

"Hey, what's wrong?" Kenna whispered to him, hoping not to wake Ripley.

"I can't sleep."

"Buddy, it's late." Kenna pulled the blankets back slowly. "You should be in bed."

"I tried, but I'm scared." Cody stood in the open doorway.

"What's wrong?" Ripley woke, sat up, and glanced at Kenna and then Cody.

"Nothing. He just can't sleep. Sorry, I didn't want to wake you," Kenna told her and kissed Ripley's temple, "Go back to sleep. I'll take him to bed."

"Will Aunt Ripley read me a story?" Cody asked.

"No, buddy. Come on, I'll read you–"

"I can do it," Ripley offered.

She slid out of bed, and Kenna followed her and Cody to Cody's bedroom, where she helped the boy back into his bed.

"Ripley reads you one story, and then it's sleep time. Deal?" Kenna asked him.

"Deal. Can it be Harry Potter?"

Kenna laughed softly and said, "If it's Harry Potter, it's one chapter."

"Chapter seventeen," he said.

"Didn't we read chapter seventeen the last time I was here?" Kenna asked him.

"I really like it." He shrugged.

"I've got it," Ripley said as she picked up the book that rested on a small desk in the corner of the room. "Chapter seventeen."

Ripley turned to the page in the book. Kenna kissed Cody on the forehead and backed away from the bed. Ripley sat on the edge of the bed at first, appearing uncomfortable. Kenna stood in the doorway of the bedroom, watching her read a story to her youngest nephew. She observed Ripley sink into the bed a little more as she turned each page. Cody's eyes grew heavier and heavier until they closed and stayed that way before Ripley could finish. His head rested on Ripley's shoulder, and she gave Kenna an adorably confused expression that told Kenna she had no idea what to do. Kenna approached, took the book from her, and helped her extricate herself from Cody's bed without waking him. When they climbed back into bed a few minutes later, Kenna kissed her on the lips.

"And you asked about the things you do for me." Kenna laughed softly. "I love you, Ripley Fox."

CHAPTER 24

"HOW have the nightmares been since the anniversary?" Dr. Clement asked.

"On and off," Ripley replied. "I've had a few, but I think they've gotten better."

"What do you think has helped?"

Ripley considered how best to respond. She was sitting on a small sofa with Kenna to her right. Her therapist, Elise Clement, sat across from them in an armchair with a notepad and pen in hand.

"Honestly, her." Ripley took Kenna's hand. "She's been a big help."

Kenna squeezed her hand back.

"Your new relationship?" Dr. Clement asked.

"I don't know how new it is anymore," Ripley said with a light laugh. "It doesn't feel new. I mean, it does..." She turned to Kenna, who smiled at her. "It does feel new in that way all new relationships do, but it also feels like I should have been with her all along. She's like a missing piece to me."

"That's great, Ripley," Dr. Clement replied and made a note. "It's important, though, that you deal with the nightmares and other things related to the fire and this pending court case independently from your relationship with Kenna."

Ripley knitted her eyebrows together and replied, "I am. I have been."

"Yes, you have." The woman nodded. "You've done a good job so far. I don't want to discount that."

"Then, what are you saying?" Ripley asked her.

"Some of the strides you've made recently are tied to your relationship with Kenna. While it's important that our partners in life support us through our issues, it's just as important, if not more so, for us to deal with our problems ourselves. What would you do, for example, if you and Kenna broke up tomorrow?"

"We're not–" Kenna started.

"It's okay," Ripley interrupted her and leaned over to kiss Kenna's cheek. "You don't have to be my protector in here," she whispered into Kenna's ear.

"I'm not suggesting you will, of course. This is just a discussion."

"I love Kenna. I don't know what's going to happen, but I know that I want to be with her. I like planning a future with her. I've never wanted to do that with anyone before. Getting married one day, having kids with her – none of that terrifies me like it used to. I'm still scared, of course. Everyone gets nervous about those moments, but I'm not so scared that I'm unwilling to try with her."

"That's great, Ripley." Dr. Clement made another note. "But, again, I'll ask the question just for the sake of our discussion. What would you do if you and Kenna broke up? Would you be able to continue to work on the reasons you're here? Would you be able to get rid of the nightmares or, at least, make them less frequent without her?"

"She doesn't have to," Kenna said. "Sorry, I don't mean to…"

"She's a little overprotective," Ripley laughed and squeezed Kenna's hand.

"I guess I just don't understand the purpose of your questions. I love her; she loves me. We're planning a life together. She doesn't have to do anything without me," Kenna explained.

"But she should be able to," Dr. Clement argued. "Would you admit, Kenna, that when we achieve things ourselves, they mean more? For example, I've seen you on the news. I assume you put a lot of work into your job."

"Of course, I do."

"If someone handed you a story that was ready to air and all you had to do was say the words they put on a teleprompter, would it mean more or less to you?"

"Less, obviously. I'm an investigative reporter. I don't regurgitate material other people have put together."

"When Ripley works through things on her own, it means more to her. There's more of an impact to us when that happens. The impact leads to progress and healing when it comes to what she's dealing with."

"What do I do then?" Kenna leaned forward on the sofa and took her hand from Ripley's to clasp with her own in her lap. "Am I causing problems because I'm helping? Am I too involved? I don't want to make anything worse for her. I just try to be there and–"

"Hey, no." Ripley placed a hand on Kenna's back and slid it under her shirt enough to feel Kenna's overheated skin. Kenna's head turned back to her, and Ripley's eyes met Kenna's concerned blue ones. "Stop it. You're not doing anything wrong." Ripley smiled at Kenna, who nodded. "What she's saying is that I need to be able to do this without you, even though I have you. Right?"

"Right." Dr. Clement winked at her and offered a proud smile. "You are very supportive, Kenna. I can already tell that because Ripley brought you here. I am glad she's told you how she feels and what she deals with. It's important she has someone else to talk to about this and that you continue to support her. What I need Ripley to do is continue to confront these nightmares, continue to remind herself the events she sees aren't real. They didn't happen, right?"

"They didn't happen," Ripley repeated.

"What did happen?"

"The dreams," Ripley answered. "And the good memories."

"Why don't you tell Kenna and I a memory of your family that neither of us knows?" Dr. Clement suggested.

Ripley thought for a moment while she drew shapes on Kenna's skin out of view of her therapist.

"We went to a carnival once," Ripley began. "My grandmother had just moved in, and we all went together. She said she'd ride the Ferris wheel with me since Benji wanted to ride with Ethan and my parents would ride together." Ripley saw it in her mind clear as day, and she smiled. "Benji and Ethan were fooling around in the car below us. My parents were in the car behind us and couldn't see, but my grandma could. She yelled down at them to cool it, or she'd climb into their car and smack them around." Ripley came out of the memory for a moment. "She didn't. I mean, she wouldn't have. She just said stuff like that sometimes. They stopped immediately, of course. After, Grandma bought us each cotton candy."

"What color was yours?" Dr. Clement asked.

"Pink. Benji and Ethan both got blue."

"And how did it taste?"

"Sweet." Ripley closed her eyes as was their custom. "There are those sugar crystals that harden before they soften."

"What did it smell like at the carnival?"

"Like fried food," Ripley answered and opened her eyes.

Kenna was staring at her. She hadn't leaned back yet, but she had turned her head to watch Ripley.

"How does it feel?"

"Carefree. It feels like anything could happen."

"Good." Dr. Clement made another note. "Now, how

have you been doing with the new developments?"

"Patrick Wilkes?" Ripley asked her.

Kenna did lean back then. Ripley lowered her shirt after removing her hand, and Kenna's arm went over her shoulder. Ripley leaned back against it, loving Kenna's presence there.

"Have you decided to testify if there's a trial?"

"I don't want to," Ripley told her. "I don't see the point."

"Because you didn't see anything?"

"I didn't. I think people assume I'm lying, that I've forgotten or just blocked it out, but I didn't see anything."

"I know that," Dr. Clement shared.

"I just don't see what I can offer. The lawyers think it's important that they hear from me, that it will help their case, but I can't see myself telling an entire courtroom what happened."

"You don't think it could help you?"

"How?"

"Sometimes, getting the story out helps."

"I have gotten the story out," Ripley argued. "Kenna knows, you know, Kenna's family knows now. The cops know, and so do the lawyers, too. Plus, my statement is on the record."

"You were eight years old, Ripley. You haven't spoken about it to anyone outside of this room since, have you? The police officers and lawyers know because the new evidence was discovered, not because you told them."

"I gave them that new evidence," Ripley defended, feeling her voice starting to get louder. That wasn't like her. "I told the investigator to turn it over so they could get this guy."

Kenna's eyes were still on her, and Kenna's free hand moved to her thigh.

"But have you told any of the people involved in the case exactly what you remember from that night?"

Kenna bit her lower lip in frustration and turned to say

something to this 'doctor.' Ripley covered the hand on Kenn's thigh with her own, causing Kenna to turn back to her. Ripley gave her a small nod.

"No, I haven't."

"Have you thought of the impact statement you brought up last time?" Dr. Clement changed the subject, which Ripley knew she did often.

"I don't plan on giving one."

"Do you know what you would say if you did?"

Ripley gulped, and Kenna gripped her hand, offering more silent support.

"No."

"While I do think it would be very beneficial for you to speak your words out loud, I can understand why you might not want to do that. It might be helpful for you to at least write them down. No one would have to read it. It would just be for you."

"Is this like the time you tried to get me to journal my feelings?" Ripley asked with an eye-roll.

The doctor laughed and replied, "Journaling is a very effective therapeutic technique that I still think you'd benefit from; and yes, it's a little bit like that."

"I don't know," Ripley said.

"Okay. We'll leave it at that for now then and revisit the topic next session," Dr. Clement suggested.

***

Kenna's mind was going a million miles a minute. As she and Ripley sat on her couch, watching some show she wasn't paying attention to, she still couldn't get her mind off that therapy session.

"You'd tell me if I was interfering with your progress, right?" she finally asked.

Ripley turned to her and asked, "Progress with what?"

"Your therapy, the nightmares; all of it."

"Oh, Ken." Ripley placed her head on Kenna's

shoulder. "You're not interfering with anything. You're helping me."

"But she said you needed to do this stuff on your own."

"I do. It just takes time," Ripley shared. "I only started going to therapy when I got out of college. She's the first doctor I've actually given a chance to help me. With the other two I had, I was still so closed off. I didn't give it a shot."

"How long have you been going to her?"

"Only a little over a year." Ripley wrapped her arm around Kenna's stomach. "My first therapist kept insisting I try hypnotherapy to reveal my blocked memories, and I stopped going after a while. I didn't think therapy could help. A couple of years later, I tried again with a different doctor. She was nice, but after a year or so, I didn't feel like I was making any progress. Dr. Clement just somehow got through to me."

"I don't want to get in the way," Kenna said.

"Honey, you're not getting in the way. That's her job. She's supposed to challenge me."

"I was proud of you, though," Kenna revealed, and Ripley lifted her head to look at her. "You stopped me from stepping in to defend you. You defended yourself. I was proud."

"Thank you," Ripley replied and kissed her. "Now, can I ask you a question?"

"Of course," Kenna said.

"Am I overstaying my welcome?"

"What?"

"I've stayed over here practically every night for the past month. I hardly remember what my own apartment looks like."

"I love having you here."

"I guess I just know that part of the reason I've been here so much is because of the reporters outside of my place, but I think they've realized I'm never there. I drove by the other day. They're gone now."

"Do you want to go home?" Kenna asked.

"I think I am home, Kenna." Ripley smiled at her. "My apartment is just where I live, but it's never felt like home. Honestly, nowhere has ever felt like home to me. Being with you, like this – that's the closest I've ever come to having that feeling I used to have before it all happened."

"Then, stay here. I don't need you to go."

"It's not too much too soon?"

"I asked you out the moment we met, remember? I think we're doing okay."

Ripley laughed before laying her head back on Kenna's shoulder.

CHAPTER 25

"KENNA, can I grab you for a second," Shannon asked her.

"Sure. What's up?"

"In Clark's office."

Kenna lowered her head and shook it from side to side before she stood up, gathered her bag, and headed toward Clark's office at the end of the hall. It was the end of her workday. That in and of itself was a new concept for Kenna. She'd rarely had ends to her workdays before, but since meeting Ripley, she didn't want to stay at the office all night. She didn't want to spend her entire Saturday or Sunday in research mode or hunting for the next story. Truthfully, she'd enjoyed mentoring a couple of the cub reporters recently, helping them plan out their stories and approaches. She had seen less screen time herself, and her reel was looking a little out of date, but she was okay with that.

"Kenna, we need to talk about this Wilkes case," Clark said the moment she entered his office.

That was his style. He'd catch you off guard, ask his questions or tell you what he wanted, and you never even had the chance to get your footing in the conversation.

"Mandy mentioned you two had a conversation. That has Shannon and I concerned," he added.

Kenna sat in one of his guest chairs. Shannon was on her right.

"I asked Mandy to let my girlfriend leave a building, that's correct," she explained. "I haven't talked to Mandy since."

"Kenna, what happened?" Shannon asked her, and Kenna was surprised at the genuine concern in her tone.

"Nothing. Did she say something happened?"

"No, I meant what happened with you? You gave up a chance at a great story, got upset that we're still pursuing it – when that's exactly what we do, turned in a subpar puff piece on social work in Pleasant Valley, and now, you're leaving early and, instead of focusing on your own work, you're spending all your time with Reggie and Stillson on their stories." Shannon turned her body to Kenna.

"I can't help how I feel, Shannon. Ripley is my girlfriend. Despite the fact that she's a private person and has asked not to be on camera or be interviewed, it would be unethical for me to report anything having to do with her."

"But not unethical for this news station to report on," Clark re-entered the conversation. "Kenna, we have an obligation to report the news. Like it or not, Ripley Fox is news these days."

"All I did was ask Mandy to leave her alone that day."

"And that was wrong of you," Clark replied. "Mandy was doing her job."

"Why am I in here now? This didn't exactly happen today."

"We gave Mandy the Wilkes case." Clark leaned back in his chair. "It's her job to pursue her leads wherever they take her. You won't get in her way again if she approaches Ripley Fox."

"I won't?" Kenna leaned back in her own chair.

"And you will ask Miss Fox for an exclusive interview. You will work with Mandy on the questions," he added.

"Excuse me?"

"Kenna, come on." Shannon gave her the look that told Kenna she was supposed to fall in line.

"What is this?" Kenna asked. "I either shape up or ship out?"

"Kenna, no one wants you to ship out." He chuckled. "But this is the job."

"And if this had to do with your wife, Clark? Your husband, Shannon? What would you do?"

"You've known this girl for two months, Kenna," Shannon said. "You're prepared to throw your career away for someone you've known for two months?"

"I was unaware I was throwing anything away. I gave a story I didn't want – and shouldn't do, for obvious reasons – to another reporter at this news station. I asked her to back off of Ripley, who wasn't going to give a comment anyway. Oh, and Mandy rapid-fired about ten questions at Ripley like a total rookie. She wasn't getting anything out of Ripley, even if Ripley did plan to make a comment."

"Your work has suffered since–"

"Since my relationship began? Are you two honestly saying you've never had a professional slump because of something in your personal life? I'm pretty sure everyone in this building has dealt with that at least once."

"You were out on Monday," Shannon added.

"I worked from home on Monday. I edited some of Stillson's stuff."

"Kenna, I am busy. I don't have time for this. I have a station to run. Help Mandy with the Fox story. This is a huge opportunity for her and for the station."

"And you want to use my relationship to get Ripley to agree to comment?"

"I want you to use your relationship with her to get us an interview, an exclusive. A comment gets us nowhere."

"And if I don't agree to do this?" she asked him. "I'm your only investigative reporter with any real experience. I'm single-handedly helping the rookies, which most reporters wouldn't even bother because it would take away from their own work."

"That's the problem, though, Kenna. Don't you see?

You're not focused on your own work anymore."

"Kenna, get Mandy what we're asking, and we'll look the other way on this whole thing," Clark finally said. "I have another meeting now."

"Are you giving me a choice here?" she asked.

"No, I'm not."

Kenna inhaled deeply before allowing her lungs to empty.

"Then, I quit."

"Kenna!" Shannon exclaimed.

"You can't quit," Clark stood.

"Yes, I can."

"Okay, we'll talk more. We don't need the exclusive." Shannon stood as well.

Kenna wiped her hands over her thighs nonchalantly before standing herself.

"I'll have my resignation on your desk in thirty minutes." She picked up her bag and added, "I'd like to be professional and still give you two weeks, but if you'd rather today be my last day, I'd understand."

"Kenna, let's be rational." Clark moved around his desk. "Is what we're asking really that out of line."

"You know it's not." Kenna walked toward the closed door, opened it, and turned back to them. "A few months ago, I would have been begging for this story. I would have done anything to get the exclusive. I would have worked twenty-four hours a day if that was what it took to get this right." Kenna paused then and shrugged. "But it's not the most important thing to me anymore. I'll be at my desk, typing up my letter. Just let me know if I need to pack my things today."

"Kenna, are you crazy?" Shannon followed her out of Clark's office.

"No, I'm actually pretty sane. I just have different priorities."

"What are you going to do? There are, like, three news stations in this town. You know Clark will blackball you at the other two. He might be doing that already."

"I'll figure something out, but I meant what I said in there, Shannon: my heart's not in the chase anymore."

"So, what? You're leaving news?"

"No, I don't want to leave news. I'm still and always will be a reporter." Kenna sat down at her desk. "But I'm not putting my relationship at risk for a story. It's too important for that. I think I just need a change of pace. If I can't keep up with what you guys need in a full-time investigative reporter, then this is best for the station, too."

Shannon crossed her arms over her chest and asked, "There's nothing I can do?"

"Be a reference? If Clark blackballs me, I might need you."

"Of course. But let's keep that between you and me."

Shannon placed a hand on Kenna's shoulder, squeezed it a little, then gave her an awkward smile, and walked off. Kenna got to work on her resignation letter.

***

"Miss Fox, one question!" Mandy, the reporter who worked with Kenna, yelled as Ripley tried to make her way toward her car after work.

"Ripley, over here!" That voice belonged to another reporter, but Ripley had begun to recognize them all.

"How does it feel, knowing Patrick Wilkes has rejected the plea deal? This case is going to trial. Will you testify?"

Ripley grabbed her keys from her bag before shifting it nervously on her shoulder. She crossed the street with four reporters, cameras, and microphones in tow. They continued to ask her for a comment, and Ripley continued to try to ignore them. It had been relatively calm and peaceful in recent days, but news that Wilkes turned down the state's offer had reached her along with the reporters. They were back now, and each wanted their own quote for their networks. Just as Ripley made it across the street, tired of hearing them all yell questions at her, she turned to them.

"No comment," she said.

It was two words. It wasn't much to the rest of the world, but to Ripley, it was something. She hadn't said so much as a word to anyone. Now, she had at least said that. She turned back around and moved in the direction of her car. The reporters stuck around until they realized she wasn't going to offer them anything else. When she finally spotted her car, she also spotted someone familiar standing in front of it. She smiled as she met Kenna at her driver's side door. Kenna smiled back and removed Ripley's bag from her shoulder.

"How was your day?" Kenna asked.

"What are you doing here?"

"Picking you up. We're going out to celebrate." Kenna slid the bag over her own shoulder and took Ripley's hand.

"What are we celebrating?" Ripley asked.

Kenna began walking, and Ripley had no choice but to follow.

"Well, there's the fact that I just saw you stand up to those reporters for the first time," Kenna offered.

"I gave them a 'no comment.' I hardly think that's standing up to them," Ripley returned.

"It's a start, babe." Kenna pulled out the keys to her own car and unlocked it as they arrived.

"Considering that's just happened, and you were already outside, waiting for me, something tells me there's something else we're celebrating."

"There is." Kenna tossed Ripley's bag into the backseat. "I quit my job today."

CHAPTER 26

"YOU quit your job?" Ripley asked the moment they climbed into the car.

"I did." Kenna put the car into reverse. "And we're celebrating."

"We're celebrating you quitting your job? You love your job, Kenna." Ripley turned to face her as they joined traffic. "What's going on? Why do you look so happy about this?"

"Because I am happy about this," Kenna stated. "Rip, I did love my job. But I haven't loved it all that much lately."

"That's my fault," Ripley replied. "It's this case, and you trying to protect me from it."

"It's not your fault I don't love my job these days." Kenna wove through traffic, which wasn't heavy but was annoying when all she wanted to do was get her girlfriend to dinner and then home in order to have her way with her. "I made a reservation for us at *Isles*. Is that okay?"

"*Isles* is crazy fancy, Ken. I'm not dressed for fancy."

"You're dressed fancy enough. I happen to think you look great." Kenna smiled at her. "We're taking dessert to go, though. I want you home and naked in bed as soon as possible."

"Kenna, slow down a second." Ripley placed a hand on Kenna's thigh.

"That's not going to help me slow down," Kenna joked.

"I'm being serious here," Ripley replied through laughter that gave her away. "You can't just quit your job. How will you pay your bills? You don't have anything else lined up." Ripley paused, and then her tone did change to serious. "Unless there's something I don't know about. Did you send your reel out?"

"Oh, babe. No, I haven't sent it out." Kenna grasped Ripley's hand for a moment before needing to take the wheel with both hands to turn them into the parking lot of the restaurant. Once parked, she turned to her and said, "I haven't sent anything out. And I have small savings I can live off of until I find something else. My condo is already paid for, and so is this car."

"Your condo is paid for?" Ripley asked.

"Rip, my mom is a part-time real estate agent. She found my condo when it was in foreclosure, got it for a great price, bought it herself, and I bought it from her. She did the same with Bella's house. How else do you think Bell could afford that nice place? Her husband is a second-grade teacher in the public school system." Kenna paused. "I paid the condo off two years ago. Keep in mind – I am four years older than you."

"But still, that's amazing. You have no debt? Really?"

"I was very lucky, babe. My parents are incredibly generous. And I got scholarships, too, so no student loan debt. I have two credit cards I rarely use but keep for emergencies, and in case I want to book an extravagant vacation."

"Wow! That's amazing, Ken."

"What's amazing is that I am now free from Channel 8 news."

"Since when did you want that, though?"

"It's not because of you. I guess it is in a way, of

course, but only in a good way. I know what I want now. Besides, they were trying to strong-arm me into giving them an exclusive with you. Clark flat out told me to use our relationship to convince you to sit down with Mandy. It pissed me off."

"Ken, I'm sorry. I–"

"No, babe," Kenna interrupted and placed a hand on Ripley's cheek. "It's not your fault. I don't want to work somewhere like that. I get chasing the story. I'm a reporter; I still have that inside me – I always will. What I don't get and do not like is them pressuring me to convince you to do something because we're dating. That doesn't work for me."

"You said you know what you want to do now. Does that mean you're going to send your reel out other places?"

"Not right now." Kenna opened the car door on her side, and Ripley did the same. They began walking toward the restaurant hand in hand. "Right now, I'm going to enjoy dinner with my beautiful girlfriend. Later, I'm going to have dessert on her body."

"Kenna!" Ripley whisper-yelled as they stood near two other couples in the waiting area of the incredibly nice restaurant.

Kenna laughed and replied, "Then, you and I will discuss what I do next."

"It's your job, Ken. You should do whatever you want."

"Rip, if we're together, we're in this together. That's what this relationship is. I don't want to make a decision about my career without you, okay?"

"Okay."

"Crawford, for two," Kenna told the hostess at the podium.

***

Ripley enjoyed Kenna's version of celebration possibly

more than Kenna. Apparently, Kenna liked to celebrate by eating delicious, expensive food, taking dessert home with them, and then doing amazing things to Ripley's body. It was all smiles and laughs from Kenna as they showered together after, and the woman was still smiling as they crawled into bed late that night.

"I don't have to go to work tomorrow," Kenna said out loud. "That's the craziest thing to me. I've always had a job. I started bussing tables at sixteen, and I've worked ever since."

"You gave them two weeks, though, Ken."

"Oh, I know. I'll be there. It's just that I don't *have* to be there if I don't want. They even told me I could work from home for the rest of my time, if I wanted. I'll be professional. Shannon is going to give me a glowing recommendation. It's the least I could do, but I'm also not someone that shirks her responsibilities, either."

"And you're sure about this?" Ripley asked for at least the fourth time that day.

Kenna was lying on her side, naked. Ripley had opted to put on a shirt and shorts to sleep in, and she was also regretting not encouraging Kenna to do the same because Kenna's body was remarkable. It was soft and smooth, toned in the right places and curvy in the others. Ripley knew her own body was in good shape, too, thanks to her morning exercises, which she had managed to keep up, despite everything going on in their lives. Kenna's condo had a gym downstairs. Ripley was a frequent user of the treadmill in the mornings and had taken to using Kenna's living room for her yoga stretches. Kenna sometimes joined her. Other times, she just watched. One time, her watching had led to Ripley flat on her yoga mat with Kenna's face between her legs. Thinking about that was not good in this moment. While they'd made love when they'd gotten home from the restaurant, that was now three hours ago. They'd behaved themselves in the shower. Now, Kenna was naked against soft sheets, and Ripley wanted her again. She gulped that thought away because she needed to pay attention to Kenna's response.

If Kenna really did want to leave her job independently of Ripley, that was great. If Kenna was only doing this because Ripley entered her life and turned it upside down, that wasn't okay. They would have to talk about it. And if that was the case, Ripley might even suggest they talk to Dr. Clement about how to handle this stuff as a couple. The woman wasn't technically a couple therapist, but she could at least handle that. Did they need couple therapy? No, they didn't. They were fine. Kenna only quit her job, and she'd done it because she wanted to quit.

"You're still worried this is about you, aren't you?"

"How'd you know?" Ripley asked.

"Because your eyebrows pinch together when you're deep in thought."

"You know me too well, Kenna Crawford. I can't have that. This relationship is over." She winked at Kenna.

"Oh, yeah?" Kenna laughed and climbed on top of her. "Was it over a few hours ago, when my tongue was–"

"Okay. Okay. Don't talk about that right now." Ripley laughed.

"Why not?" Kenna kissed her neck. "Is there a problem?"

"Yes, one of us has to go to work tomorrow because she doesn't have a choice. The other one is doing it out of professional courtesy," Ripley said.

"Oh, I see." Kenna kissed the spot behind her earlobe, knowing it was a favorite of Ripley's. "I guess I can let you off the hook then."

"Can you also put on clothes?" Ripley asked.

Kenna lifted herself up and stared down at her with wicked eyes.

"Problem?"

"Yes, it's a problem." Ripley laughed again. "You're sexy as hell, Kenna Elizabeth Crawford."

"Middle name? Really, Ripley Lynn?" Ripley's smile

faltered, and Kenna caught it like she always did. "Hey, where'd you go?" she asked as she touched Ripley's cheek.

"That was my grandmother's name," Ripley answered. "I don't know where my first name came from, but my middle name was for my grandmother."

"That's right." Kenna seemed to recall. "It's a beautiful name for a beautiful woman." She kissed Ripley's lips gently. "A beautiful woman I love more than anything."

"We should get some sleep," Ripley said. "I have two home visits tomorrow, and I don't expect either of them will be good."

"How are these people allowed to be foster parents?" Kenna rolled off Ripley.

"Because there aren't enough really good people out there who register to foster. Everyone generally wants their own kids, and the added time and expense of fostering on top of that is usually too much."

"Maybe that's what you and I will do," Kenna said. She stood, moved to her dresser, and threw on a pair of shorts with underwear and a shirt. "We could be foster parents one day."

"What?"

"Just an idea," Kenna offered as she slid back under the blankets.

"Instead of us having our own?"

"Or, in addition. I know it's far off and not something we need to talk about anytime soon. It was honestly just a thought. I don't think I'd mind having one or two biological ones between us, but I'd also be okay with adopting them. There are so many kids out there that need good homes. I've only glimpsed into your world, babe, but I can see that. We could foster, too. I don't know. I'm just thinking out loud."

Ripley turned to her girlfriend, placed a hand on her cheek, and said, "I would love that."

"You would?"

"I told you the kids thing is a new topic of

conversation for me when it first came up, and that's true. I guess, though, I always kind of had it in the back of my mind that if I did have kids one day, I'd ideally foster or adopt."

"Then, when we get ready for that step, we'll talk about it, okay?"

Ripley smiled into the kiss she gave Kenna. Never in her mind had she entertained the idea that Kenna would want to foster kids who needed homes. She hadn't even thought Kenna would be interested in adoption. She loved this woman she was falling asleep next to every night, and she wanted nothing more than to share the rest of her life letting Kenna surprise her with how much they seem to complete one another.

CHAPTER 27

KENNA was on a mission. No, that wasn't right. Kenna was on several missions. She had no idea how she would manage to achieve all of them, but she was going to try her best. She wouldn't be assigned any new stories because of her resignation, and she wouldn't offer any of her own to Clark, given how he had treated her. She had a list of stories she'd take with her wherever she decided to go. Since she was in the office, though, she'd help Stillson and Reggie, their two youngest reporters, as much as she could with their stories while she was still on staff. That had been her favorite part of her job in recent weeks anyway.

She'd also work on those missions. There were three of them. First, Kenna had borrowed Ripley's phone the other night, and she had downloaded all the pictures on Ripley's phone to the cloud. She then sent the files she'd chosen to a printer; mission one was in progress. The second mission would be a little more challenging, and it would also take time.

"Mal, thanks for coming in," Kenna greeted the investigator as she met him in the small café that was housed in the lobby of the station.

"Why are we meeting down here?" he asked as he sat across from her.

"Because this isn't for the station. It's for me."

"Oh."

"And you may not have heard, but I've resigned from Channel 8. Next Friday is my last day."

"What?" He leaned forward in the cheap café chair. "When did this happen?"

"The other day. I wasn't sure if you'd heard or not."

"No, I haven't. What the hell, Kenna?"

"I need a change. It's for the best. Anyway, I'll be paying you myself for this one. Whatever your going rate is, just let me know. And, technically, it's two jobs."

"Two jobs?"

"I need your investigative skills on something. I could try to do it on my own, but it would take longer. It's also about Ripley, and I don't want her to know I'm working on it."

"I thought you were all up in arms over anyone having anything to do with her and this case."

"It's not about the case." Kenna sipped on the coffee she'd ordered before Mal's arrival. "And it's not bad. It's something I want to do for her, but I don't want her to know in case there's nothing to be found."

"Well, now I'm intrigued." Malcolm clasped his hands together on the table. "Let's call this one my going-away present, then. I'll do it on the house."

"You don't have–"

"You're the reason the network has me on retainer, to begin with, Kenna," he reminded. "I kind of owe you thousands of dollars for that."

"How about you give me the first ten hours on the house, but I pay for the rest of your time?"

"Now you're doubting my skills?" Malcolm pressed his palm to his heart in mock-offense. "What do you have for me that's going to take more than ten hours?"

***

"Ripley, I am begging you here. I don't beg."

"I don't plan to testify," Ripley said.

"Wilkes has asked for his trial to be moved up. It's his right to a speedy trial – and while we have problems in

Pleasant Valley, we don't have a lot of homicide trials; the judge granted his request. We have less than three months to prep. That was by his attorney's design and was a smart move. We need all the help we can get."

"You have experts that can testify and people who can talk about Wilke's as a person. You even have that witness that came forward saying they saw him with kerosene in his truck before one of the fires."

"Circumstantial," the ADA replied.

"I don't have physical evidence hiding in my pocket," Ripley reminded.

"You have the story. You have what you remember. You can tell us about your parents, your brothers. You can talk about how much they had to live for."

"No, I can't," Ripley reminded him of that as well.

She missed Kenna. She had taken this meeting alone because it was Kenna's last day at work. She wished she could have postponed it in order to have the woman here, with her, holding her hand and taking some of these questions, offering strong replies. In Ripley's most recent solo session with Dr. Clement, though, her therapist had again encouraged her to attempt to handle as much as she could on her own.

"I know this is hard."

"No, you don't. You have no idea how this feels for me," Ripley told him.

"I know you want Wilkes locked up so he can't do this to anyone again," the ADA said.

"Of course, I do."

"I know you want to do what it takes to make that happen."

"I'm here, aren't I?" she asked, referring to his stuffy brown leather office. "I'm willing to meet with you, talk to you, but I'm not going on some stand to talk about what my family missed out on."

"Why not?" he asked. "This is your chance, Ripley."

"Because I don't know what they missed out on," she

said as she stood. "I don't know." She grabbed her bag and slung it over her shoulder. "I was eight years old. For all I knew, my parents were bank robbers who hid it really well. Ethan was friends with Patrick. Maybe they were in on it together, and it went horribly wrong. I don't know. I will never know because I was asleep, and I was eight years old. I played with stuffed animals, read picture books, and thought my brothers were the coolest kids in the world, my dad was Superman, and my mom was Wonder Woman. I don't know what they were really like. I don't know if they were good people. I don't know."

***

"You said that?" Kenna asked as they sat next to one another on her sofa, recounting their days.

"Everyone wants me to talk about them, but the truth is, I don't know anything about them."

"Honey, you didn't want to know anything about them," Kenna reminded her. "You shut yourself off from it. I understand; I do. You were in the system. You didn't exactly have a lot of opportunities to learn more than people told you. But even as an adult, you still haven't tried to learn more about your family."

"What do you think this case is all about? I told you to give them the information. Patrick Wilkes is on trial because of it."

"Babe, that's not your family. That's the fire. They're two different things."

"Can we just talk about your last day at work, please?"

"No, Rip. This is important," Kenna reasoned and turned to her on the couch. "Don't you want to know more about them; know your mom's favorite color or your dad's favorite hobby? Don't you want to know where your name comes from?"

"I won't ever know those things, Kenna. They're gone. All I have are questions," Ripley stated firmly.

"Then, it's time to ask them."

"Why? I won't get the answers."

"Maybe not to everything, but I know the answers to all those questions I just asked you. I'd like to share that with you if you let me."

"What are you talking about?" Ripley squinted at her.

"Your mom's favorite color was teal. She painted your nursery that color the day after she found out she was having a baby girl. Both of your brothers had a pale-yellow nursery, but your mom changed it just for you because she wanted you to have her favorite color surrounding you, her little girl." Kenna ran a hand through Ripley's hair. "Your dad's favorite hobby was camping. Anything outdoors would work, but he loved camping. He especially loved taking his family during the summer."

"What are you—" Ripley gulped. "How do you know this?"

"You were named after William Ripley. He came from Yorkshire, England, to Boston in 1638 with his wife, Jane. Jane Ripley had three daughters. William had no brothers. The Ripley name died when those daughters married their husbands. Your great-grandfather was William's grandson. His name was Benjamin Foxley. When his father was found guilty of desertion in one of the many wars in this damn country, Benjamin changed the family name to Fox to get some separation. He had two daughters and one son, and that son's name was Ethan. Ethan was your grandfather on your dad's side. Your parents named each of their children after someone in the family. You were also named after your grandmother, as you already know. Ethan's middle name was Henry. Henry is a distant cousin who died in the Civil War. Benjamin's middle name was John, and John was the name of William's father who remained in England when William settled in Boston." Kenna paused as she stared into Ripley's watery eyes. "I have it all written down for you. It's confusing, I know. You can read all about it, though, sweetheart. It's all there for you."

"How?"

"I wanted you to know your history, Ripley. It's so important to know where you come from." Kenna slid Ripley's hair behind her ear as a tear streaked down Ripley's cheek. Kenna wiped it away. "Your parents were good people. They worked hard, they took care of their family, and they loved you, Ripley."

"How?" Ripley repeated.

"I did some investigating," Kenna answered. "Please don't be mad. I asked Malcolm to help because I couldn't do it myself." She smiled. "By the way, John Ripley was in distant relation to the royal family. You, my dear, are technically something important in England."

"What?" Ripley laughed through her tears that fell in earnest now.

"He was an Earl. I don't exactly know how all that works, but that technically makes you Lady Fox, I believe. Maybe you own land over there."

"Kenna," Ripley leaned in and placed her forehead to Kenna's. "You did all this?"

"I was planning on giving you everything tomorrow anyway. Why don't you go into my office?"

Kenna stood first, pulled Ripley up by the hands, wiped at her tears again, and pulled her toward the office. She opened the door and ushered Ripley in before following behind.

"What is–"

"Sit down," Kenna said softly. "Sofa's for you."

Kenna pointed to the sofa, which had boxes on it. She wheeled her desk chair over and sat in front of Ripley, who stared at the boxes.

"I'm supposed to open these?"

"The one on top first." Kenna pointed to a small box she hadn't had the time to wrap. Ripley lifted the lid to reveal the gift inside. "I know you have them on your phone, but I thought you should have a real photo album of them, too."

Ripley flipped through the photo album, which contained all the pictures of the children she had helped.

"Kenna…"

"I had a few framed for you. They're inside that box." Kenna pointed to the box on the floor. "You can open that one later. I just thought you should have pictures of the good things you do around you, Ripley. They shouldn't just be on your phone."

"We'll talk about you snooping in my phone later." Ripley winked at her.

"Open that one now."

Ripley followed Kenna's gaze to another unwrapped box. Ripley lifted the lid and peered inside.

"Another album?"

"Babe, this one's different. Open it," Kenna instructed softly. When Ripley did, Kenna knew she'd made the right decision. Ripley's face lit up before she immediately burst into tears. "I did some research. I found a few of your parents' friends and asked them to scour their own photo albums, emails, files, and anywhere else they might have stowed pictures away. I had copies made and put them all in here for you."

"This is my family, Kenna." Ripley cried.

Kenna moved to her side, wrapped both arms around her, and pulled Ripley close. The album remained open in Ripley's lap.

"Yes, it is. This is your family, sweetheart. They were good, honest people, and you've always known that. You don't need proof. You knew them, Rip. You knew them," she consoled. "There aren't that many in there, but there were at least enough to fill a small album. I have them all stored on the cloud for you, along with two external hard drives, just in case. Those are both in my fireproof safe in my desk for now, but I thought you could get a safe deposit box if you want and put one of them in there. You'll have them forever."

Ripley pulled back and turned her attention back to the

photos in her lap. Kenna massaged the back of her neck as Ripley turned page after page. Kenna hadn't been all that lucky. Many of the pictures featured the friends or their families in the foreground with the Fox family in the background, but Ripley didn't seem to mind. She ran her fingertip over the plastic that was protecting the images. She laughed at one picture of Ethan and Benji playing soccer behind a picture of three young boys who were the subjects. They were all in matching soccer uniforms. There were a few, though, that featured her family. Then, there was the one picture Kenna had lucked into. It didn't include Ripley's grandma, but it did have Ripley's parents, her two brothers, and Ripley front and center with Ethan's hand on her shoulder. Kenna didn't know where it had been taken, but it was outside. The family looked happy. Kenna wagered this was the only surviving family photo.

"Kenna, this is the best gift you can ever give me. You know that, right?"

"I do," Kenna replied, deepening her massage.

"I could have found this had I tried," Ripley said without looking from the picture.

"It doesn't matter, babe. You found it now."

"No, you did."

"What I did was help you start," Kenna replied. "You have to finish."

"Finish?" Ripley looked away from the picture and met Kenna's eyes. "Your parents had a few close friends. Two of them still live near Pleasant Valley. One of them has a son Ethan's age. They were friends. They've all said they'd be happy to talk to you whenever you want. They'll tell you everything they remember about your family, Rip."

"They're here?" Ripley asked. Kenna nodded. "Why didn't they–"

"They didn't reach out because you never did. They didn't know if you'd want to hear from them. It's still up to you. If you don't want to talk to them, that's okay. They're the ones that told me about your mom's favorite color and your dad's love for the outdoors. Megan is the one that knew the color. She lit up when she talked about your mom, Ripley. She told me how much your mom wanted you. She loved her boys, but she'd always dreamed of a girl." Kenna paused. "You should hear the whole story from her, though. She tells it well."

"I don't know what to say, Kenna."

"The last box has the genealogy research Mal did for me. You can read through it whenever you want," Kenna said. "There's one more thing."

Kenna stood, pushed empty boxes out of her way, and helped Ripley carry the two photo albums with her to the bedroom. When Ripley sat on the bed without noticing Kenna's other surprise, Kenna nodded in the direction of the table on Ripley's side of the bed.

"You had it framed?" Ripley turned to see the 8x10" photo of the family.

"I did. I have one of my whole family on my side, and I thought you should have one on your side." Kenna sat next to Ripley as Ripley reached for and caressed the photo with such reverence. "Rip, I thought it could stay there permanently."

"Okay."

Ripley was too enamored to realize what Kenna was saying. Kenna rubbed Ripley's back and smiled at how happy Ripley seemed right now.

"Babe, I'm asking you something."

"You are?" Ripley turned to her.

"I want the picture there permanently because I want you here permanently. I'd like you to move in with me." Kenna watched as Ripley's expression changed to surprise mixed with terror mixed with excitement. "It's a lot. I shouldn't have done this all at once. I'm sorry." Kenna moved back about a foot. "I think that's apology one hundred from me at this point." The woman tried to laugh off.

"I'm looking forward to the next hundred," Ripley

smiled at her, wiped a tear, and met Kenna's eyes. "From here." She pointed at the bed.

"Does that mean you're moving in?" Kenna asked hopefully.

"How can I not? I somehow found the most amazing woman in the world, and she wants to live with me."

"But do you want to live with me?"

"This is my home, Kenna. Wherever you are, that's my home."

Kenna smiled, leaned in, and pecked her lips.

"Good. Now, I'm going to leave you alone."

"What?" Ripley asked, mystified.

"You need some time with this stuff, babe. I'm going to go pick us up some dinner. I'll stop by *Brinkley's* on my way back."

"You don't have to do that. You've done so much." Ripley stood and placed her hands on Kenna's shoulders. "I don't know how to repay you for this, Kenna."

"You don't ever have to repay me for this. Babe, I did this because I love you. It makes me happy to see you happy."

"Still..."

"You know what you did for me?" Kenna asked, placing her hands under Ripley's shirt on her back.

"What?"

"You helped me realize there are way more important things in life than work. You helped me realize that I had dreams outside of being a reporter. You helped me realize that I can have all those things, too. I can still be a reporter, but I can be happier at the job by finding the right place for me, and I can have the woman I love here with me all the time. We can build a life together in whatever that means for us. I can have all that because I have you, Rip."

"You do have me." Ripley kissed Kenna's forehead. "I'm yours."

CHAPTER 28

"WAIT! You're living together now?" Bella asked.

This time, when she questioned Kenna about Ripley, Ripley was sitting right next to her.

"Mom, can Aunt Ripley please play now?" Brady asked, tugging on Ripley's arm.

"Brady, go play with your brother. I'm talking to Aunt Kenna and Rip–" Bella stopped herself and giggled. "And, I guess, your *Aunt Ripley*."

"They just started calling me that. I didn't tell them to or anything," Ripley said.

"It's okay." Bella waved her off. "Brady, go." She pointed at her son and then to the living room. "Play video games or something; pollute your brain; leave the adults alone for ten minutes." She turned back to Kenna and Ripley as he walked off. "I don't know how my husband spends all day with kids at school and then comes home to this."

"Your kids are awesome, Bell." Kenna wrapped her arm around the back of Ripley's chair.

"They are. I love the crap out of those little devils." Bella smiled at the two boys before returning her glance to her sister. "So, moving in?"

"I asked, and she said yes."

"And when is the big moving day? Do you need help?

213

I have a big strapping man who can help, and two scrawny boys, too."

"There's not really much to move," Ripley shared. "I don't have much stuff, to begin with. What I do have, we're not keeping."

"Mostly boxes of clothes, books, and a few other odds and ends," Kenna added. "She's getting rid of everything else."

"I guess that makes it easier."

"I still want us to make it our home, though," Kenna said while looking at Ripley. "It's my stuff; I want it to be our stuff. Maybe we can go shopping in a few weeks or something."

"I like it the way it is," Ripley told her as she shrugged. "I like your stuff. It's one of the reasons I felt so at home there, to begin with."

"So, that had nothing to do with me?" Kenna lifted an eyebrow at her.

"No, it's always been about your stuff."

Bella watched their back-and-forth, and when Kenna met her sister's eyes, she knew what Bella was thinking.

"You're right, you know?" Kenna said to her.

"About what?" Bella asked.

"That this is me happy." Kenna leaned into Ripley.

"How did you know that's what I was thinking?" Bella laughed.

"Because I know you. I know that look." Kenna pointed at her sister.

"How are you doing with Patrick Wilkes? I heard the trial is right around the corner."

"He's trying to make it so the prosecution can't prepare by speeding it up. It'll be his downfall, though," Kenna said.

"I was asking *Aunt Ripley* over there." Bella pointed at Ripley.

"Oh, I'm okay. I stay out of it, mostly. He was in court the other day for some preliminary hearing. The ADA asked me to go, but I had to work. I think it was good that I wasn't there, though. I don't particularly want to see him."

"But you'll be at the trial, right?"

"I will. I at least owe that to them." Ripley tensed a little under Kenna's arm. "But I don't know if I'll testify."

"Don't know?" Kenna asked.

"Yeah, I don't know."

"You've never said that before."

"I haven't?" Ripley asked her.

"Mom, Brady stole my controller!" Cody yelled from the living room floor.

"I did not!" Brady yelled back.

"I'll go play with them." Ripley kissed Kenna's cheek and moved into the living room.

Kenna couldn't hear what she said to the boys because Ripley spoke softly and only to them. She did watch Brady hand Cody back the controller and turn back to Kenna and Bella.

"Mom, I'm sorry I yelled."

"Thank you, honey," Bella replied to Brady. Then, she looked to Kenna. "Can she move in with me?"

Kenna laughed and turned to see Ripley sit on the floor next to Cody, who rested his head on her shoulder. He passed her his controller, and she joined Brady in his game.

"She is going to make an amazing mom someday," Kenna told Bella.

"I can tell," Bella said back. "So will you, you know? I kind of envy those kids you two will have."

Kenna turned back to her sister and asked, "Will have?"

"I wasn't just noticing that you were happy earlier, Ken. I was noticing that you seemed... I don't know... Complete?" Bella softened her voice. "You were always just flailing about. You hunted women like you hunted for the right story."

"I did not hunt," Kenna objected.

"Well, they hunted you, then." Bella glared at her.

"Either way, you were just out there untethered. Even with work, I always wondered when you'd come to tell me you got some new job in a much bigger city. This is the first time I've ever seen you settled, and I mean that in a good way."

"It feels good."

"What are you going to do about work, though? You can't live off your savings forever."

"She and I still have to talk about that, but I've only been jobless for a week. I'm kind of enjoying my little staycation. I mean, look at my hot girlfriend... Wouldn't you want to take time off to be with her?"

"I would. I already asked if she could move in with me. Did you think I was kidding?"

"Keep your married hands off my girl there, Bell." Kenna pointed at her playfully.

"She's all yours, baby sister."

***

"Hey, can we talk?" Kenna asked.

"Now?" Ripley toweled off her face.

She had been in the downstairs gym. Normally, she would do her workout in the mornings before work, but recently, she had changed at least a few of them a week to after work. It gave her a chance to unwind from her day before she and Kenna would have dinner. She'd needed those morning workouts before she met Kenna. They had helped her get through the day. She'd found, though, that waking up next to someone, sometimes having a quick round of morning sex, and then climbing in the shower was a nice way to help her get through the day as well.

"I was just thinking about what you said at Bell's the other day. I never really followed-up on it."

"Followed-up?" Ripley flopped down onto the floor in front of the couch, not wanting to get the fabric covered in her sweat. "You're sounding like a reporter again there, Crawford." She winked at Kenna and took a long pull from her water bottle.

"I guess it's this job search," Kenna replied. "You said you didn't know if you were going to testify."

"Oh, that. Yeah, I guess I did."

"Before that, you'd said you weren't going to. I guess I was wondering what changed."

"I don't know. Maybe it was just a misuse of words." Ripley toyed with the now empty water bottle.

"Rip, do you want to testify now?" Kenna asked her gently.

"I don't know. Maybe." Ripley shrugged. "That was, like, a week ago, at Bella's. I was kinda hoping you didn't remember."

"I'm an eagle-eyed investigative reporter. Of course, I remember." Kenna squinted at her playfully.

"I called Megan." Ripley changed the subject.

"Who?"

"Megan Harris, the old friend of my mom's."

"Oh, right. You called her?"

"When I was at work the other day." Ripley spun the bottle on the floor. "She didn't answer. I left a voicemail."

"I'm sure she'll call you back."

"Maybe."

"She will, babe. She was so helpful with all that stuff. She's the one that told me you could call."

"Maybe she changed her mind," Ripley suggested. Kenna moved to the floor, where she smacked the water bottle away and straddled her girlfriend. "Ken, I'm all sweaty."

"I know. It's hot." Kenna leaned down and kissed her. "Also, I don't have anywhere that I need to be all dressed up for. Now, listen to me, Ripley Fox."

"I'm listening." Ripley moved her hands around Kenna's back and stilled them.

"She will call you back. People get busy. Just give her a few days and try again."

"Okay." Ripley laughed at her.

"And, in the meantime, you can have sex with your reporter girlfriend on the floor of our living room. It's clean because I've had a lot of free time to make this place dust-free."

Ripley laughed wildly at that and replied, "How did you turn this conversation into one about sex?"

"It's your fault. You come in here looking all hot after a workout, and you're wearing a sports bra and that see-through t-shirt. Wait… Did anyone down there see through your t-shirt, Rip?" Kenna glared down.

"I was the only one in the gym," Ripley answered.

"Good. And I'm buying you new shirts to wear down there."

"Jealous?"

"Yes," Kenna replied and kissed her before she pulled back and said, "And I am very proud of you for making that call."

"What about the testifying part? Is it okay that I still don't know?"

"Whether you testify or not is up to you."

"But what do you think I should do?" Ripley asked as she ran her hands up and down Kenna's back.

"This one is on you, babe. Like the doctor said, I'm here to support you in whatever you decide. Either way, I'm here when you come home at night. You have to be the one that makes that decision, though."

CHAPTER 29

"WE told you about this before, Miss Fox."

"I just don't see the point," Ripley replied.

"It's not your decision. It's a capital case."

"I'm aware that it's not my decision, but you said I'd have input," she told the ADA.

"And you do. I'm taking into consideration everything you say, but this is coming all the way from the major. He wants Wilkes gone. The death penalty does that for us."

"Yeah, in ten or more years. I've read up on how all this works. He gets appeals, and those take forever."

"Rip, where's the bad here?" Kenna asked.

The three of them were sitting in the ADA's office. Now that Kenna was out of work, she could attend every meeting. It had been a few weeks since their conversation about whether or not she thought Ripley *should* testify. Today, they were meeting with the ADA to firm up whether or not Ripley *would* testify. If she agreed, they'd need to plan out their questions and her responses.

"I don't see the point. He could just as easily be locked away forever."

"Miss Fox, Wilkes has murdered at least seven people that we know about. I'm sure there were more. When we told him we were charging his mother with conspiracy and that if he talked to us, we'd leave her out of this, he laughed at us. He wasn't even interested in saving his mother; the woman who saved him."

"Rip, is this a death penalty issue?" Kenna turned and asked.

"I told you before, I don't have an opinion either way."

"Then, what's the problem, Miss Fox?"

"Nothing." Ripley shook her head.

Kenna glared at her, expecting her to say something else, but Ripley just let go of Kenna's hand and stared out the window to her right. It was pouring down rain outside. The gloominess of the weather matched her mood.

"We're at that point now: we need to know if you're going to get on the stand. I can't tell you how important it is that you do this, Miss Fox. I honestly believe that regardless of the evidence, this is the only way we will win this case."

Ripley continued staring out the window. She felt Kenna's hand on her own but didn't move her fingers to link them together. She wondered about her parents then. She asked herself what they would want her to do. Even with everything Kenna had given her to bring them closer to her, Ripley still didn't know what they would do if they were in her shoes. Maybe Ethan should have been the one to make it out. He probably would have had no problem with any of this. He would've made it out of the system intact. He probably would have gone to college, made a ton of friends, had a couple of serious girlfriends, and ended it with a perfect job. She'd seen him in the picture, smiling widely. He'd been such a happy kid. He'd only just gotten to the beginning of that brooding-teenager phase. Ripley guessed he would have made his way out of that just fine. He would have liked work, loved his wife, and probably had his kids. He would have been a productive member of society who mowed his lawn every Saturday, took the kids to soccer, and had a date night with the wife every week to make sure they spent time on them and not just on the kids. Ripley was only just now starting to get her life together. Ethan definitely would have been better at this.

Still, as she sat there and watched the rain pound against the window, Ripley didn't see them like she did in her nightmares. She hadn't in weeks. Since Kenna's gift, she'd only seen them in a few dreams. It had been a welcomed relief for the first time in her life. It was as if now that she had pictures of them and could see them as they really were, Ripley's imagination stopped making things up. She'd been sleeping better. She'd been working better. She'd been falling in love more every day with the woman sitting next to her.

"I'll testify," Ripley finally said.

Kenna's hand instantly squeezed her own, and Ripley turned her palm up. Kenna slid her fingers between Ripley's and squeezed again. Ripley's heart raced at her statement. She knew she could take it back if she wanted to, but she wouldn't. She'd do this. She would speak on behalf of her family regardless of how much it hurt or how many extra sessions she'd need with Dr. Clement.

"Excellent," the ADA returned. "We'll begin working on your answers tomorrow if that's okay. I have time in the afternoon."

Ripley squeezed Kenna's hand hard. Then, she turned to Kenna and gave her a look that must have told Kenna everything the woman needed to know before Ripley's eyes returned to the grayness outside.

"I've got a better idea," Kenna stated. "Rip, tell me if this isn't okay." She paused. "It's better if you don't rehearse this. Her reactions will be more visceral if she doesn't know the questions or have time to prepare how to answer them. That's what you want, right?" she asked him.

"This is already so hard for her; I fail to see how this will make things better," he said.

"Because I can't tell the story over and over," Ripley answered.

"I see," the ADA replied. "It's not how we'd normally do things."

"It's what I can do," Ripley offered and turned back to face him. "It should have been Ethan."

"What, babe?" Kenna asked.

"Nothing," Ripley said for the second time that meeting.

***

"You've never lied to me before. Why did you start today?" Kenna asked the moment Ripley closed the door behind her.

"What?" Ripley turned around to face her. "What are you talking about? Also, hello. I literally just walked through the door."

The meeting had been in the early afternoon. Ripley had gone back to work after, while Kenna had gone home. Kenna had been waiting for Ripley to get home. She hadn't started on dinner, and she hadn't done any job-hunting. She had been sitting in their living room, staring at the lamp they'd just bought to make the place a little more their home instead of Kenna's. She'd stared, and she'd waited.

"You lied in that meeting." Kenna stood in front of the dining room table, crossing her arms over her chest.

"I didn't lie. Where is this coming from?"

"I asked you about the whole death penalty thing. You lied; I could tell. You don't lie to me, Ripley. You never have. It's one of the things I love so much about you."

"Can we talk about this later? I'm starving, and I'd like to change my clothes." Ripley moved to walk past her toward the bedroom.

"Ripley, why did you lie?"

"I didn't fucking lie, Kenna!" Ripley yelled. "God, what is wrong with you tonight?"

"You've brought up Wilkes being put away for life at least five times that I remember. That's not nothing, Rip. You said that today; you said it was *nothing*." Kenna raised her voice.

"What does it matter? It's out of my hands."

"Why do you want it in your hands?"

"I don't want to fight about this. I want to change my clothes and eat dinner. Now, I'd kind of like to eat dinner alone, given I came home to whatever this is."

"*This* is a fight, because you're not being honest with me," Kenna explained.

"I don't want to fight with you," Ripley said and moved into the bedroom.

"Why not?"

Kenna followed close behind her but stood in the open doorway when Ripley moved to slide her shoes off in the closet. She emerged a moment later.

"Because I don't fight, Kenna. I don't fight." Ripley undid the buttons of her shirt. "I've told you that. I didn't fight. I didn't cause problems because–"

"Because people wouldn't let you stay?" Kenna's voice softened.

"Why are we talking about this?" Ripley removed her shirt, leaving only a black bra covering her.

"Do you think if you fight with me, I won't let you stay?" Kenna asked with genuine concern.

"Kenna, I'm exhausted."

"Ripley, tell me," Kenna insisted.

"I don't know. Maybe. Maybe that is something I've thought about."

"Is that why you still have your apartment?" Kenna asked, but her tone had changed. She was worried now as she sat on the side of the bed near Ripley. "Rip, is that why you still have your apartment even though you moved in here?"

"Kenna, I still have my apartment because it would cost me more to break the lease than it did to just keep it."

"And that's the only reason?"

"I am so confused." Ripley took her bra off, tossed it into the closet somewhere, pulled a t-shirt out of one of her drawers, and covered her skin. She undid her slacks, let them fall to the floor, stepped out of them, and stood there. "You accused me of lying in the meeting today, and now we're talking about my old apartment."

"Fights aren't always linear." Kenna shrugged.

"Why are we fighting?"

"Because there's something you're not telling me." Kenna held out her hand for Ripley to take.

"But you want to hold my hand?"

"I want you to sit down next to me so we can talk."

"But we're fighting."

"You've been able to avoid fighting with people in your life, and I can understand why you did that when you were in the system, but, Rip, this is our life together. We're going to fight. You can't avoid it."

"What happens if we don't make up? What if the fight doesn't end?" Ripley asked.

She took Kenna's hand and sat next to her on the bed.

"As long as we keep talking to each other and keep listening, we'll be fine. My last girlfriend – if I can even call her that – told me the reason she didn't want to be together was that, when we fought, I always accused and yelled, but I never listened to her side," Kenna revealed and chuckled at the memory.

"So, you have a habit of accusing women of things?" Ripley lightened the mood.

"I'm learning," Kenna said. "I told you, you have this effect on me. You make me want to yell and fight because that's sometimes what you do when you're in a relationship: you have things that need to be worked out. Fighting is sometimes the only way that happens." Kenna paused. "But, Rip, you also make me want to listen. You make me want to stop to hear what you have to say. One of the reasons you're able to do this to me is that I know you're telling the truth."

"I do tell you the truth." Ripley placed her head on Kenna's shoulder. "But I do worry that I might mess this up. I guess today, it hit me that I'm still a little messed up from everything that's happened and what's going on now. I didn't want to fight about it because I don't want to cause problems for us, Ken. I don't want this to end."

"Babe, this isn't ending because you're a little messed up. We're all a little messed up." Kenna wrapped an arm around Ripley's waist. "Can you tell me what happened today?"

"The whole death penalty thing?"

"Yes."

"It's crazy," Ripley added.

"I don't care." Kenna laughed.

"He hasn't spoken yet. He hasn't confessed. He hasn't given any details or explained why."

"That's true."

"If he dies, Kenna, the possibility that he might tell me *why* dies with him."

"Oh, Ripley." Kenna kissed her temple. "You want him to be alive in case one day he decides to talk?"

"Yes. It's all I can think about whenever they talk about executing him. I guess he could confess right before they shove a needle in his arm, but what if he doesn't? What if he dies and I lose the chance?"

"What if he never says anything?"

"I know. I know it's a big possibility that I will never get those answers. I just thought that the more time he has, the more likely he gets bored in prison. Maybe, when he doesn't have his outlet of lighting fires, he would need to try to torture me with the details of my family's death. Maybe he'd ask me to visit just so he can see my face as he tells me what happened. I could deal with that. I could give that to him if he could just tell me *why*."

Kenna squeezed Ripley tightly and said, "I get it."

"You do?"

"Why didn't you say that today?"

"They've made their decision, and I understand why they think it's important. I guess all I can hope for now is that deathbed confession."

"What if that never comes? What if there is no reason? What if there is, but he doesn't share it? Will you be okay with that?"

"I guess I'll have to be."

CHAPTER 30

PATRICK Wilkes was a small man. He had light red hair that bordered on strawberry blonde. It had been shaved down to nearly nothing. His glasses, she'd seen in pictures before, had been replaced with prisoner glasses. The one-size-fits-all approach to frames did nothing for his face, which was thin and bony. It wasn't as if this had all happened in prison, though. Patrick had always looked like this. Ripley remembered him as a scrawny kid. She'd also seen pictures of him throughout the years. This was definitely Patrick Wilkes. Ripley wondered if maybe he was bullied or somehow mistreated in school, but that didn't make sense because of what she knew of Ethan. Her brother had been popular, or at least, it had seemed so to her. He always had friends around, and Patrick had been one of them.

Maybe he'd been abused by his father. Likely, his mother wouldn't have been the culprit since she'd rescued him time and time again. But what did Ripley know? She wasn't a psychologist. Maybe it was just that sort of behavior that caused Patrick Wilkes to set fires and kill people. As a witness, Ripley hadn't been allowed to be in the courtroom until the time of her testimony. Kenna had gone in, though. She had sat in the room every single day, and she'd come home and tell Ripley all the details. Ripley was grateful for her girlfriend because Kenna understood what she'd want to hear and what she'd prefer to never know. She knew they'd show pictures of the house and probably the bodies, or what was left of them. Ripley did not want to see pictures.

When the time came for her to sit on the stand and answer questions, it had been an eleven-day trial already. Ripley didn't know if that was long or short, but it had included jury selection. The ADA said it was normal. She gulped and played with a tissue in her lap that the jury couldn't see, while the ADA picked up his notebook and placed it on a podium.

"Miss Fox, I want to thank you for coming today to tell us your story."

"Your Honor, is counsel testifying?" the opposing attorney stood and delivered.

"Counsel, ask the witness your questions," the judge said to the ADA.

"May I call you Ripley?"

"Yes." Ripley leaned into the microphone to deliver.

"Thank you, Ripley. Now, I'd like you to take us through that night if you would, please. Let's start at the beginning. Who was at the house?"

"My grandmother, mother, father, and my two older brothers."

"Ethan and Benjamin?"

"Yes. We called him Benji, like the dog. He liked the movie." Ripley smiled at the thought.

"Benji was only eleven? Ethan, thirteen?"

"Yes."

"How old were you?"

"Eight."

"Eight years old." The ADA repeated and moved to the side of the podium. "What did you do that night?"

"We had dinner," Ripley began. "My mom made us chicken nuggets. My dad was in his office. My mom had me take him a plate because he didn't come out for dinner. He did that sometimes. Ethan spent most of the evening in his room. I remember walking by it when my mom made me wash up for dinner. He was on the phone."

"Ethan was on the phone?"

"He was on the landline. I remember he saw me, stood up, and closed the door so I couldn't hear."

"Do you know who he was talking to?"

"I don't know. He sounded upset."

"What happened after that?"

"I went to bed before the boys. My bedtime was earlier. I think they stayed downstairs and watched TV with my mom, but I don't know."

"Did you hear anything strange after going to bed that night?"

"No, I was asleep. My mom told me I was a heavy sleeper once. She said a tornado could spin through my room, and I wouldn't wake up." Ripley realized that was the first time she'd ever said that out loud.

She glanced past the attorney to find Kenna sitting in the front row of the gallery. Kenna smiled a proud smile and gave Ripley a wink.

"What happened next?" he asked.

"I woke up to the fire," Ripley replied as her voice broke a little. "I remember the heat and the smoke. I don't know how long the house had been burning. I remember the fireman coming into the room and picking me up off the bed just before the flames reached me."

"Is it true you have small burns on the tips of your toes?" he asked.

"How did you–"

"Your medical records indicate you were treated for burns on your feet."

"They healed, mostly." Ripley met Kenna's eyes again. "There are a few you can still see, though."

Kenna's smile faltered but only for a second before it was back, encouraging her to continue.

"Ripley, let's talk about Patrick Wilkes for a second – the defendant. Did you know him back then?" He pointed to Patrick Wilkes.

"Yes." Ripley didn't look over at Patrick.

"How did you know him?"

"He was a friend of Ethan's."

"How long was he a friend of Ethan's?"

"I don't know. I don't remember when he first came to the house."

"But he did come to the house?"

"Yes, at least a few times."

"Can you recall if he and your brother ever fought?"

"I think once, while playing football," Ripley recalled. "Ethan caught a pass and ran, while Patrick was on the other team. I remember him knocking Ethan down when Ethan scored a touchdown. Ethan got upset. I think they yelled a few times before my parents broke it up."

"Nothing else?"

"I don't think so."

"Okay. Let's talk about your family for a minute."

'Here we go,' Ripley thought. She let out a deep breath, closed her eyes, and tore at the tissue in her lap.

"Tell me about your parents. What do you remember?"

"My parents were good people. They worked hard to take care of us. My mom was my Brownie troop leader. I was in Girl Scouts, and she helped me sell cookies that year and let me have sleepovers with my friends. She went to every game Ethan and Benji had and to every one of my dance recitals."

"Dance?" he asked.

"I was in ballet at the time."

"What about your dad?"

"My dad loved to camp. He took us every summer. He'd help us make s'mores, and he made sure to spend extra time with me since he spent so much time with the boys because of their sports."

"Let's talk about your brothers."

"Your Honor, is she giving a victim impact statement during the trial?" the defense attorney said.

"I'll grant some leeway, but wrap it up soon," the judge told the ADA.

"Yes, Your Honor." He nodded at the judge. "Your brothers, Ripley?"

Ripley's eyes welled with tears, and she did everything she could to keep them focused on Kenna.

"My brothers were children. They loved sports and getting dirty. They had friends. They had a younger sister that idolized them." She looked away from Kenna, feeling slightly more confident. Her eyes met Patrick Wilke's face, and he must have felt her gaze because he lifted his eyes to meet her hazel ones. "Ethan wanted to play soccer forever. He loved his friends. He stood up for me and Benji. Benji was a great brother. He read stories to me before I learned how, and he even practiced ballet with me when Ethan wasn't looking." Ripley let a few tears fall. "You took that away from me."

"Objection! Your Honor?"

"You took them away from me," Ripley repeated.

"Sustained," the judge said.

"Ripley, can you tell me what happened to you after the fire?" the ADA asked.

Ripley was still staring into the cold, dead eyes of Patrick Wilkes, but before she could tell the next part, she needed to look away. She didn't want him to see her eyes as she talked of the consequences of his horrible actions.

"I didn't have any other family. I ended up in foster care." She wiped her eyes with a new tissue she pulled from the front of the witness stand.

"Were you ever adopted?"

"No, I aged out of the system."

"What does *aged out* mean?"

"When you're eighteen, and in foster care, you're an adult. The government doesn't take care of you anymore."

"What was it like in foster care?"

"I'd prefer not to talk about that." Ripley sniffled.

"Very well." The ADA walked a few steps toward her.

"Ripley, can you tell us how this fire, how the loss of your family has affected your life?"

"Again, Your Honor. Objection."

"Sustained. Counsel, do you have any other questions for this witness?"

"No, Your Honor. I think everyone in this room understands how the defendant's actions impacted this young woman."

"Objection!"

Ripley climbed down and made her way down the middle aisle. Kenna stood and followed her out. Ripley heard the attorneys were still engaged in their debate, but she couldn't listen anymore. She made her way out into the hall but kept going. She exited the building only to find a large group of reporters outside.

"No comment!" Kenna yelled from behind her before placing her hand on Ripley's back.

The reporters swarmed around Ripley. They shouted questions at her. Ripley heard none of them and all of them at the same time. Her tears were drying, but the evidence of them was written all over her face. She looked down at the ground for a moment, took in a deep breath, and lifted her head.

"I'll speak to all of you for a moment." She turned to Mandy. "Except for Channel 8."

"Ripley, I—"

"You heard her, Mandy," Kenna said, not missing a beat.

Mandy backed away but stayed close enough so as not to miss what Ripley would say. Ripley didn't really care if Mandy heard what she was about to say. She mainly wanted to make a point to Clark about how he'd treated her girlfriend.

"A little over twenty years ago, I went to bed after having a normal night with my family. The next morning, I was an orphan. I lost everything." She paused and felt Kenna's hand stroking the skin of her back. "Patrick Wilkes took everything from me. It's time justice was served. Thank you."

She moved swiftly through the crowd, and Kenna followed. Ripley reached back without looking, and Kenna took her hand. When they made it to Kenna's car, Ripley burst out into tears. Kenna let her cry herself into silence until they made it home. Then, Kenna helped her to bed, wrapped her in a blanket, and then wrapped herself around Ripley's body.

"You are amazing, Ripley Fox. I am so proud of you. Your parents would have been so proud of you. Ethan and Benji would be proud of you, too."

"It's over, right?" Ripley asked as she stared at the picture on the table.

"Today is over, yes. If you don't want to go back in there ever again, you don't have to."

"I do have to, though." Ripley rolled in Kenna's arms. "I have to, for them."

"Don't do it for them, sweetheart." Kenna kissed her forehead. "Do it for yourself."

CHAPTER 31

KENNA sat in the office of Channel 6 news. It was one of the other two local networks in Pleasant Valley, and they didn't technically have a position open, but Kenna had scored an interview anyway, based on reputation. The station seemed like a duplicate of Channel 8. The standard hustle and bustle of a newsroom was apparent, as was the near-silent section of the floor where the fact-checkers and researchers were seated. Kenna had been taken straight to the station manager's office, where she'd sat in his guest chair, and they had some obligatory small talk.

"What happened over at Eight? You've been there a long time. If I'm not mistaken, we tried to snatch you up a few years ago, and you turned us down," the burly station manager said.

"We had some creative differences with a story," she replied honestly.

"That comes with the territory, though. Can you expand on that?"

"I had a lead on a potential story, so I started digging, met with the woman who would be its focus, and I fell in love with her." Kenna shrugged. "I asked my station not to run with it, given my relationship and the fact that she didn't want a story done about her, and they decided to put another reporter on it. When I objected to that, they sat me down and told me they were not only going to do the story, but that they expected me to get an exclusive interview because she's my girlfriend."

"It's interesting how you tell it. Clark gave it to me another way."

"I'm sure he did." Kenna scoffed. "Look, I understand that news is news. My relationship shouldn't stop a story from going out. My problem wasn't that they still wanted to pursue the story – other networks did, too. They still are. My problem was with the fact they expected me to use my relationship to get them an interview. It was clear that declining wasn't an option."

"So, you're here now hoping I'll add you to my roster?"

"I'm here now because you took my call." Kenna leaned in toward the desk. "My girlfriend lives here. We have a home together. I'd like to stay in Pleasant Valley and work. The way I see it, I have two options: I get another job at a station, or I try my hand at teaching journalism at a community college. I'd like to avoid that second thing."

"You know I don't have anything right now. We're staffed in features. We have our anchors and our field guys. I could maybe reach out if anything changes, though."

"I don't want a reporting gig, Ross. I want a producing one."

He sat back at that and said, "Producing?"

"I was the best investigative reporter at Channel 8, and I've worked hard honing that craft, but I've also been teaching their cubbies how to do the job. I've basically been producing my own stuff these past few years. That's what I want now: I want to produce."

"Kenna Crawford, the producer," he said it as if just trying to see how it sounded. "I thought you'd go anchor one day or hit a bigger market. Are you sure you want to produce locally?"

"I want to produce; I don't care where. And I need to be here, at least for now. If it works out, I'll stay."

"I know you know I don't have any producing slots open," he replied.

"I know. I checked. Plus, I know your people." She smiled at him. "We've gone out drinking, and they've complained about you," she joked.

"I bet they did," Ross said while laughing. "Kenna, I'd love to have you on board, but I don't have anything right now; unless you want the online side."

"Online?"

"Our online pieces. We don't have a producer slot for that. We have an editorial slot, though."

"Editing online pieces?"

"It's mid-level. We have an exec-editor, but if you're looking for something different than investigative reporting, you could throw your hat in the ring, and I'll get you an interview with the exec."

Kenna considered that offer for a moment. She had never thought about being an editor. This was for their website. It would maybe have video snippets here and there but would likely just be the writing itself she'd be editing. She liked writing, and she wrote a lot of stuff for her own pieces, but she wasn't sure this was the avenue she wanted to pursue.

"Thanks, Ross. I don't know if that's for me, though."

"Well, think about it, at least. The position is posted online. Take a look at the description, and if you decide you want to talk more, shoot me an email. I'll set it up."

Kenna left the interview feeling a bit deflated. Clark had spoken with the other networks as Shannon had predicted. Channel 4 hadn't even given her an interview, and Channel 6 only had the editorial opening. She'd consider it as she'd promised Ross, but she knew she wouldn't take it. It wasn't at all the direction she wanted to go. The only problem was that for her to go the direction she wanted, she'd likely have to leave Pleasant Valley.

***

Ripley stood outside the house for a good fifteen minutes before she even walked to the porch. She stood there for another five before the front door opened without her knocking. A woman stood there, holding on to the doorknob, smiling at her.

"Hi, Ripley," Megan greeted her.

"Hi," Ripley replied.

"I was wondering if you were ever going to ring the bell."

"Sorry, I was a little early. I didn't know if I should," Ripley returned.

"Come on in," Megan offered and motioned with her hand.

Ripley had waited the few days before calling Megan again after her initial attempt. It turned out, Megan had been out of the country on a vacation, and she had turned her phone off. As soon as she turned it back on and got Ripley's messages, she called Ripley.

"I'm so sorry I missed your calls. I could have sworn I told Kenna I was going to be out of the country for a few weeks. My husband and I took our two grandbabies on a Disney cruise. Then, we stayed with our daughter in Arizona for a bit."

"That's okay. I appreciate you calling me back."

"Sit. Sit."

Megan moved into the comfortable-looking living room while Ripley followed. As she did, she thought about the fact that Megan had grandchildren. Her parents would have grandchildren right now. The way things were moving with Kenna, she'd likely be a parent one day. Ethan and Benji may have been fathers already. Ripley sat on the sofa. Megan sat next to her and turned to face her.

"I guess I was just wondering how you knew my parents. I don't remember you myself, but I was young."

"I can understand why. Would you like something to drink?"

"No, thank you."

"Well, I met your mom in college. We were in the same sorority."

"My mom was in a sorority?"

"Kappa Delta Nu all the way," Megan said as she smiled. "I was a year ahead of her, but we were close. We lost touch when I graduated but caught up later, right around the time when she was pregnant with you." Megan paused. "I wasn't around when she had your brothers. I don't know how she was, but with you, she was so happy, Ripley. I went over to the house when she was about seven months along. She was painting your room herself while your dad was out of town. She said she just couldn't wait."

"Teal?"

"Her favorite color," Megan added. "It was half-yellow when I got there. I picked up a roller and helped her for a few hours. We stayed in touch for a few years. I remember you as a toddler. I actually went to your first ballet recital. My daughter is a few years older than you, and she took dance as well."

"I don't remember her."

"I didn't expect you would. She was six when you were three." Megan paused. "I actually have something if you want to see it. I cued it up for you just in case." She leaned forward on the table, picked up a remote control, and passed it to Ripley. "Just press play. I'll go make us some iced tea and give you a moment."

"What is it?" Ripley asked.

"I found it after Kenna came by and asked for pictures. I honestly forgot I had it. I know you were young, so it's hard for you to remember how much your parents loved you, but they did, Ripley. I know they did. I hope this helps you see that a little more, too. We did this thing that night where I filmed you so they could just watch, and they filmed my daughter so I could do the same. Then, we copied and exchanged the videos. I thought you'd like it."

Megan left the room. Ripley hesitated before turning toward the large flat-screen TV. She held the remote in her sweaty hand, took a deep breath, and pressed play. A few moments later, a shaky video came on the screen. It showed a small stage and a woman introducing the three-year-old ballerina class. Six toddlers waddled more than walked into the stage. Music began, and they started dancing. Well, a few of them danced. A couple of them tried to dance, got distracted, and waved to the audience. One of them really danced. She danced overenthusiastically, wildly even, and smiled as she did. The camera zoomed in, and Ripley recognized herself. She was the one dancing like no one was watching.

Ripley couldn't believe it. She didn't remember doing it. She did remember taking dance lessons for a few years but had no recollection of whether or not she actually enjoyed it. On that stage, though, she could tell she had enjoyed dancing. She had enjoyed it a little too much, considering how off-rhythm she was. Then, Ripley heard it. It was a sound she hadn't heard in over twenty years.

"She's having fun. That's what matters," her mother said as she chuckled.

"Obviously," Megan's voice joined. "She's adorable."

"She's my little Road Runner," her mother added, still laughing.

Road Runner. Ripley remembered now. Her mother used to call her that. She was Ripley the Road Runner. How had she forgotten that? She was always running somewhere, trying to keep up with her brothers and their much longer legs. Her mother called her that all the time. Sometimes, she just called her runner. The camera panned away from the stage, and Ripley saw them. Her mother sat closest to the camera. Her face was beaming. She was laughing, and there was a tear in her eye. She was so happy. Her father sat next to her. His dark hair was perfectly mussed. He smiled, too. The camera moved back to Ripley on the stage, but Ripley wanted it to go back. She didn't want to see herself dancing like an idiot; she wanted to see her parents. She wanted to see them move, hear them speak. The song and the dancing ended, and Ripley hit rewind. She pressed play just before the camera panned, and she watched again.

"Sweetie, I'll give this to you. You can watch it whenever you want." Megan had re-entered the room with two iced teas. "I only wish I had more to offer you."

"This is…" Ripley couldn't turn away from the TV. "This is more than I've ever had." She felt her tears falling. "I haven't seen them move or heard their voices in twenty years."

"I have one of your dad with your brothers in the backyard, too. He was teaching them how to head a soccer ball. I'll make sure you have both."

"Thank you," Ripley said and finally turned to her. "Thank you."

"You don't have to thank me. I should have given you this stuff long ago." Megan sat next to her again. "I don't know if you have to go, but I'm happy to tell you everything I can remember about them or about your brothers."

"I'd like that. Thank you."

CHAPTER 32

"WHAT are you thinking right now?" Ripley asked her.

"That I'm starting to get bored," Kenna replied.

"What?"

Ripley moved from between Kenna's legs and stared up at her.

"No, no." Kenna caressed Ripley's cheek. "Not that, Rip. I don't mean with that or with you."

"I just went down on you."

"Actually, you went down on me about ten minutes ago, dear. You've been hanging out in that area kissing my thighs ever since, which I'm not complaining about. As I enjoyed the afterglow of my orgasm, you and I were silent, which is one of my favorite things about us, by the way. You asked what I was thinking about."

"Favorite things?" Ripley moved to lie next to her on the bed.

"We get each other. I think we get each other in all ways, but especially in bed. We don't have to say anything. You just know what I want. You know when to go slow, when to speed up, and when to stay between my shaking legs, kissing my thighs, while I enjoy the pleasant sensation of my sated body and mind."

Ripley smiled down as she kissed Kenna's lips.

"That was beautiful." She pecked Kenna's lips again. "Now, do you mind telling me what's got you so bored?"

"My unemployment." Kenna kissed Ripley's lips this time, tasting herself on them.

"You decided not to apply for that editorial thing. Is there something else you're interested in?"

"I really want to produce, Rip. I guess I might not have a choice. This place isn't exactly New York or LA or even a mid-market – I don't have that many choices. I looked within fifty miles around Pleasant Valley. There were a few reporting jobs, and I sent my reel to one of them yesterday."

"Fifty miles?" Ripley asked.

"It's not ideal, I know, but I could commute."

"But you don't want to report; you want to produce."

"I know, but nothing's available around here, babe." Kenna ran her hand down Ripley's chest between her bare breasts. "If I get a reporting gig, I can always work my way into producing."

"And you'll be happy doing that? Commuting? Reporting?"

"I'll be happy doing you right now." Kenna's hand slid between Ripley's legs.

"You're changing the subject." Ripley gasped when Kenna entered her.

"Then, tell me to stop," Kenna whispered in her ear.

Ripley didn't tell her to stop, and Kenna rolled them over until she was on top of Ripley. She pushed high and deep while Ripley grasped her ass to push Kenna into her farther.

"God, you're gorgeous," Ripley complimented her. "Those eyes are gorgeous."

"Have you seen *your* eyes?" Kenna asked as she thrust into her. "Rip, sometimes I think they're looking all the way into me."

"That's because I see all of you," Ripley grunted as Kenna thrust and then curled her fingers. "I see your feisty side." Kenna thrust again. "Your sweet, soft side." Kenna stroked her gently, pulling out, and sliding her fingers over Ripley's clit before returning inside. "And I love all of you."

"I love all of you," Kenna replied, staring into her eyes.

"I love how we can talk, too." Ripley moaned when Kenna used her thigh to apply more pressure.

"I want to taste you," Kenna said.

"Wait." Ripley placed her hands on Kenna's cheeks. She held her there while Kenna stared at her. *"She didn't need to be saved. She needed to be found and appreciated, for exactly who she was."*

"Rip?"

"It's from a book; J. Iron Word," Ripley said, and Kenna stopped moving inside her. "I didn't read the book, but I saw the quote online. I waited, Kenna. I waited, and I thought I'd never have anything resembling love of any kind in my life, but there you were. And you love me. You love all of me. You don't try to fix me. You don't force me to do things I'm not ready for. You're there for me, and you just love me."

"You don't need to be saved, my love." Kenna kissed her. "But I did find you. I found you, and I am never letting you go. So, I will appreciate you and love you for as long as you let me because I waited for you, too."

Ripley's eyes shone with unshed tears now. Kenna kissed her lips before moving her mouth down Ripley's body and nestling her head between Ripley's legs. She started stroking Ripley with her tongue while her fingers began moving inside again.

***

"Will you watch something with me?" Ripley asked Kenna while twirling Kenna's hair.

"What do you have in mind?" Kenna asked playfully.

"Not that." Ripley laughed.

"What's *that?* Where did your dirty mind go?"

"Don't say 'dirty mind' when I'm asking you about this." Ripley laughed again.

Kenna lifted her head from Ripley's lap and met her eyes.

"What's wrong, babe?"

"Nothing's wrong." Ripley tucked Kenna's now rogue hair behind her ear. "When I went to Megan's last week, she gave me something. I've watched it over and over when you weren't here."

"What is it?"

"My parents." Ripley shrugged. "She had a couple of short videos of them."

"She did?" Kenna brightened. "You've watched them without me?"

"I needed some time alone with them. It's the first time I've seen them move. I haven't heard their voices in so long. I just needed to watch them by myself."

"I understand. You don't have to share them with me if you don't want."

"I do, though. I want you to watch them with me."

"Then, let's do it." Kenna turned to the TV. "Where are they?"

Ripley and Kenna were on the couch in the living room. Kenna had been gone the entire day while Ripley had worked from home. Kenna's interview in the neighboring Mason had been for Channel 12 news. It had gone well, according to Kenna, but the commute had been long and exhausting. With traffic, it had taken her an hour and a half to get there. Ripley knew Kenna wasn't looking forward to that part of the job if she did get it. The drive home had been even longer. Ripley had cooked them dinner, and they'd shared it at the dining room table while Kenna had regaled her with the details of the interview. Ripley could tell the woman's smile wasn't meeting her eyes and that this wasn't the job Kenna really wanted, but she didn't know how to tell her that. They'd been lying on the couch, talking, for the better part of an hour. Ripley explained how she'd gotten a young girl into a better foster home that day, and she had added her to her phone photo album and showed Kenna the picture.

"I already put them on. They're really short. They're, like, two minutes. Two minutes and thirty-two seconds, both of them combined. It's not that big–"

"Ripley, baby, I want to watch them. Come here."

Kenna held out her arm, and Ripley slid against Kenna's side. She turned the TV to the proper input and pressed play. They sat together and watched the two short videos. When the second one ended, Kenna took the remote from Ripley's hand and pressed play again. They watched the videos over and over again until Ripley finally turned the TV off.

"Are you ready for tomorrow?" Kenna asked.

"I'm getting there," Ripley replied.

***

The courtroom was completely silent. Ripley and Kenna sat in the front row of the gallery. The only sound came when the side door opened. Three officers entered along with Patrick Wilkes, who was in handcuffs and leg shackles. Ripley could hear the clanging of metal on metal as he waddled uncomfortably to the table. An officer unlocked his handcuffs, and Wilkes sat in the chair he usually occupied. The officer then bent down to unlock and remove the shackles.

Wilkes wore a suit and tie. It made him look human. He had worn a suit every day of the trial, and Kenna had explained it was likely his mother was bringing him new clothes for each day. It helped the jury to see him as a person and not as the monster that he was. His tie today was blue. Blue was the color of honesty and loyalty. The ADA had explained to them earlier in the process that Wilkes would likely wear blue in some way every day of the trial. Wilkes had worn a blue tie, a blue shirt, a blue jacket, a blue handkerchief in his breast pocket, and one day, he had worn a blue pin on a brown suit jacket. Ripley hadn't been able to make out if it was a symbol or had words on it.

Today, Wilkes had a blue tie and blue jacket with a crisp white shirt. His prison glasses had been exchanged with his old glasses, which did make his face look at least a little more relatable. His eyes, though, still showed nothing. Their coldness showed through the lenses he wore. His hands were clasped together on the table as if he had nothing to worry about. In reality, today was the day he'd learn if he would be set free or if he would spend the rest of his life in prison. Sentencing would come later, but if found guilty, it would be either life without parole or death. There was no other option for what he'd done.

Ripley hadn't entertained the possibility of him being found not guilty. She couldn't. It wasn't possible.

In reality, of course, it was possible. The jury could find that there wasn't enough physical evidence tying him to the crime. These days, with everyone watching CSI and other shows like it, they expected DNA evidence in every case. Ripley had been warned about that possibility. She had hope, though, that the jury could see past that.

Kenna held her hand tightly as the jury entered the room. Ripley couldn't look at them. She had been told by different people what it meant if they looked down at the floor when they walked in versus if they met the defendant's eye. She didn't know if Kenna was looking at them. Ripley glanced at the hands in her lap. Both of her hands were clinging to Kenna's as the judge entered. They stood briefly before sitting again. The hands returned to her lap. Kenna leaned over and kissed her temple.

"I love you," she whispered. "And no matter what, it will be okay."

About ten minutes later, it was all over. Ripley stood first, and Kenna followed, still grasping her hand. Ripley moved out of the room before everyone else, rushed down the hall with Kenna in tow, and headed to the bathroom, where she finally let her tears fall. Kenna pulled her close. She held on to her and let her cry on her shoulder. She whispered things into Ripley's ear that told her to let it out. She told her it was okay. She massaged the back of Ripley's neck, played with her hair, and kissed her cheeks, her forehead, and then her lips. She kissed her gently, sweetly, several times over until Ripley's sobs slowed. They ceased altogether as Kenna pulled her back into herself. Then, Ripley splashed cold water on her face. She dried herself off with paper towels and tried to put herself back together while Kenna watched on. When they emerged from the bathroom, the ADA stood there, waiting for them.

"Sentencing will be next week. Normally, it could be months, but the judge granted early sentencing. I think everyone wants this whole thing to be over as soon as possible. Technically, the right to a speedy trial doesn't apply to sentencing, but I didn't argue with their request. This should all be over for you soon, Miss Fox," he explained.

"Thank you," Ripley replied hoarsely.

"You'll be asked if you want to give your victim impact statement. It's not a requirement. It's completely your choice. I don't want to pressure you either way."

"Good," Kenna replied, rubbing Ripley's back.

"I found something this morning. It came in too late to be useful in the trial, and I can't bring it up at sentencing, either, but I wanted you to have it." He handed her a piece of paper. "These are the phone records from your house that night."

Ripley took the paper and asked, "The night of the fire?"

"You mentioned your brother was on the phone," he said. "It took a while to get this. The phone company has merged with another company since then. Their records from twenty years ago aren't exactly easy to get a hold of. We didn't know about the phone call back then. I got this sent to me last night. It shows one call that night from Bethany Wilke's home number to your house."

"Patrick called Ethan?" Ripley asked.

"We have no way of knowing that for sure, but it seems likely. You said your brother was on the phone, and this is the only call your house made that night."

"What did they say?" she asked.

"I don't know. The only person that knows that is Patrick Wilkes, and he's not talking."

"So, I may never know?"

"Hey, what's important is that he is guilty. He's going to go away, and he can't do this to anyone else again, Rip. He's going to have to pay for what he did to your family."

"I guess."

"Can we have a moment?" Kenna asked the ADA.

The man nodded, shook their hands, and then walked outside to the courthouse step where he would give a statement to the waiting press.

"Babe, it's over," Kenna told her.

"No, it's not," Ripley said.

CHAPTER 33

"YOU'RE going to take it, aren't you?" Bella asked.

"I'd be okay for the next few months, financially. If I got crafty, I could probably last a whole year without working. Now that Ripley moved in, she insists on paying for half of everything. It's cute, but unnecessary. We've worked out a thing where she pays for the internet and groceries whenever she shops, but that she uses what she was paying for rent at her old place to pay off her student loans faster instead." Kenna paused. "But it's not the money part I'm worried about."

"You're bored, aren't you?"

"Crazy bored, yes," Kenna replied. "I had a nice few weeks off where I was fine, but now, I'm going nuts being around the house. I think I have cleaned it top to bottom at least ten times. Rip probably thinks I have OCD. I have reorganized my office, bought another desk so she and I can share it, I've researched, I have stories lined up… I just need a place to pursue them." She smiled. "For the record, not having a job and having a live-in girlfriend, that sometimes works from home, has been nice for my sex life."

"Gross, Ken!"

"What? Like you hadn't told me how hot it was when you two first got together." Kenna pointed at a picture of Bella and her husband that hung on the wall. "I seem to recall that honeymoon story."

"God, I remember that," Bella replied wistfully. "We need another honeymoon. He hasn't done that to me in forever."

"Gross, Bell," Kenna returned. "But can I be serious and not graphic with you?"

"Sure," Bella said as she laughed lightly.

"Bella, she's amazing in bed. I don't mean that she – you know – gets me there all the time. She does, and that is amazing, but it's that we seem to get each other in a way I haven't experienced before. She's what I need in that department."

"Isn't she what you need in all departments?" Bella lifted an eyebrow.

"I'm growing old with her, Bella. She's that person for me."

"Hey, what's wrong?" Bella asked when she noticed a change in Kenna's tone.

"I think I got my hopes up on the producing thing," Kenna answered honestly. "I know I'm ready. I know I'd be good at it."

"What about other markets? You had your heart set on getting out of here."

"Maybe one day," Kenna replied.

"Why not now?"

"Because I have Ripley. We just moved in together."

"In a condo that's paid off. You could sell it fast, take the money and run."

"She's got a job here, Ken. Plus, she's got a lot going on right now."

"The trial's over. Couldn't she get a job anywhere? She's amazing at it from what you've told me."

"She is amazing at her job. And the trial's over, but sentencing is next week, so it's not *really* over yet. Plus, I don't know that it's going to be over for her for a while. The stupid ADA told her about a phone call the night of the fire. I get that he was trying to help. I understand that, in theory, it's important for her to know what happened that night. It's a freaking phone call between her murdered brother and the 'friend' that killed him. For all we know, it was just two teenage boys talking about the next time they could hang out. They could've been talking about some girl in school. It could have been nothing, but she's hung up on it now. She's wondering if Patrick got so upset with Ethan about something, that he broke into their house and killed the whole family."

"Do you think that's what happened?"

"I don't know, but neither does Ripley. That's the problem."

"And Patrick Wilkes is the only person who knows what they talked about?" Bella asked.

Kenna had an epiphany then. She stood quickly from the dinner table she shared with her sister, kissed the top of Bella's head, said a hasty goodbye, and ran out of the house.

***

"Ripley, it's important that you deal with the fact that you may never know what Patrick and Ethan talked about that night," Dr. Clement said.

"I was thinking about asking Patrick for a meeting. I've been told he hasn't had any visitors outside of his mother."

"Do you think that's best?"

"I don't know." Ripley put her face in her hands out of frustration. "I just feel like I need to know what happened. It's so strange." She lowered her hands and met the doctor's kind eyes. "I never needed to know before."

"Before what?"

"Before all this; before they found the evidence. Now that I know about Patrick, that he did this, it's like I need to know everything."

"Is that a good thing or a bad thing?" Dr. Clement made a note in her notepad.

"I don't know. Honestly, I don't know."

"Can I tell you what I think?" Dr. Clement put down

her pen and clasped her hands in her lap.

"That's what I'm here for, right?"

"I think it's a good thing, Ripley. You seem more engaged in your life than you were before. You were going through the motions with everything outside of your job; and I'd argue you were even going through the motions there. The kids you impacted were your primary focus, and that is noble, but it's also not healthy. What you've done now is taken positive steps to improve your life, to find love, to try to move on from what happened to you so long ago."

"So, I should meet with Wilkes?"

"Only you can answer that for sure. I think there's another question you have to ask yourself, though. What happens if Wilkes does agree to meet with you, but you don't get the answers you're looking for? Would that be better or worse than how it is right now?"

***

"Babe, I have to talk to you about something," Kenna said as she lifted Ripley's legs on the couch and sat down under them.

"Okay." Ripley lowered the case file she had been reading.

"I had an idea. Normally, I would go out on my own, ask my questions, get my answers, and make my story. This time, though, they're not my questions; they're not my answers. And it's definitely not my story."

"Kenna, what are you talking about?"

"Your toes are cute. Have I ever told you that?" Kenna rubbed Ripley's bare feet.

"You're stalling." Ripley removed her feet from Kenna's lap and sat up.

"Maybe, but I really do think your toes are cute."

Ripley lifted an eyebrow at her and said, "Funny how you never mentioned that before I mentioned the burns when I was testifying."

"There's a sentence I never thought I'd hear," Kenna replied. "I never noticed them before, and I've spent a lot of *very* focused attention on every inch of your skin." Kenna gave Ripley her sexy smirk.

"If what you want to talk to me about has to do with getting me turned on, you're accomplishing your task, Ken."

"Keep that in mind for later, but sex is not what I want to talk to you about."

"Please don't tell me you want to talk about the sentencing hearing. I don't know if–"

"I want to talk to you about Bethany Wilkes."

"Bethany? Why?" Ripley rested her elbow on the back of the couch and her head on her hand.

"She's facing criminal charges."

"I know that."

"I had an idea that I wanted to run by you. If you say no – the answer is no. I'll drop it. We move on."

"Kenna, spit it out already," Ripley insisted.

"She covered for her son over and over, including that night. It's no guarantee, but there's a chance Patrick told her why he did this. Even if he didn't tell her why, exactly, maybe she knows about the phone call."

"She won't talk to me," Ripley returned.

"What if you went to our ADA *friend* and asked him to make a deal?"

"What kind of deal?"

"If she meets with you and answers your questions truthfully, he gives her a shorter sentence. Maybe he even offers her probation."

"Kenna, I don't know."

"Babe, like I said, this is up to you." Kenna smiled at her and laughed a little. "Honestly, it's kind of killing me, not just doing it. I thought about going to his office today and telling him he's offering her a damn deal so that my girlfriend could get the answers she deserves. Since that Wilkes asshole isn't giving it up, his messed up mother will have to."

"Ken, you—"

"I didn't. I'm here, aren't I?" Kenna interrupted. "I believe what Dr. Clement said, Rip: this is something you have to decide to do yourself. If you don't want to talk to her or ask for a deal on her behalf to get the information she might have, that's fine with me."

Ripley met Kenna's eyes for a moment before she turned away toward one of the pictures they had added to the living room side table. It was a photo of young Ripley with her father. One of the friends Kenna had spoken with had located it for her. Ripley had framed it recently, and it now rested next to the couch.

"I'll call him tomorrow," Ripley finally said.

"Yeah?" Kenna asked, her excitement showing.

"I'd like to try. If she doesn't cooperate, there's nothing I can do, but I have to try."

"I think that's good, babe."

"Me too." Ripley smiled at her.

CHAPTER 34

"THE deal includes what I asked for?" Bethany Wilkes asked three days later. "My lawyer's read over this?"

"Your attorney is right outside and can come in at any time. He's reviewed the document and has approved it. Once you sign that document, you are obligated by law to tell us everything you know regarding the Fox Fire. If we find out you've lied to us or left anything out, the deal is void. You'll go on trial for conspiracy after the fact."

Ripley listened to the ADA as she sat across from Bethany Wilkes in a conference room downtown. She could see Patrick in his mother's face. Their eyes were the same color, but Bethany's weren't cold. The woman actually looked sad. Ripley didn't know if that was for herself, for her son, or for the hell she had put Ripley and others through by covering up for him. Bethany signed the form, slid it across the table toward the attorney, and faced Ripley fully.

"I want you to know how sorry I am for what happened to you. I'm sorry about your family."

For the first time, Ripley realized she didn't need Kenna there. She could do this on her own. As she stared into Bethany Wilkes' eyes, she believed the woman was genuinely sorry for her. Ripley also believed she could get the answers she needed by using the one thing she'd always been good at. She smiled softly as she realized the thing she'd always been good at was asking questions to get the answers she needed. It was, strangely enough, also a strength of a certain reporter she knew.

"Bethany, I appreciate your apology," she began. "I know you had nothing to do with what happened to my family that night."

"Nothing I say in here can be used against Patrick, right?" Bethany asked the lawyer standing in the corner of the room.

"Your son was found guilty of murder. That's over. Our deal states I won't go after him for anything you say in here."

"I didn't know." Bethany turned back to Ripley. "Back then, I didn't know he was like this."

"But you suspected, didn't you? Thought he might be different?"

"He struggled to make friends where we were from. His father wasn't much help, and I was just starting out in the fire department when he was born. My schedule wasn't great. I was on three or four days at a time and then off for one or two, but I was always so tired. He's my only child." Bethany had tears forming in her eyes. "When I realized he needed more from me, I pursued arson investigation since that schedule was more regular. I got the position here, and he seemed to be doing so well. He had a couple of friends at school, and he played basketball on the weekends." She paused and wiped at a tear on her cheek. "When the little fires started, I didn't know it was him. I swear, I didn't know."

"I believe you," Ripley said. "I know my brothers probably did a lot of stuff my parents didn't know about."

"He was on his own a lot once I left his father. Maybe it was my fault, what happened. I don't know. I thought I raised him okay."

"I think that's all parents. There's a woman I'm trying to help at work, and she has a young daughter that's run away from home a few times now. I know her mom is doing everything she can to make sure she knows how loved she is."

Ripley left out the part about the said mother bringing her abusive boyfriend into the house as the cause of the girl's actions. She also felt the bile rising in her throat. She hated having to be kind to this woman, but she knew it was the best way to get what she needed out of her today. After this, she'd never have to see her again.

"Patty had a problem. Once I recognized it, I sent him to live with his father. His father was much better at disciplining him than I was."

"But that was after the night of the fire at my house, right?"

"Yes."

"What happened that night, Bethany? Can you tell me what you did to save Patrick?"

"I did try to save him. I thought he'd made a mistake. I sent him to his father. His father was supposed to punish him."

"For the fire?" Ripley pressed.

"Yes, for the fire. For everything. When Patty got home that night, he smelled like smoke and kerosene. Those are two scents I knew very well. He told me he'd been out walking and saw the fire. I believed him at first, but when I went to wash his clothes later, I felt something come over me – I don't know how to explain it – I had these goosebumps on my arms. I went into his bedroom and found him watching TV." Bethany paused and wiped at another tear. "He was watching the news." Her eyes welled up even more. "The fire was on the TV. He was watching it. He was lying on his bed, and he was…" She sobbed.

"It's okay. Take your time," Ripley tried to console. The bile rose in her throat even more, and she wanted to vomit. "Take your time."

"He was touching himself. He had his hands inside his underwear, and I could tell what he was doing. He was watching the screen and doing *that* to himself." The woman sobbed louder. "I knew then something was wrong, but he was my son."

"You had to protect him," Ripley said.

"I didn't know how bad it was. He said he saw the fire. He didn't say it burned the whole house down. When I saw the TV screen, though, I knew how bad it was. I knew I'd be called. I cleaned his clothes, told him to tell me what happened, and went to work."

"What did he say happened?"

"He repeated the story a few more times. This was after I left his room. He yelled at me for going in without knocking." Bethany leaned in and whispered, "I think he finished... I think he finished what he was doing before he got dressed and came downstairs. It was that important. He had to finish."

"What happened when he came downstairs?"

"He was so angry. I knew he'd never do anything to me, but in that moment, when I saw his face and his reaction to me interrupting him, I thought he just might. He's my son," Bethany repeated. "He told me he saw the fire, and he thought your family was inside. I could tell he wasn't telling me everything, so I asked him if he had anything to do with it." She wiped more tears, and the ADA dropped a box of tissues in front of her. Bethany pulled one out immediately and blew her nose. "He said no, but his eyes were cold. He sat down so calmly at the kitchen table and said he liked the colors the fire made. He liked how when it was really hot, it glowed almost purple. He said he liked the smell of kerosene, and he liked watching the smoke. He liked fire. He liked how hot it got, how it made him sweat a little, and how it felt to burn his skin just enough to leave a mark that goes away after a few days."

"That's when you knew?"

"Yes." Bethany wiped her eyes with another tissue. "I didn't know what to do. He was only thirteen. When I got the call to go to the scene, I wrote it up correctly. I swear, the report is accurate. I didn't omit any details of what I saw there."

"But you also didn't tell anyone about Patty?" Ripley asked, using the familiar name.

"He's my son. I couldn't. I sent him to live with his father after that. I did the best I could."

Ripley felt the liquid boiling at the back of her throat. She knew she couldn't last much longer in this room, listening to this woman talk about what her monster of a son had done, and how she'd covered up for him; how she had allowed him to do this to other people through her negligence.

"There was a phone call between your house and mine that night. Do you remember if it was you or Patrick?"

"It wasn't me. I don't think I ever called your parents."

"Did Patrick tell you about the call?"

"No, the last thing on my mind was a phone call." She dropped a third used tissue on the light wood of the table. "Why?"

"I saw my brother in his room that night. He was talking on the phone, and he looked upset. He closed the door, but I remember his expression to this day. That was the only phone call made to our house that night."

"Patty didn't talk on the phone much, but I do know he called Ethan a few times. I don't remember if he called that night, though."

"He never told you about it?"

"No." Bethany looked at the ADA, who was standing in the corner with his arms crossed over his chest. "I swear. I didn't know about a call. I've been honest here."

"It's okay. I know you are," Ripley said. "Was Patty angry with Ethan for some reason?"

"Are you looking for why?" Bethany asked. "Are you trying to find out why he did this to your family?"

Ripley decided to be honest with her and replied, "Yes, I am."

"I don't know why. I tried to figure it out after it

happened. I tried to find out where I'd gone wrong. What made him want to play with fire? Was it me? Was it because I was a firefighter and then an arson investigator? Was it because I wasn't home a lot when he was young, and he was trying to get back at me? I don't know. I'll never know. He's never told me why he did it. I don't know if your brother upset him that night or any other night. If I did, I would tell you."

"Why do you say that?" Ripley asked.

"Because I want this deal. I want to see my son."

Ripley turned to the ADA and gave him a confused expression.

"Her deal includes a clause that states that her son will be sent to Heights once we know his sentence. It's the closest maximum-security prison to Pleasant Valley. She's getting two years at the local minimum-security and will be on probation for another five after that. Once she serves her sentence, she'll be permitted weekly visits with her son, and they'll be able to touch," the ADA explained to her. "In a death penalty situation, it's normally behind glass." He paused. "I knew this was important to you."

"Thank you," Ripley said and then turned to Bethany. "Is there anything else you can tell me?"

"I'm sorry I don't know more. My son isn't normal. He doesn't work like you and I do. I don't know how that happens." Bethany placed a hand on top of Ripley's on the table. "I can only hope you don't keep searching for the why because I don't think there is one."

When Ripley left the room moments later, she rushed to the bathroom, pushed herself into an empty stall, and promptly vomited.

CHAPTER 35

"I CAN start in two weeks."

"And this is what you want?" Ripley asked.

Kenna nodded and looked down at her hands that were holding on to the bucket of popcorn in her lap.

"Want some?" Kenna lifted the bucket to Ripley's side.

"You wanted that." Ripley laughed at her. "Set it over there if you're done."

The theater was relatively empty. It was Thursday afternoon. The sentencing hearing would be the following morning. After Ripley's meeting with Bethany Wilkes, they had both wanted to do something that could take their minds – particularly Ripley's – off the case and Patrick Wilkes. Ripley had left the office early that day. It had been her idea to take on an early afternoon showing of one of the new releases. Neither of them cared about the actual film. It was just nice to get out of the house and do something together that didn't involve the job hunt or Patrick Wilkes.

Kenna placed the half-eaten popcorn bucket into the empty seat to her right. With Ripley on her left and no one else around them, it kind of felt like they had the place to themselves. There was one couple near the front of the theater and over to the left edge, and there was one man in the middle of the rows and to their right. Ripley had chosen the very back row and wanted to sit in the center. She said that seat gave the best view of the screen. Kenna wanted the best view of Ripley. She planned on spending at least some of the movie making out with her girlfriend.

"I say, for the next two hours, we don't talk about anything big in our lives. We just sit here, enjoy the movie, and talk." Kenna turned a little in her seat toward Ripley as the lights dimmed. "And maybe make out."

"You want to make out with me in the movie theater like we're teenagers?" Ripley turned her face to Kenna.

"I didn't get to make out with you as a teenager. Sue me." Kenna wiggled her eyebrows at Ripley.

"Before that two-hours thing starts, though, tell me one thing." Ripley moved a little closer to Kenna and placed her hand on Kenna's thigh.

"Okay."

"This job, is it really what you want?"

"We said no talking about–" Kenna stopped dead in her tracks when the lights went completely dark, and the instant they did, Ripley's hand moved to her center, cupping it over the jeans Kenna had worn. "What are you doing?"

"You wanted to make out in a movie theater like we're teenagers, but we're adults, Ken. The room is dark. No one can see us," Ripley whispered into her ear. "Can you be quiet?"

"Yes," Kenna whispered back as Ripley's index finger slid up and down over the heavy fabric that suddenly felt very tight.

Ripley slid her hand up, unbuttoned Kenna's jeans, and as the first commercial played loudly in the theater, she slid down Kenna's zipper. She heard Kenna let out a long breath. Ripley smirked as she nibbled on Kenna's earlobe. She slid her hands inside Kenna's panties and cupped her again.

"Like this?" she asked.

"Harder."

Ripley pressed her palm harder into Kenna, and Kenna's hips bucked slightly in response. Ripley licked the outside of Kenna's earlobe before attaching her lips to

Kenna's neck.

"What now?" Ripley asked in a whisper as the next commercial began to play.

"Touch my clit," Kenna replied.

Ripley used two fingers. She dipped them between Kenna's lips and felt the wetness that had already begun to pool there. She slid them up once, down again, and held them in place.

"Now?"

"Inside just a little," Kenna's responses were getting quieter and coming between short gasps.

Ripley dipped inside her as much as the angle would allow before pulling up and stroking Kenna fully. She moved her hand up and down slowly before picking up speed. Kenna's hand gripped the other armrest while her arm wrapped around Ripley's shoulder, allowing Ripley to move closer. Ripley's lips moved to Kenna's jaw, and Kenna turned her head to connect their mouths. She moaned as Ripley's tongue met her own. Ripley's fingers picked up in speed even more. She could tell Kenna was getting close, so she stopped her fingers and pulled back her mouth.

"If you want this to continue, I want an honest answer."

"What?" Kenna breathed out. "Rip, that's–" Ripley stroked her once more and stopped.

"Tell me you don't like when I do this. Tell me you don't like when I make you wait a little."

"I do like it, but you're–" Kenna stopped when Ripley entered her again.

"Ken, please tell me the truth."

"I don't want it."

"Want what?" Ripley asked.

"The job." Kenna pressed her hand to Ripley's and tried to coax it to move against her. "I don't want it, but I do want you to continue. I'm so close, Rip."

Ripley stroked Kenna again. She kissed her lips, her ear, her neck, and stroked her clit until Kenna came in her hand. When Kenna's tremors ceased, Ripley pulled her fingers out, turned Kenna's face to her own, and slid her fingers inside her own mouth, sucking on them for a moment before she slid them out and into Kenna's, allowing her to do the same.

"Are you ready for the movie now?" Ripley asked with a pleased smirk on her face.

***

"Do you want to tell me what that was about?" Kenna asked the moment they were outside the theater.

Two more couples had entered the small theater to watch the movie just as it had begun. One had, for some reason, sat in the same row as Kenna and Ripley, while the other couple moved right in front of them. This made talking during the movie difficult. She'd had to wait until they were outside and headed to the car.

"What?" Ripley asked.

"You just fingered me in a movie theater, babe." Kenna unlocked the car with a press of a button.

"Kenna!" Ripley whisper-yelled as her head swiveled to see if anyone was nearby.

"If you're going to do it, you should be able to talk about it." Kenna pointed at her. "Let's go for a walk."

"I thought we were going home," Ripley replied as she opened the door and then closed it at Kenna's declaration.

"Let's walk and talk. We can grab dinner." Kenna held out her hand for Ripley to take. Ripley walked around the car and took it. "Now, let's talk about that little display in there."

"I felt like touching my girlfriend."

"In public?"

"I've never done that before, if that's what you're asking," Ripley told her as they walked.

"But you wanted to today?"

"Yes."

"And that little trick you pulled to get me to talk?"

"Why did I have to trick you into talking?" Ripley shot back as she smiled.

"When did you get so good at asking questions? I'm the reporter." Kenna laughed lightly.

"I guess I realized what I do with the kids sometimes is very useful in my life," Ripley said. "It's how I got Bethany Wilkes to talk."

"Are you trying to use your trickery on me too there, Rip?" Kenna squeezed her hand.

"I'll ask again. Why did I have to?"

"Come on, Ripley. You know there's nothing close for me here. The commute is a bitch, and it's not exactly what I want, but they told me if I give it a few years, I can probably get into producing full-time. It pays well, and they've ensured me I'm in control of my stories. Plus, it's a slightly bigger market."

"But you don't want it?"

"It's not that big of a deal."

"Why are you taking it then?" Ripley stopped walking, causing Kenna to stop as well. "Be honest, Kenna. Please."

"I've only reached out for jobs somewhat near Pleasant Valley."

"Because of me?" Ripley asked.

"Because of a lot of things." Kenna paused and looked around for a moment. "I own a home here, Rip. My sister and her family are here, and I love living so close to them. I have friends here. I have history here."

"All that was true before, but you were still planning on looking at larger markets. You had your reel ready to go. What changed?" Ripley pressed.

"You know the answer to that," Kenna told her.

"Were you even going to ask me?"

"Ask you what?"

"What I wanted," Ripley explained.

"What you wanted for me at work?" Kenna sounded confused.

"Kenna, you never asked me if I wanted to stay here."

Kenna looked at Ripley, and in that moment, she realized that Ripley was right: Kenna hadn't thought to ask her girlfriend if she wanted to stay in Pleasant Valley or if she'd be willing to move if there was a good reason.

"I guess I just assumed. Your job is here, Rip."

"And that's it." Ripley placed both hands on Kenna's waist. "Come here." She let go of Kenna and took her hand back instead. They walked a short distance in silence before they turned the corner onto a residential street. "Do you know what street this is?"

"Yes."

"I haven't been back since that day you drove me here and we parked." Ripley pulled Kenna along.

"Come on. Let's go get some dinner," Kenna said.

"No, it's okay." Ripley walked them along the sidewalk until they arrived in front of the house that had been built over the ruins of her former home. "Kenna, there's nothing here for me. I go to work, and I do my best to help those kids, but I can be a social worker anywhere. This place used to terrify me, and I avoided it at all costs because I couldn't stand to see where it had happened. Now, I can stand here with you and talk about it." She turned to Kenna. "And I'm okay. I'm not a hundred percent, but I'm okay."

"I'm proud of you, Rip." Kenna leaned in and kissed her forehead.

"I'm proud of me, too. It's taken me a while, but I think I'm going to be okay."

"And you'd be interested in moving if I applied for a producing job and got it?"

Ripley sighed and wrapped her arms around Kenna's neck, pulling the woman in for a hug.

"Kenna, I love you, and I want to be where you are. I've never even really left Pleasant Valley," Ripley said against Kenna's neck. "You know, after the fire, the home insurance company didn't pay out because it was arson. That, apparently, wasn't covered in their policy. They had life insurance, but that covered the cost of the funeral arrangements. It didn't leave much. When I entered the system, what money was left to me ended up disappearing into the hands of a distant relative, who has since passed away."

"Babe, I'm–"

"I told you that because I want you to understand what I mean when I say I've never had anything before that was just my own. When I was in the system, I didn't even have a toy that belonged just to me. My textbooks in school were rentals, for crying out loud." Ripley pulled back to meet Kenna's eyes. "My apartment was rented, and my furniture was secondhand and falling apart. My car was used when I got it. My laptop belongs to work. I've never had anything I could call my own." She paused and stared deeply into Kenna's eyes. "But I have you now." She ran her hands through Kenna's hair. "And I love that you're mine, that you understand me, that you support me, and that you considered staying here and taking a job you didn't want just because of me. I love that, but I also hate that because I never want to hold you back from something you want. And I especially don't want to do that because I have no reason to stick around Pleasant Valley. This place only has bad memories for me."

"Outside of meeting me, of course." Kenna needed to lighten the moment because this moment felt big.

"Of course." Ripley kissed her gently. "You're the best thing that's ever happened to me, and I want you to do what's right for you in your career. I want you to know that I don't need to stay here. There's nothing keeping me here anymore."

"Are you sure? You've gone through so much recently, Rip."

"And I think that's why I feel like I can leave, and it would be okay. I was actually talking to Dr. Clement about this in my last session. I still have a lot of guilt to deal with, but I've started taking steps."

"Guilt?" Kenna's arms circled Ripley's waist. "Like a survivor thing?"

"No, it's more about the fact that I never tried to find out who did this to them. I never pursued it. Once I got caught in the system, I let it go. I only looked into it a little, and then I just left it because I couldn't deal with it."

"You shouldn't feel guilty about that, babe."

"But I do," Ripley replied. "I'm working on that. The important thing is that I think not doing all this made me feel like I couldn't leave Pleasant Valley. Now that things are happening, and we know Wilkes did this, I can stand outside this house and remember more good things than bad things. That's a big deal for me."

"And you'd really be willing to move somewhere else if it came to that?" Kenna asked with hope and concern in her tone.

"If you go, I will go with you."

CHAPTER 36

"I UNDERSTAND we are foregoing the victim impact statements at this time," the judge said as she sat on her bench and moved papers around.

"That's correct, Your Honor," the ADA replied as he stood.

Ripley sat behind him in the front row of the gallery. There was a moment when she considered tugging on his jacket and calling him to attention to correct the judge's comment. She could make a statement. As Kenna sat next to her, squeezing her hand tightly, she did consider it.

"Very well. We'll proceed with sentencing then. The defendant will stand," the judge instructed.

Patrick Wilkes stood. He buttoned up his jacket, as did his attorney. Today, Patrick wasn't wearing blue. Today, he was wearing a brown suit that fit him terribly. The arm length was much too long for him. The jacket was bulky on his small frame. His prison glasses had returned for some reason, and his black tie did nothing to convey honesty.

***

"Are you okay?" Kenna asked the moment they were alone in the car.

"I will be."

"You still want to go?"

"Yes," Ripley replied instantly, covered Kenna's hand that had landed on her thigh, and turned to face the window.

Kenna squeezed her thigh, put the car in drive, and took them to their destination. Ripley climbed out of the car first. She nodded to Kenna to follow, and Kenna did so hesitantly, likely trying to give Ripley an out if she needed to do this alone. Ripley didn't want to be alone anymore. She wanted Kenna beside her forever and in everything. They walked down the endless rows to the destination Ripley was very familiar with. When they arrived, she took Kenna's hand, squeezed it, and then let it go again to remove the piece of paper from her pocket. She looked straight ahead for a moment.

"Hi, Mom," she said. "Hi, Dad, Ethan, Benji." She pointed behind the row of tombstones. "Hi, Grandma." She glanced at Kenna. "She's buried next to my grandfather." Ripley turned back to the tombstones in front of them. "There's someone I want you all to meet," she began. "This is my girlfriend, Kenna. Now, I know what you must be thinking." She turned to Kenna. "Kenna is not a man."

Kenna burst out laughing and said, "Oh, my God."

"I never exactly had the chance or a reason to come out to them before." Ripley smiled at her and realized that was the first time she'd ever smiled while standing in this cemetery.

"You're so cute sometimes." Kenna turned to the tombstones. "Your daughter, granddaughter, and sister is really freaking cute sometimes. I hope that's okay for me to say."

Ripley watched as Kenna spoke to the gravesides as if the people were standing right there in front of them. She loved Kenna a little more then.

"Kenna and I have been together for a few months. God, that's crazy!" She turned back to Kenna.

"I know. It feels like a lot longer."

"And not even that long…"

"At the same time," Kenna added. "That's a good thing, I think."

Ripley turned back to the graves and said, "I love her. You'd love her, too, I think. She makes me happy. She challenges me and makes me think. She also drives me nuts when she leaves glasses on her nice coffee table without coasters under them."

"Our," Kenna stated.

"What?"

"It's *our* coffee table, Rip."

"Oh, yeah." Ripley lowered her head a little before raising it back up to smile. "We live together; I probably should have mentioned that. I moved out of that crappy apartment and into Kenna's condo. It's much nicer. Plus, she's there." She wrapped an arm around Kenna's waist, pulling her in closer. "She's who I hope you guys would have wanted for me. Dad, I think you'd really like how she understands finances and tries to teach me how to manage my 401k. I don't know why I think this, but I've always had a feeling you were the kind of dad that would bother me about having enough money to retire." Ripley chuckled at herself. "We never got that far, did we?" she asked. "Anyway, Kenna actually has a financial planner that's now looking over my stuff, too. Ethan, I still suck at soccer and basketball, as you probably know, but Kenna's nephews are trying to teach me some new tricks. Maybe I'll be as good as you guys were one day." She tightened her arm around Kenna. "Mom, Kenna cooks. She made the best chili for me one night. And when I told her you used to make this pork dish I actually liked, she tried to make it for me. It was pretty close."

"I didn't have your recipe. I did the best I could," Kenna said.

"We do the best we can for each other. I think that's what matters," Ripley shared.

"Agreed."

"Anyway, you're probably wondering why I'm here,

when it's not anyone's birthday, and I was just here for the anniversary," Ripley spoke to the graves again. "Today, Patrick Wilkes was sentenced to death for setting the fire." She paused to gather herself. "I didn't want that. I would have preferred he be sentenced to life with no possibility of ever getting out, but it wasn't my call." Ripley paused again as she lay her head on Kenna's shoulder. Kenna's arm went around her shoulders. "I was hoping he'd be around for years and years, just in case he ever wakes up one day and wants to explain why he did this to you; why he did this to me. I guess there's still time. He'll appeal and appeal. Maybe next week, next month, or next year he'll want to tell me why, but I know I can't rely on that. I know I can't wait for it like I've been waiting my whole life. That's what I've realized recently: I've been waiting my whole life to know what happened and why. Now that I finally know *what*, I have to just deal with the fact that I might never know *why*."

"Is that okay?" Kenna asked in her ear as if not wanting Ripley's family to hear her.

"Yes," Ripley stated. "And no," she added. "If he wanted to tell me right now, I'd want to know. I can't pretend that's not the case." She turned to Kenna purposefully, tucked the paper back into her pocket, took both of Kenna's hands in her own, and met her blue eyes. "But I won't let it hold me back from living my life."

"I'm proud of you," Kenna whispered to her and smiled.

"Guys, I might be leaving Pleasant Valley one day, and it might be one day soon. I might not be able to come back here for every birthday or on the anniversary, but I think that would be okay with you. I think you'd want me to live." Ripley continued to look into Kenna's eyes as she said, "And I want to live. I want to live with Kenna and have a family with her." She smiled as Kenna smiled. "I wrote something." Ripley turned then and dropped one of Kenna's hands. She reached for the piece of paper again, looked down at it, and placed it on top of the tombstone someone else had picked out years ago for both her parents to share. "When someone gets sentenced for a crime, they let the victims make a statement before sentencing. At first, I didn't want to give one because I knew I couldn't handle it. Then, Dr. Clement told me I should still write it down, even if I don't actually say it out loud. I wrote this last week. This morning, in the courtroom, I realized I could stand up in front of the room and tell them." Ripley breathed a sigh of relief. "I could have done it, and I would have been okay. I've come that far that I would have been okay. I didn't, though. I decided Patrick Wilkes doesn't care about the impact he made on my life. And, honestly, I don't care about the impact my statement could have made on his. When I wrote this, I thought it would be all about the negative things that happened to me because of the fire and because of what I lost." She met Kenna's eyes again. "But as I wrote, it turned into something much more than that. I started writing about how I became a social worker to help kids that were like me. That was my calling. I started writing about how I met Kenna because of what happened to me. And I love her. She's the person I'm supposed to be with." Ripley rested her head on Kenna's shoulder again. "I kept writing, though, and when I finished, I realized it wasn't a victim impact statement; it was an update on my life more than anything. It was a journal entry that tells you how far I've come. So, I've brought it here, and I will leave it here as well. I want you to have it. I'm going to go home now, and it might be a while before I come back. I just wanted you to know that I'm okay. I'm okay, everyone."

"You are okay," Kenna stated.

"Yeah, I am," Ripley agreed.

"And we'll be okay," Kenna added.

"Yeah, we will be."

EPILOGUE

"KENNA, we can't."

"Actually, we can, and we have." Kenna kissed Ripley's neck. "Like, a million times."

"Your sister and brother-in-law are going to be here any minute," Ripley replied.

"Bella is always late. We'll be fine. Besides, this is the last chance we have to do this here before we move."

"You said that last night, babe," Ripley argued as Kenna's hand slid under her shirt to cup her breast.

"And I meant it last night. But now, it really is the last time we'll get to do this in here. We're leaving as soon as everything's out of here," Kenna returned and unbuttoned Ripley's jeans.

She also pulled back then as she stared into Ripley's hazel eyes. Kenna watched as Ripley's expression turned from playful to smoldering, and that was a change Kenna knew all too well by now. She slid her fingers into Ripley's belt loops and lowered the jeans down to Ripley's ankles. Then, she knelt and pulled them off completely. Ripley's legs were exposed now, and she loved Ripley's legs. They were toned and nearly always smooth. Since Ripley had taken up to going to the gym downstairs, the woman had shaved almost every day, telling Kenna she didn't want anyone in the gym to see her with hairy legs. Kenna wasn't complaining. She nibbled Ripley's skin up to her thighs. When Ripley tore off her own t-shirt, Kenna knew they were in business. Her hands pulled Ripley's white boy shorts off her legs. Kenna had bought them for her and loved how Ripley looked in them. Sometimes, Ripley walked around the house only wearing those boy shorts and a tank top. Every time that happened, Kenna had to have her up against the wall, on that dining room table, or on the floor. Once, they'd managed to make it all the way to the bed.

Today was the last day they'd be in their condo. Bella and her family would be arriving soon to take them to lunch. All their earthly possessions were in a moving van that was being driven by the moving company they'd hired. They'd sold Ripley's car and would buy her a new one once they arrived at their new home. They'd begin their drive as soon as they wrapped their farewell lunch.

Kenna knelt in the middle of the completely empty living room, save one suitcase and a messenger bag near the front door. Ripley stood nearly nude in the middle of the now expansive space. She unclasped her own bra and tossed it to the floor just as Kenna took her into her mouth. Kenna's tongue started first before her lips sucked Ripley softly between her lips. Ripley's hand went to the back of Kenna's head to coax her to continue, and when Kenna slid one hand between Ripley's legs, Ripley spread them wider. Kenna slid two fingers inside and looked up to see Ripley using her free hand to play with her own nipple.

This was possibly Kenna's favorite sight in the world; she loved watching Ripley express herself this way. And Ripley touching herself while Kenna buried her face between Ripley's legs was also Kenna's biggest turn on. As she stroked her in time with her tongue, Kenna's eyes remained open. Ripley's eyes opened as well, and they lowered to watch Kenna watching her. Ripley smirked down at her, and Kenna licked her then, causing Ripley to gasp at the sight probably even more than the action.

"Tell me what you want," Kenna said in a husky tone.

"The floor," Ripley replied.

Kenna smiled up at her and backed up for only a second while Ripley moved to lie on the hardwood floor. Kenna slid on top of her, sucked Ripley's nipple into her mouth, and pushed her fingers back inside. They moved slowly at first before Kenna picked up speed. She switched to the other nipple, toyed with it, using her teeth, and kissed down Ripley's stomach. When her mouth reconnected with Ripley's clit, Ripley came while pressing her hand down onto Kenna's head to apply more pressure.

Kenna made sure Ripley's tremors had ceased before she stood, stripped off her own jeans and panties, and then straddled Ripley's waist. Only a moment later, Ripley's hands were on her hips, encouraging her up farther. When Kenna straddled Ripley's face, she let out a loud moan. Ripley's tongue slid inside her first before it pulled out and repeated the action. Then, it stroked Kenna's clit, flicked it back and forth, and Ripley sucked it hard into her mouth. It didn't take long for Kenna to come as her hips moved erratically over Ripley's face. Just as her hips started to slow, the doorbell rang.

"Shit," Kenna whispered and stood.

"Kenna!" Ripley sat up. "I told you they'd be here soon." Ripley stood, completely naked, and gathered her clothes from the floor. "Your nephews are out there."

"They don't know we have sex, Rip." Kenna slid her underwear back on and pulled her jeans on over them.

"I can hear you two moving around. Open the door," Bella said through the door.

"Coming," Ripley offered as she slid her jeans on over her boy shorts.

"I just did," Kenna added with a smirk.

"I'm going to the bathroom. Jesus, Kenna! Wipe your face," Ripley commanded.

Kenna chuckled as she reached for Ripley's messenger bag where she knew Ripley had tissues. It wouldn't do much, but it was all they had, since they'd packed up everything else, and it was currently being driven to its destination. Ripley hurried off to the bathroom, where they had left toilet paper, at least.

"Hey, Bell," Kenna greeted as she opened the door.

Bella immediately gave her a once-over and said, "I'm glad I left the kids in the car with their father. Your damn jeans aren't buttoned or zipped, baby sis." She pointed at Kenna's pants. "Ripley, you can come out now, as long as you're fully clothed," the woman yelled. "Here." Bella reached inside her overly large purse. "I carry these around for the kids, but you need them more than they do."

Bella passed Kenna a small package of wet wipes, and Kenna could only laugh. When Ripley emerged from the bathroom somewhat put-together, Kenna tossed her the package.

"She figured us out," Kenna said.

"What do you mean?" Ripley tried to cover at the same time she pulled out two wet wipes, wiped her hands and her face, and handed Bella back the package.

"Gross. Let's go. Do not hug me, touch me, or try to kiss me on the cheek until both of you have cleaned yourselves up at the restaurant bathroom."

Kenna and Ripley could only laugh at Kenna's sister's antics. Kenna took Ripley's hand, and they looked around the condo they'd already handed over the keys to. It had been their first home together, technically, but the place had been Kenna's first. Where they were going would be their first real home together. Kenna pulled the handle of their small suitcase, and Ripley slid her messenger bag over her shoulder. Kenna then noticed Ripley didn't play with the strap, shift the bag around, or commit one of her other nervous tells, as was her usual custom.

"I can't wait to get there," Ripley said after Bella had walked off down the hall. "I'm excited for you to start work. Hell, I'm excited for me to start work."

"That's because you love your work," Kenna said.

"We have a home now. We get to start over."

THE FIRE

"We do," Kenna agreed. "You're not nervous, are you?" she asked Ripley, slightly mystified.

Kenna had never been nervous prior to meeting the love of her life. Since meeting Ripley, though, she found herself nervous somewhat regularly and to varying degrees. She knew it was because Ripley was the one thing in her life she could never live without. Her work could come and go, her friends could pass in and out of her life, but Ripley was the one person she needed. Because it mattered more than anything, Kenna got nervous. She was even nervous now, standing next to Ripley in their condo, getting ready to say goodbye-for-now to her family before their eight-hour drive to the city they'd call home. She was particularly nervous now because she'd asked her mom for her grandmother's ring to give Ripley when the time was right. Bella had wanted her own engagement-ring-and-wedding-band set, but Kenna had always wanted to give her grandmother's set to her future wife. When she and Ripley started discussing their potential move, Kenna knew she needed to get it from her mom because Ripley was the woman it was meant for.

"No, I'm not nervous. I'm ready," Ripley stated.

"Then, I'm ready, too," Kenna added.

Made in United States
North Haven, CT
28 October 2022

26056489R00171